I0549528

Judas Island

Also by Joan Druett

A PROMISE OF GOLD
Judas Island
Calafia's Kingdom
Dearest Enemy
Finale

THE MONEY SHIP
The Launching of the Huntress
The Privateer Brig
The Dragon Stone
The Midwife's Apprentice

WIKI COFFIN MYSTERIES
A Watery Grave
Shark Island
Run Afoul
Deadly Shoals
The Beckoning Ice

OTHER FICTION
A Love of Adventure (Abigail)

NON FICTION
The Notorious Captain Hayes
Eleanor's Odyssey
Lady Castaways
The Elephant Voyage
Tupaia, Captain Cook's Polynesian Navigator
Island of the Lost
In the Wake of Madness
Rough Medicine
Hen Frigates
Captain's Daughter, Coasterman's Wife
She Was a Sister Sailor
Petticoat Whalers
Fulbright in New Zealand
Exotic Intruders

A Promise of Gold

Book One

JUDAS ISLAND

JUDAS ISLAND

THE FIRST IN AN OLD SALT PRESS TRILOGY published by Old Salt Press, a Limited Liability Company registered in New Jersey, USA.

For more information about our titles go to www.oldsaltpress.com

ISBN 978-0-9922588-7-8

Copyright © 2016 Joan Druett

Publisher's Note: This is a work of historical fiction. Certain characters and their actions may have been inspired by historical individuals and events. The characters in the novel, however, represent the work of the author's imagination. Any resemblance to actual persons, living or dead, is entirely coincidental.

All rights reserved. No part of this book may be reproduced or transmitted in any form or by any means, electronic or mechanical, including photocopying, recording or by any information storage and retrieval system, without written permission from the author, except for the inclusion of brief quotations in a review.

Cover and interior art copyright © 2016 Ron Druett

ONE

THERE was a scent of ancient murder in the air.

Captain Dexter stood at the rail of the *Gosling*, frowning as he tried to track down the source of his deep sense of misgiving. The weather was fair. The ebbing tide muttered about the hull of his brig, but the *Gosling* merely bobbed and rolled, held securely by her anchors, which were in good holding ground. The wind was so slight as to be almost imperceptible. High in the pale late afternoon sky the clouds were moving fast, but the surface of the sea was only disturbed where breakers rolled against the feet of the tall cliffs of Judas Island. Gulls screamed deafeningly, circling over the patch in the water where Bodfish, the steward, had thrown a bucket of potato peelings, but their cries weren't the kind that presage a gale.

Which was lucky, Dexter mused, because there were only three men besides himself on board, and one of those was the steerage boy, while the other two were the steward and the boatswain. Six of his fourteen men were on the darkening heights of Judas Island, and five, with his mate, had taken the whaleboat to visit the whaleship that lay in the entrance to the open sea, half a mile away.

Tomorrow afternoon he would bring the men back from the island, he decided, and give up the hunt—yet again.

Meantime, though, there should be just time enough to take one hundred barrels of oil on board. Dexter studied the whaleship again.

The whaler had come into sight at the head of the bay in the mid afternoon, a sturdy bluff-bowed vessel with stout sticks and slung boats and short sails. She was low in the water — full to the bunghole with oil, judging by the way she moved. Oil fetched 225 cents per gallon in the Valparaiso market, and the captain of the whaleship would be lucky to get 90 cents for the same in New Bedford. The holds of the brig were empty except for a half-cargo of lumber, and Dexter had traded, and that most profitably, in oil before. Accordingly, he had flown a signal, and had sent his first mate in the brig's whaleboat when the other ship cooperatively lay aback.

But he hadn't expected the visit to take so long. The officer and his boat's crew had been gone for two hours, which was twice as long as it should have taken to bargain for a few barrels of oil. Dexter thought with irritation that he really should have gone himself. But, as usual, he wanted to avoid the society of a shrewd New Bedford skipper. Not only was there a chance that the spouter master would remember the Dexter name, but he must be feeling uncommon curious to know what the brig was a-doing in such an unlikely corner of the world. Dexter had not felt in the slightest like listening to probing questions about what attractions the island held, and then devising plausible replies. Charlie Martin was as capable of making up answers as he was.

Was it the whaleboat's long absence that was nagging at his mind? Dexter thought not, because he knew all too well how sociable his first mate could be. He looked again at the island, where his six men were digging. It was an ominous shape, hunched against the sky, with tall cliffs and yet flat-topped. It must be its history that was weighing on his soul, he decided. The wreck ... if there had been a wreck ... had been a long time ago, and the screams of the drowning and the tortured had faded into silence long since, but there was still that aura of ancient evil that hung about Judas Island. He shrugged away superstitious misgivings, and strode to the door in the break of the poop that led down into the unusually luxurious afterquarters of the brig.

Because the poop deck was six feet higher than the amidship deck, Dexter had to duck only a little as he trod onto the first of the three steps that led down to the passage. Once in the corridor he stood fully upright, as the headroom was so generous. Two doors to his right—on the larboard side—led to two little staterooms. At the sternward end of the passage there was a lobby, which led to his private quarters in the stern. Instead of going there, however, he opened the elaborately carved, mahogany double doors that stood to his left, and walked into a spacious mess cabin. A large table with a bench along each side and an armchair at the sternward end ran fore and aft beneath a broad skylight, which was high enough to hold two hanging lamps and a hanging rack with glasses and decanters. The low sun that slanted through the skylight glinted on the facets of old, fine crystal.

The cabin was empty, as was the pantry that ran off it. Evidently Bodfish was in the between decks quarters where he berthed with the sailmaker, the boatswain, the cook, and the steerage boy. Dexter could smell baked beans, and when he poked his head into the pantry, it was to find that the steward had left a pot of beans simmering over a spirit lamp. No doubt they were intended for Mr. Martin, along with his two junior mates ... but Charlie Martin had been gone a long time.

With no compunction whatsoever Dexter filled a plate, and carried the plate to his place at the head of the table. He sat down in his special armchair, then began to eat with enjoyment. He ate with his hat on.

The hat was made of worn and comfortable leather, and

suited Dexter to perfection. It was a very old friend and Dexter like to wear it with eloquence, to match his mood. Now, as he heard boots coming across the deck and down the steps and through the corridor he tipped it back in a gesture of optimistic inquiry.

The double doors opened to reveal his first mate, who looked extremely animated. Charlie Martin had recently cultivated a huge lot of curly adolescent beard, which he tugged when excited. Now, he looked set to haul it out by the roots.

Dexter said, "Well?"

"They suspicioned we was pirates, when they first raised us, sir."

"They did?" Dexter was amused. It took a crafty old skipper, he thought, to appreciate the privateer lines of his brig. Then he wondered if the Dexter name had been recognized.

"They had muskets ready to shove in our chest if we said the wrong word, and the old cook informed us that he had two kittles of water a'bi'lin' on the galley stove and we wouldn't be advised to try bad business. They was all so reassured to find that our mission was innocent that the reception turned extreme 'ospitable."

The brig chose that moment to roll a little. Charlie stumbled in time to it, and had some little bother regaining his balance. Or so Dexter observed. And now that he knew about it, he could smell Charlie's aura of brandy.

He said, "The cook became friendly?"

"The cap'n, sir! Cap'n Smith, whaleship *Humpback*, forty days out of Auckland, New Zealand. A bald-headed old customer, he, naught but half as long again as the sea-boots he wore." Charlie was beaming, lost in what to Dexter seemed to be unstoppable eloquence. "Mrs. Smith were there, twice as wide, twice as tall, three times as foreboding, but a first-rate brandy and generous at that..."

"And he agreed to sell the oil?"

4

"That he did, sir, that he did."

"At our price?"

"Aye, sir."

"Jehovah," said Dexter, delighted at the prospect of a nice little profit. "You have done well."

"Thank you, sir." Then, to Dexter's surprise, Charlie Martin looked about and lowered his voice, saying, "But he asked a favor in return, though he vowed he would see us paid proper for it."

"What?" said Dexter, abruptly very suspicious.

But before Charlie could answer Dexter heard light steps in the corridor. Then the double doors opened. A blonde girl looked through the gap, and walked in. She was very young, less than twenty, but as fat as a dowager.

She sighted Dexter at the end of the table, smiled brilliantly, and said in a clear English voice, "I am delighted to meet you, Captain Dexter!"

When Dexter rose slowly to his feet, she swished towards him in a multitude of skirts, holding out her hand to shake. The girl seemed wider than ever when he looked down at her. A voluminous cloak did little to hide a most unfortunate figure—and yet she did not seem like a prim and proper New England wife, because her face was so elfin. This girl—for she was definitely just a girl—had thick, disordered, wheat-colored hair, and a pale face with fine-boned cheeks that seemed hollowed with hunger, an effect that was dramatically emphasized by dark-brown, long-lashed eyes, and fine, dark, arched eyebrows.

Dexter did not shake the proffered hand. Instead, he hooked his fingers in his belt and said forbiddingly, "Mrs. Smith?"

"Mrs. Smith?" The girl dropped her hand with a grimace. "My God, no, never. My name, Captain Dexter, is Miss Harriet Gray."

Then she smiled expectantly, her head a little on one side, as if she assumed he would know the name. He did not. Dexter shot a questioning look at Charlie Martin, who simply shuffled and blushed.

Looking back at the girl, Dexter said, "And your reason for coming on board my ship, Miss Gray?"

"I've come to ask you to carry me to Valparaiso, Captain Dexter," she replied, adding with bright confidence, "Captain Smith and Mrs. Smith were quite sure you would be amenable, once they told you their problem. Indeed, they were positive that you would be helpful. And I am persuaded that once you hear my story you will agree at once to do it."

Dexter said dangerously, "I will?"

"Of course! Well, sir, so I am assured. I bought passage in the *Humpback* in Auckland, you see—passage to Valparaiso, and *more* than the market rate, I promise, more than I could really afford, Captain Dexter, but my errand there is so *urgent* I had no choice. It's absolutely essential that I get there by the end of June, and Captain Smith *promised* that he would honor our bargain. I relied absolutely on Captain Smith's promises! But now he has changed his mind. He has decided to head straight for Cape Horn, to get to New Bedford in time for the market—whatever the *market* might be. Of course I protested—vehemently, I assure you!—because surely he must have known about that *market*, sir, before he agreed to carry a passenger. Then, when Mr. Martin came on board after some oil, well, Captain Smith decided that you could carry me to Chile more easily than he could. He's coming in his boat to confirm the bargain, and pay the fair share of the passage money I paid…"

Dexter interrupted, "So this is the favor." Swinging round on his mate, he barked, "And what did you say, sir, that gave Captain Smith the strange impression that I would be party to such an arrangement?"

Charlie went red and gulped, but the girl forestalled his excuses, saying quickly, "Oh, please, Captain Dexter, please don't blame Mr. Martin. He was merely being polite—and you won't be out of pocket in the slightest, and I shan't be the slightest trouble. I am never seasick, and—if you don't like to put into Valparaiso, any other Chilean port will do. Just as long as I can get to Valparaiso by the end of the month and ... and I truly wouldn't ask, except that Mrs. Smith assured me that you have a faultless reputation, the reputation of a *gentleman*, sir, that you are respected far and wide..."

Dexter's eyes widened. Then he shouted, "Whatever my reputation, madam, I do not run a packet ship. I do not carry passengers, and Mr. Martin should have told you that!"

"Oh, please, do not blame Mr. Martin!" she cried again, while Charlie Martin gazed at her adoringly. "Captain Smith and his wife overruled everything he said, they were absolutely positive that you would listen with sympathy to my request."

Dexter glared at Charlie, who went more beet-red than ever. Never had Dexter seen calf love written so plainly on a silly young man's face. He turned his inimical expression back to the girl, and snapped, "I don't buy oil when a condition is strung to the sale, Miss Gray. In fact, I don't make bargains with strings attached at all! And I most particularly don't make bargains with shifty Yankee merchants who think to use me as a means to get quit of their obligations!"

He knew he was shouting, but didn't care. *Faultless reputation*, he thought angrily, *respected as an obliging man*. Then he wondered if this intrusive waif thought him the most easily flattered of fools, and his lips set more tightly than ever.

He turned to Charlie Martin, and snapped, "Oblige me, sir, by returning Miss Gray to the whaleship."

"But, sir..."

"And please inform Captain Smith that I no longer wish to buy his oil."

7

"But, Captain Dexter!"

This cry was from the girl. He ignored the desperation in her voice, saying curtly, "Mr. Martin, please do it"—and there was tap on the door.

Dexter shouted, "What is it?" and swung round, fully expecting to see the presumptuous and shifty whaleship captain himself. However, instead of a short, bald spouter master, Bill the steerage boy stepped into the cabin.

Dexter glowered at him. The urchin was the misbegotten product of a Yankee beachcomber and a Tahitian girl, whose father had deserted him after the Tahitian girl died. An ageing missionary couple had tried to bring the boy up decently, but had given up on the thankless burden, and when Dexter had called at their mission station on Capricorn Island they had begged him to take the boy away. Dexter had done them the favor, had been kind and obliging, had taught the boy his ropes and his tables, and now he shouted, "Well, you little scoundrel, what is it?"

Bill's olive-skinned face was creased up with a knowing smirk. "Nothing more than this, sir, which I was ordered to carry to the cabin," he said in his mission-educated voice, and pointed downward, directing Dexter's glare to what lay by his grubby bare feet.

Those feet and the bare ankles above them protruded from patched dungarees that had grown all of a sudden far too short, and by those feet rested two valise-shaped wicker baskets, the kind that were commonly used for carrying magnums of champagne.

Dexter said impatiently, "Well?"

"I do believe they are the lady's duds, sir," said Bill, and had the sauce to fetch a grown-up leer. "A boat from the whaler come and left them, and the officer in charge of the boat put them in my care, sir, and ordered me to deliver them to your passenger, who was in the after quarters already, according to what he said."

Dexter said blankly, "What the hell?" But, before the boy

8

could answer, Miss Gray said in the most agitated of tones, "Oh, dear God, surely they haven't gammoned me?" Then, picking up her skirts, she flew through the double doors, dashed down the passage, and pelted up the three steps that led to the deck.

Dexter pelted after her. A detached part of his mind admired her ankles as she arrived on the deck ahead of him, neatly shod in little ribboned slippers, admirably slim and elegant, and surely wasted on that cumbrous form. Then she was at the starboard rail, where she leaned outwards so far that his hands went out of their own accord to catch her before she fell.

She shouted, "Goddamnit!" His hands dropped without touching her. For a moment he felt shocked, particularly as the curse was enunciated so clearly, in a cultured English accent. Then he saw the source of the girl's sudden fury. The sea was empty. Where he'd expected to see a whaleboat returning to a ship there were a couple of gulls flying low over the lonely waves.

Then he saw the whaleship. The *Humpback* was a good two miles off, filling for the horizon with every evidence of haste. "What the hell?" he said. He couldn't believe that the whaler had got so far in so short a time.

Charlie arrived, took one look, and shouted, "I'll kill him!"

"What?"

"That little bastard, Bill! I'll slaughter the boy, sir, I swear I will. They dropped off their passenger's baskets and paid him to keep shut about it until they were safely away, I know it!"

Dexter was certain Charlie was right. Fury seized him — impotent fury, for there was nothing he could do about it. The *Gosling* had the legs of the whaler, but six of his men were on the island, and he couldn't make sail without them. And it was his own bloody fault — he should have gone to the *Humpback* himself, instead of sending this callow young fool. The guilt made him even more furious.

Miss Harriet Gray dropped back from the rail, and turned and faced him. Dexter watched her straighten her shoulders. Then, having braced herself, she said very calmly, "Well, Captain Dexter, it seems we have no choice. I've been abandoned on your ship, left to your mercies, and you have a passenger, like it or not."

"Is that so? I am your servant, ma'am?" With savage irony, Dexter swept off his hat, took her slender hand, bowed low, and kissed it. He felt it tremble, but she didn't snatch it away. He let go, straightened, set his fists on his belt, and waited, glaring down at her.

Miss Harriet Gray did not seem intimidated. In fact, Dexter could have sworn he saw her lips twitch. The dark eyes definitely danced ... and in that moment he was in danger of finding her interesting. He almost began to wonder who she was, and why he should have known her name, what she'd been a-doing in New Zealand, and why it was so important she get to Valparaiso urgently... But it was just the effect of the starlight, and the silver of the moon, he decided, because when she moved a little so that her face was back in the shadow the moment of danger was over.

She said, "I am as sorry about this as you are, Captain Dexter. Captain Smith and his wife have made a fool of me, as well as gammoning you."

Fool. He didn't need reminding that a crafty old whaleman had gammoned him, or that he'd been tricked into taking this self-assured young minx into his care. Dexter sourly contemplated the implications. At least her presence would distract his men from their luckless hunt for pirate treasure on the island, he supposed, but snapped, "You should never have consented to accompany Mr. Martin to my brig!"

"But it's for only a week, a few days at the most..."

He shouted, "It will be less than that, Miss Gray! You'll be put on board the first vessel I speak, and I don't care what

10

kind of floating hulk it might be—it can be a barge, a scow or a—a dung-carrying *guano*-ship, for all I care, because I refuse to be made a fool of for even one week!"

She cried, "You can't do that to me, Captain Dexter!"

"And why not, pray?"

"I can't sail on a vessel where the master might be a notorious rogue!"

Dexter took a deep breath, bereft of words for a moment, and the ironic humor of the situation almost took over. He almost laughed. Not a notorious rogue? How little Miss Harriet Gray knew.

But then fury surged again, and he shouted, "And when you concluded—for some unfathomable reason—that I am not a notorious rogue, ma'am, did it not occur to you as an unaccompanied female that it was not just unwise, but also imprudent and improper to board a strange ship?"

She said blankly, "I beg your pardon?" Then, to his complete exasperation, she laughed. "Oh, don't be such a prig, Captain Dexter. Of course I knew there was no impropriety."

He lifted his brows, and said, "And what gave you that very strange idea?"

"Well, I believed, for a start, that Captain Smith was following on my heels. After all, he was the one who had to complete the oil sale. And Mrs. Smith assured me you are married."

"I'm ... *what?*"

"And that it's commonly known that you carry your wife to sea, Captain Dexter."

He stared, thunderstruck at first, then incredulous that she should be taken in so easily. He said flatly, "My God, you really are a fool," and headed for the door in the break of the poop.

He heard the busy rustle of her voluminous skirts as she pursued him, and Charlie Martin's shouts as he chased Bill about the decks. He had a glimpse of the imp tearing up the mainmast shrouds, but ignored it, and ignored Miss Gray, too, until she caught him up as he set his foot on the first stair, and stopped him with a hand on his arm.

She said, "Captain Dexter, what do you mean?"

"You were gammoned yet again, Miss Gray."

"What?"

He turned away, pulling his arm out of her grip, went the rest of the way to the mess cabin, and headed for his armchair at the head of the table. When he looked up she was standing at the other end of the table, with the light of the hanging lamp fully on her pale face, accentuating the hungry hollows in the smooth cheeks. She really was beautiful, he thought reluctantly. Like the slender ankles, that elfin face surely was wasted on that clumsy form.

She met his stare unwaveringly. "Mrs. Smith was loud in her praises of Captain Benjamin Dexter. She called you a gentleman of the sea. Was she lying?"

He let out a bark of mirthless laughter. "And who the hell is Benjamin Dexter?"

She stared. "*What?*"

"I've never heard of him. I doubt that he exists."

She blanched, and whispered, "Oh, dear God," and put a finger distractedly to her lips. As he watched she nibbled the tip of it in a nervous gesture … and for the first time he felt sorry for her, as if he really were the gallant and kindly gentleman of the sea that the Smiths had described.

She said wildly, "Then who the devil are you?"

"Jahaziel Dexter, ma'am," he said, and went back to eating his beans. They had gone cold, he noted with regret, but they tasted good, so he cleaned up his plate while she silently watched.

Let Charlie Martin deal with the problem of the inconvenient and unwanted passenger, he thought.

TWO

JAHAZIEL, thought Harriet, watching Charlie Martin pack up his duds and give his stateroom a quick tidy, preparatory to handing it over to her. *Jahaziel.* It was one of those quaint New England names taken out of the Bible, which Englishmen found so amusing. She wondered what Jahaziel Dexter's friends called him, but was certain at that moment that he had no friends.

What an unkind man … and those beans had smelled so delicious. She'd had trouble suppressing the wistful rumbles of her stomach as she'd watched him fork them up. She had missed supper, and midday dinner on the whaleship had been the usual weevilly pea soup with equally vermin-ridden hard ship's bread. Those beans … she could still smell them … and Mr. Martin's brandy breath, too, the brandy that had been lavished so generously while he and she were being gulled. Captain Jahaziel Dexter didn't seem to be able to comprehend that she and Mr. Martin were victims, too, she resentfully thought.

Then the perspiring Mr. Martin backed out with his duds, and she heard him throwing things around in the room next door, where he was evidently taking over some-one's berth—the second mate's, probably. She didn't hear

13

anyone arguing about it, so either the rightful occupant was completely cowed, or he was somewhere else. On the island? What the devil were they doing on the island, anyway? And how long would she be here, before the brig set sail and passed her onto the next vessel Captain *Jahaziel* Dexter spoke. Barge, scow, or guano-ship, she remembered, and sat down on the edge of the single narrow berth, contemplating her two baskets as she brooded over her impossible situation.

Finally, she heaved a great sigh, and stood up to tidy her dress — or, more accurately, to undress. The capacious cloak came off first. She shook it out and laid it on the bunk, where it would serve as her blanket, because Mr. Martin had taken his blanket away. Under the cloak she was wearing three shawls, and she took off all three and put them on top of the cloak. Folded, one would serve as her pillow, she thought. Then she pulled off her gown, revealing that she was wearing another gown underneath. After folding the gown she had removed, she reached under her skirt, and began to discard petticoats. At the end of the process she was back to her usual very slender self, wearing just underclothes, a petticoat, and a fine silk gown.

This wearing of most of her wardrobe was a family trick. In the past, it had made it easier to get away from boarding houses in a hurry, when her father didn't want to face the embarrassment of having to pay an extortionate bill. It was a heritage of life in England — so why had she worn so much of her wardrobe when she left the whaleship? What instinct had warned her to revert to this old, devious habit? She had sensed that the unpleasant Smiths weren't trustworthy, she realized now. Somehow, deep down, she had expected to be stranded on this brig. Such nasty, dishonorable, devious, underhand people, she thought.

Harriet sat down again. There was a little desk at the head of the berth, and on top of it lay a tall blue book. Without any qualms at all, she opened this, and turned to the beginning. "Comes in fine weather," she read, and "Light winds from the north." It was the brig's logbook, she knew then, and Mr. Martin would collect it in the morning, ready to make the next entry at noon.

It was bound to be boring, she thought, but she read on, because it helped to take her mind off her righteous anger. And, suddenly she found she was enjoying it, because the journal turned out to be so much more fascinating than she had expected. She read exotic names like Manila and Canton, and the names of marvelous cargoes, too — *bêche-de-mer*, pearl shell, silk taffetas, and spices. This brig had sailed on some very strange errands, and had taken poetic-sounding goods from other vessels, as well as discharging exotic cargoes at night, on coasts with unfamiliar names. This was no ordinary ship, she thought. Keeping her finger on the book to mark the spot where she had finished reading, she frowned into space as she remembered what the *Gosling* had looked like from the deck of the whaleship — what a romantic and dramatic picture this ship had made as Mr. Martin's boat pulled towards her.

Not a ship. A *brig*. A ship had three masts, but this brig had only two — two very tall masts, towering into the sky, and raked ... just so. The rake of her masts had made her look very much more piratical than any other vessels Harriet had seen. Her stern had had a beautiful swooping sheer as it rose above the waves, and above the sternboard, where the brig's name flourished in gilt, a gallery of many-paned windows had gleamed greenish in the sun. The name *Gosling* meant a baby goose, but the brig looked so much more dashing than a clumsy young bird. Swift, she thought, as if the *Gosling* often needed to escape from something. She had a white streak painted along each of her black sides, with squares to look like gunports — which was common enough, except that the *Gosling*'s gunports looked as if there were real cannon behind them, instead of being mere squares of black paint. The quarter deck was very long, she remembered, and had she glimpsed the glitter of two long-barreled guns at the stern? *Chasers*, she thought. Were they ever fired in anger, or to give a timely warning? What the devil, she thought, did Jahaziel Dexter do for a living? It didn't seem like ordinary trading and freighting at all.

Two hours later her reading stopped. She'd read the last entry. It was for 8 June, ten days before. The creaking quiet of the brig surrounded her. The night was warm, but she felt an uneasy shiver. Folding her arms tightly, she rubbed at the gooseflesh on her forearms. The logbook ... there was something wrong with the logbook, which covered more than two years.

Not only did the *Gosling* sail on very strange ventures, but at no time had the brig returned home to New England. Again, she shivered. When she stood up the hem of her skirt brushed the floor, and her movements seemed loud.

Mr. Martin had mumbled something about a place to wash, which was off the short lobby at the sternward end of the passage. He had also warned her that the door at the far end of the lobby led to the captain's private quarters in the stern, so not to go further than the washroom if she didn't want to intrude on his presence. The *head*, as he called it, in seafaring fashion, was the private head for the captain and the officers. The seamen and the petty officers had their own head, forward, so she didn't need to worry about them. Wryly, she thought that the possibility of blundering into the unfriendly captain was worry enough.

Harriet picked up a towel and half-opened the door of the little stateroom. When she peeped cautiously through the gap, the passage was empty. There was no sound from anywhere in the afterquarters, just the tread of whoever was on watch on the poop deck above, and the creak of the brig as she lay at her anchors. Harriet went across the passage and looked through the double doors into the mess cabin, and it was empty, too. The table had been cleared—by whom? — but there was still that homelike smell of baked beans.

Strange, she thought, and tried to shake off a dreamlike sense of delusion, because the brig rocked like a ship, but did not feel like one. The whaleship had been a working vessel, unmistakably, with all the damp and bilge that the term implied. Harriet had never lost consciousness of the fact that there were just a few planks between her and a watery eternity. What, she wondered, made the difference? It was the domesticity, she thought ... and yet there was no sign of a woman's touch. Jahaziel Dexter did not carry his wife, she remembered with a grimace.

She went back into the corridor, and tiptoed to the door at the end. She opened this very cautiously indeed, inch by inch, remembering the warning that the captain's private domain lay beyond. As Mr. Martin had described, it opened into a small lobby, with a door to her left. The light from a lamp diffused through the darkness, perhaps from a lantern in the captain's sitting room, but it was otherwise very dark. She felt for the latch to the door, opened it quickly, made sure there was no one there, and slipped inside. To her relief, the little room was lit, though only dimly, by a single small lamp hanging from a wall bracket.

The fixings were surprisingly domestic, as domestic as the mess cabin. There was a china basin with a drainpipe to let the water out, a china pitcher of clean fresh water in its own little niche, a towel on a hook, and a bar of yellow soap. The lavatory was a civilized one, with a wooden seat and a lid. Everything was very clean, and so she had no hesitation in going about her toilet.

Nonetheless, Harriet did everything very quickly, nervous that someone would come in, and was still drying her face as she left the room. Half-blinded by the towel, she stumbled, and caught up against a hard, warm frame. It came as a shock, as there had been no sound to warn her that there might be someone in the lobby, and she gasped,

17

jerked away, and almost fell. Large hands steadied her, and then held still, almost circling her narrow waist. She stood rigidly, trapped with the man in the little lobby, listening to his quiet breathing, unable to get to the door to the passage. Then she felt the long fingers shift upward, and sensed rather than heard the man's quick breath of surprise.

The circling hands moved up, up, spreading over her ribcage until they were halted by the swell of her breasts. She was in danger, she thought, *in danger*. A slow heavy pulse of time, and if she moved … if she moved…

The brig rocked softly, and the lamp in the other room swung, casting a halo of light, which fell across the intent face of the man who held her. It was Jahaziel Dexter. She saw him blink slowly.

Then he grinned lazily, and said, "So this was what was hidden underneath that cloak. Miss Gray, you surprise me."

She already knew that, and said nothing.

"You should take more care."

She thought, *Yes*, but still did not speak. Then she felt the intimate grip slacken and become casual. Another heartbeat, and then he backed away, opened the door, and held it for her.

Dexter said, "Good night," and even bowed a little, in his sardonic fashion. As she sidled past him, she kept her back very straight. Then she was in the passage. She heard the door shut behind her.

When she turned, to her vast relief the corridor was empty. Jahaziel Dexter had gone back into his own quarters. He had left her alone.

THREE

DESPITE her worries and problems, Harriet slept the heavy sleep of the utterly exhausted. Curled under the comfort of her cloak, she didn't stir until dawn, when she was wakened by busy sounds on the quarterdeck above her head.

She lay still, listening to footsteps and the bumping of heavy objects, wondering groggily where she was, because this did not feel like the whaleship. Then came the creaking sounds of the lowering of a boat, followed by a splash, and all at once she remembered what had happened. When she heard the clop and splash of oars nearby, she knelt up on the bed to peer through the nearest of the two portholes that were set into the top of the bulkhead by the side of her berth.

A boat bobbed into view, a halfboat that had been made by cutting a whaleboat in half and patching on a blunt transom to make a dinghy. She recognized Mr. Martin's back as he sat working the tiller. There were two oarsmen, who stared right at her, and she became uneasily aware that they could see her face, disembodied like a goldfish in a bowl. One of the oarsmen was a crab-faced fellow, who frowned with displeasure, and the other winked broadly, and pouted his lips in a travesty of a kiss. Harriet hurriedly slid down and got dressed. This time, she put on just the normal number of clothes, but chose an everyday gingham dress, instead of the more revealing silk gown.

While she pulled it on, she wondered how many men lived on the brig, and what they were saying about her, and how in the name of all Providence she was going to manage to keep them at bay. It had been bad enough in New Zealand, after she had been left alone to live off her wits, but this was worse. If only, if *only* the captain had been the gentleman of the sea the Smiths had promised. Anger stirred, and she brushed her hair with unnecessary vigor. Then a cock crowed—a rooster!

Where? From the stern, she was certain. Then she heard the clucking of hens. Did Captain Dexter have eggs? Perhaps she heard pigs, in a pen. Did the brig have bacon? Her stomach rumbled in most unladylike fashion. Then she wondered if he would be callous enough to deny her breakfast. She was horridly sure that he would—but then she smelled coffee! Captain Dexter must have a steward, she thought—and perhaps the steward was kinder than his master. With luck, the captain was on deck, and she could cajole the steward into pouring her a mug. Before she could think to stop her feet, those feet carried her pell-mell across the passage and through the double doors into the cabin.

One step inside, and she lurched to a stop. Too late, Harriet had realized that the table had occupants already. Two boys sat there. They were mere lads, young men who were less than twenty, she thought. Surely not old enough to be the brig's second and third officers? But they must be the mates, because life on the whaleship had taught her that only officers ate in the after quarters. Both were handsome, in a dashing sort of way, but were otherwise opposites of each other. One had lint-colored hair, and the other had long black ringlets, and an olive complexion.

The one with pale hair grinned, and the dark one studied her with melting eyes, obviously considering himself a ladies' man. Harriet contemplated them with a cool expression, but was nervously aware that they had been talking to each other, and that the chat had stopped when she opened the door.

The two boys smiled on, not at all deterred by her haughty air. So Harriet changed tack. She took a deep breath, smiled brilliantly, and exclaimed in her clear English voice, "Good morning!"

Neither boy answered. Harriet wavered on the brink of dashing back to the stateroom—but then she was saved by the sudden opening of the pantry door.

A tall thin man came out, and looked all around. "Do I hear no politeness?" he demanded. "None of our far-famed courtesy?"

The boys leapt to their feet. The one with tow-colored hair said, "Sorry, ma'am, good morning, Miss Gray," while the one with the black ringlets fetched a bow, one that was not mocking at all, but redolent with Old World courtesy.

"And I too, Miss Gray, am much obliged," said the tall thin man.

Harriet looked back at him, thinking that *she* was the one who was obliged, because his was the first really friendly face she had seen in weeks. As she gazed up at him, he beamed down at her. He had luxuriant gray sheeplike whiskers but was mostly bald on top, so that his face seemed upside-down.

He said, "We on the brig *Gosling* are generally known for our good manners, but our boys have let us down, Miss Gray, and I apologize deeply, on their behalf."

Harriet smiled and waved a dismissive hand, though she was starting to find it vexing that they all knew her name, but she knew none of theirs.

As if he had read her mind, the tall, thin man cried, "Introductions! Introductions! This, Miss Gray, is Mister Valentine Fish, and this"—*this* being the lad with black ringlets—"is Mister Crotchet."

Crotchet? Good lord, thought Harriet.

21

"*À votre service*," said the dark boy in an unfamiliar kind of accent, and fetched another bow.

"I'm a Massachusetts lad," contributed Valentine, "and Crotchet hails from Lower Louisiana."

"And I," said the tall, thin man, "if I may make so bold as to introduce myself, am Bodfish. Steward of the brig *Gosling*," he added.

Harriet said nothing, because she was feeling rather hysterical. Bodfish and Fish, Fish, Bodfish and Crotchet. It sounded like a musical turn. Then the steward thrust forward his hand, and she found herself shaking a long, bony palm.

"Coffee?" he said.

"Oh, yes," sighed Harriet. "Yes, please, Mr. Bodfish." She wondered where Captain Dexter might be, and hoped he wouldn't turn up until she had safely breakfasted.

"Then please be seated." A rag appeared like magic in the bony hand, and was swept over one of the benches that ran down the long sides of the table.

Harriet sat down, and Mr. Fish and Mr. Crotchet sat on the bench opposite. Mr. Fish winked, but Harriet ignored the saucy boy. It was much more pleasant to watch the battered coffee pot that that was produced as dexterously as the rag, and tipped over three enormous mugs.

"You may be surprised," said Mr. Bodfish indulgently as he poured, "to find a steward in such a person as myself—and why not, for I'm amazed, too! I shipped in Lahaina in December," he said. "As a foremast hand. Imagine that!"

Harriet indeed found it hard to imagine, and Mr. Fish let out a muffled snort.

"I have done better in the past, and I don't mind admitting it. Clerk at times, purser at others. Commerce, most surely, is more in my line. But when the chance came to ship with Captain Dexter, I grasped it, not caring how lowly the position might be. Men apply in their dozens to ship with Captain Dexter, you know."

"They do?" said Harriet politely. She didn't believe him for an instant. Even in her most landbound innocence she knew that captains and agents had to stoop to connivance and crime to fill the forecastles of their ships.

"'Tis on account of the grub," said Mr. Fish.

Bodfish had disappeared into the pantry again. Harriet said nothing, satisfying herself with one haughty glance, and Bodfish reappeared with a plate of warm soft bread.

Fresh bread! There was butter, too, good butter that was as astounding on a ship as the good sugar in the bowl. Harriet closed her eyes as her teeth sank into the deliciousness, luxuriating in taste and smell and texture. When she opened them again, still blissfully chewing, the steward was watching her.

"Good?" he benevolently asked.

"Oh — *excellent.*"

"I did have my qualms about being steward, and I don't mind admitting it. But no sooner had I learned to furl the main royal all by myself, and no sooner had I worked off my share in the *Gosling* Company, than Captain Dexter held a meeting, on account of the steward not wishing to be steward any more. He wanted to shift to the foc'sle, Miss Gray, so Captain Dexter called for a volunteer. It was a challenge indeed, for if the captain's high standards not be met then it is squally times and no mistake. But before I knew it my feet had stepped me forward."

Harriet looked at those feet. They were very long and thin, no doubt as bony as his hands, encased in elastic-sided boots.

Then she said, "Share? In the *Gosling* Company?"

"Yes. You find my bread acceptable?"

"Oh, yes!" She looked about for another slice, but Fish and Crotchet had demolished the lot.

"Bread needs a routine, I've found." The steward's long face was tilted ruminatively, while one hand whisked his rag about as if of its own volition. "Like any growing thing, yeast needs its sameness. Every night I go to bed betimes, and the flour, ready sieved, and the yeast, ready mixed, do the same. I rise early in the morning, and so does the bread. We have soft bread twice a day and hard biscuit every meal, all hands the same, coffee twice, tea twice. Irish Cookie and I pride ourselves on our culinary expertise, Miss Gray, and Captain Dexter commends us, so surely that ain't self-praise?"

"Of course not," she said, and he smiled benevolently, and disappeared back into the pantry.

Putting on her sweetest voice, she said to the towheaded boy, "And where were you when you shipped on the brig, Mr. Fish?"

"In Charleston, nigh on a year ago."

"And ... Crotchet?"

"Crotchet," he said, "hails from Lower Louisiana, and I—"

"Yes, yes—but surely Crotchet is an unusual name?"

"Crozet—André Crozet," said the boy with black ringlets, and smiled bewitchingly.

"Crotchet shipped in the same port, naught but five months after me, only I dunno that we can call him *shipped* for he joined us by accident," said Valentine Fish. "We were four hours out when we found him curled up and snoring drunk in a coil of rope amidships, wearing nothing but his drawers and a gold Harland watch—"

"Mr. Fish!" ejaculated Bodfish, coming out of the pantry. He sounded as affronted as a society matron—but Harriet did not pause to feel amused, for she scented what he was carrying.

Fish, freshly caught, freshly fried fish. Despite the bread she was hungry again. There had been fish served on the *Humpback*, salt fish, boiled fish, fish heads staring from chipped and dirty plates, all of which had been the opposite of appetizing, but this fish was moist and fragrant, cooked

24

by the lightest of hands.

Bodfish heaped her plate and then gave the rest to the boys. Valentine and Crotchet fell to at once, eating with adolescent appetite, and Harriet ate heartily herself, for who knew when—or where—she would eat again? The food on a barge, scow or guano-ship was certain to be suspect— though Captain Dexter was unlikely to speak one while his brig was lying at this island, she meditated.

Again, she wondered what he was doing here. According to the logbook, the brig had arrived on 8 June, and surely it didn't take ten days to take on wood, fresh water, and fruit?

She said to the boys, "Do you know when the brig will weigh anchor and make sail?"

"Oh, today, I should imagine," said Valentine Fish in his confident way.

Oh dear, she thought. There could be any number of scows and barges to speak, once they left this anchorage, because they were on the trade route to South America. "Are you sure?"

"No, we ain't, ma'am," said Crotchet in his soft French-accented Southern voice. She looked at him attentively, much preferring him to the self-assured Mr. Fish. "The Company has to discuss the matter yet," he told her. "But I'd wager, ma'am, if you'd care to put a bet on it, that we will set sail this very day, for even the most hopeful of men are ready to give it up."

Give up? Give up what?

Harriet said cautiously, "You do business here?"

"Yes, ma'am, but not the great business we thought we would do," he said, and filled his mouth again.

Harriet watched him, frowning. She had looked a long time at the island the day before, from the rail of the whaleship. It was strangely intimidating, with massive cliffs that rose vertiginously from the sea. People lived there, she had observed—she'd seen glimpses of chimney tops and tiled roofs, domesticated orchards, and even the spire of a church. Men had been working near the edge of the cliffs, tilling the soil at the top of the rock, laboring to make the dirt produce.

Perhaps other men made a living fishing off the rocks, she thought. This very fish might have been bought from the inhabitants ... but what was this business the *Gosling* men were doing on the island, the business that hadn't worked out well? Trading with the natives? Or smuggling something onto shore?

She said tentatively, "I saw a boat leave for the island this morning."

"That was Mr. Martin," said Valentine Fish, and his saucy grin widened. "Miserable he be this morning, like the last three days of a very wicked life. He'll hassle them boys, I reckon, they'll get a tongue-lashing like what they didn't expect. I'll take a boat there myself, in a few minutes, or thereabouts," he added.

"But I wager that we'll be away by sunset, ma'am," said Crotchet. His smile was coaxing. "You wouldn't care to put some money on it?"

"Certainly not," said Harriet.

And the fancy mahogany double doors flew open, and Jahaziel Dexter strode into the cabin.

FOUR

THE two boys left. She had never seen young men move so fast. One moment they were there, and the next they were not, and she was left alone with their skipper.

Harriet watched that skipper very warily, but he merely twinkled at her as he sat down in his armchair. When he smiled his lean brown cheeks creased up, faunlike in a face that had a natural lopsided humor. He was freshly shaven, and the sun through the skylight emphasized his quizzical eyebrows in an expression that she reluctantly found attractive.

He said, "Please don't leave the table on my account, Miss Gray."

She stared back resentfully, finding no trouble at all in hating him, for she'd had no intention of leaving the table, at all. Or not, at any rate, until she was more certain of her future.

Now that he had delivered his first broadside, however, Jahaziel Dexter ignored her. The steward brought in more fish, more coffee and more bread, and Harriet watched Captain Dexter eat, determined not to speak until he did.

It did not seem to embarrass him in the slightest that she watched him. In fact, Harriet had the distinct impression

27

that he was enjoying it. He cut up his fish with a fork and piled the glistening flakes onto bread. Then he ate with his fingers, with the neat swift movements of a cat, to all appearances as if she weren't there.

Those hands were strong, with businesslike palms and long fingers, the flat clean nails sunk into the skin with years of grappling with wet rope and canvas. She wondered how old he was — twenty-five? His appetite was youthful, but years had gone into the creasing up of his face, and the set of his shoulders was broad with experience. He was wearing a striped shirt and buckskin trousers tucked into rawhide boots, and a soft thin leather weskit, unbuttoned. He smelled of leather, too, a clean smell of leather and soap.

Then she heard bumps up on deck. Mr. Fish was lowering his boat, she thought, and tilted her head to look at the skylight. When she looked back at Captain Dexter he had finished eating, and was watching her.

He smiled and said, "Did you enjoy your breakfast?"

She scowled back, certain he begrudged her the food. "It was excellent, thank you."

"We do ourselves well here."

"You do, indeed." If the men of the brig ate as well as they had done this morning, she thought, then Captain Dexter was robbing the owners blind.

"A good appetite," he mused, "is, in my opinion, a virtue."

She had eaten rather a lot, she thought uneasily.

"Even in an uninvited guest."

She stared at him with simmering dislike, and snapped, "I intend to pay for my passage."

"What passage?" he inquired, and grinned.

"Captain Dexter, I am as anxious to quit your brig as you are to be rid of me," she returned heatedly. "But that seems impossible as long as your brig is lying here. Barges, scows and guano-ships don't call here very often, I'm sure."

"That's true," he admitted, and his eyes glinted, almost

28

on the verge of laughter. For the first time she registered that his eyes were green. His hair was an unremarkable brown color, but his eyes were a bright hazel green.

She waited, but he merely twinkled at her, so she said very cautiously, "But you're still determined to put me on the next ship you speak?"

To her surprise he laughed, a full-bodied laugh of genuine amusement. "No, no," he said. "I wouldn't do that, not even to a waif who is as inconvenient as you. I was in a passion when I made that threat. Now, in the light of day, I've repented. How could I live with my conscience if I left you in the care of some notorious rogue of a guano-ship master? My conscience might be tattered, but it really wouldn't let me do that."

Harriet watched him very suspiciously indeed. He didn't look the least repentant, and she didn't trust him an inch. "So what will you do?"

"Ah..." He paused, while she simmered in suspense. He watched her face; he looked up at the skylight; he sipped his coffee, and all the time she wished she could shake him. Then he said idly, "I'll steer for Capricorn."

"Capricorn?" She'd never heard of the place.

"It's an island, just a couple of days away. Beautiful place, very friendly natives, but I won't drop anchor there. There's only one gap in the reef, you see, and the risk of getting windbound is too great. I'll send you ashore in a boat."

Half of what he'd said did not make sense to her, but the import was plain enough. She said, horrified, "You're going to *maroon* me? On an *island*? What the devil do you think I am, sir? A *pirate*?"

"Oh, you won't be there long," he assured her with a chuckle. "Not a pretty girl like you. Lots of whaleships anchor in the lagoon to take on freshwater and coconuts ... bananas ... breadfruit. It might take a few weeks, but you should have no trouble at all in persuading some skipper to carry you to his next destination."

"Oh, my God!" She was on her feet, trembling with rage. "You can't do that to me, Captain Dexter!"

"I can't?" He seemed to think about it, because he then said musingly, "Then you will have to stay with us until we get to our next port."

For an instant, hope flickered. "Next port?"

"Auckland, New Zealand."

"What!" Horror rushed through her, chilling her heart. "But I can't go back there, I can't!"

"As an uninvited guest, you have very little choice, my dear Miss Gray."

"Do I not?" she cried, flying into a panicked rage. "Don't be so sure of that, Captain Dexter! The reins of my fate are still firmly in my hands! Your brig has proved a most uncomfortable refuge—despite the excellence of the rations! I might be—what was it?—an inconvenient waif—and one, furthermore, with a most inconvenient appetite!—but I coped alone in New Zealand, Captain Dexter, and I can cope alone here!"

She was shouting in her passion. Bodfish popped out of the pantry, the very picture of alarm at her noise, but Captain Dexter, to her utter exasperation, merely looked the picture of a most diverted man. "Tut," he murmured. "Such a temper —and what the devil do you mean, Miss Gray? Cope alone here? Cope alone where?"

"I mean that you can leave me here, sir! Why put up with my unwanted presence for the two days it would take to get me to Capricorn? I am happy to go on shore at *this* island, sir—and in fact I insist on it!"

"Jehovah," said he, sounding most astounded. Then, to the further detriment of her temper, he let out a roar of laughter. "Such eloquence," he said, when he had calmed down. "And what a tantrum. Is this why Captain Smith was so keen to get rid of you?"

For a moment she was truly afraid she would lose the

last shreds of control, and hit him. He discerned as much, she saw, for his grin widened even further, and he unfolded his arms and began to duck. She stamped her foot and left the cabin in a furious rush of skirts, dashing headlong up the stairs to deck, where she informed the astonished Valentine Fish that she would be obliged if he would wait a little, as she was coming in his boat to shore.

FIVE

MR. Fish's boat was another halfboat. Harriet sat tensely in the stern by the tiller, watching the island as the two silent oarsmen pulled toward it, both of them staring at her with riveted round eyes. She was wearing most of her wardrobe again, and her two baskets leaned on her knee, but the heat of her temper was cooling fast, its vigor quenched with foreboding. The island looked ... menacing, and she had just remembered its name.

Judas Island. There were fleeing mares' tails of clouds crossing the sun, causing shadow and light, but Judas Island seemed shadowed all of the time. There was no reef and no lagoon; the island rose precipitously from the sea, and the water at the base of the cliffs was dark and secret, full of serpentlike writhings of kelp.

The boat knocked against the rocks. Great rusty chains hung down from iron rings set into the granite. Harriet reached up to grasp one to steady herself as she stood, and the metal crumbled into a gritty handful of rust. For some strange reason, she was chilled with a shiver of foreboding. Horizontal shadows in the cliff face marked rough terraces that unknown people had cut in the past, and there were shallow caves and piles of discarded shells to show past feasts.

The boat bobbed up and down wildly, but she jumped on shore by herself, disdaining the oarsmen's offered help. She did allow Mr. Fish, however, to carry her baskets. Picking up her skirts, she trudged determinedly after him, up the narrow, zigzag track to the top. They were heading, she thought, to the place where the islanders had been tilling the soil. She wondered what language they spoke and thought it must be Spanish. But Spanish hospitality, she remembered, was famous. And there would be women in the village, she was certain. The thought was wonderfully bracing. Then all at once she arrived at the top.

She turned, looking around the scene that had opened out. Below her — the brig, floating, as beautiful as a dream in the blue-green of the bay. As she watched, the whaleboat that was slung from the stern was being lowered. Captain Dexter was coming, she thought with distaste, and looked away, along the top of the island.

Rolling grassy hillocks undulated inland toward the trees and the rooftops she had seen from the whaler. On the tilled ground immediately before her, men straightened from their digging to stare. For a long moment she couldn't understand why they looked familiar, and then she recognized Mr. Martin, his face red and grimy. He, like the others, was holding a shovel. They were all seamen, she abruptly deduced — *seamen from the brig*. Holes pocketed the ground, joined by strings stretched from stakes, as if to mark out a crazy playground.

She said blankly, "What the devil are you doing?"

Charlie Martin stalked toward her, looking not at all like the amiable soul who had been gulled by the Smiths, and had borne her so gallantly on board the brig. He rubbed a forehead that obviously hurt, and said stiffly, "I'm not at liberty to tell you that, Miss Gray. But what I want to know is what the h— what in tarnation you are a-doing here. Mr. Fish, please explain yourself!"

34

Valentine Fish said, "She insisted on coming, sir, and there was nothing I could do about it."

"You didn't ask the captain's permission before letting her into your boat?"

Harriet snapped, "Mr. Fish didn't need to ask permission. It was my own decision, and mine entirely."

She glared, and Mr. Martin rolled his eyes up as if appealing to Providence. Then she heard a peevish voice say, "She enticed our cadet, that's what, she seduced him with her female wiles, she give out unseemly orders to an officer of our own vessel, and she but a passenger and female at that, who ain't but got no right to make decisions."

She swung about, and met the rheumy stare of the crabfaced fellow who had pulled an oar in Mr. Martin's boat that morning. She snapped, "I am not a passenger, I have resigned the position. So whine on, do, for your whining means naught to me."

It was almost soothing to see the man's mouth sag open. Then she heard Charlie say in tones of utmost consternation, "But what are you a-going to do if you're not our passenger any more, Miss Gray?"

Harriet paused, her pose consciously melodramatic. She looked about, at the holes, the strings, the raptly attentive seamen, the rolling hills and the distant rooftops—and all at once the sun came out. The grim scene was abruptly friendly, the short grass a kindly green.

She turned back to him, smiled graciously, and said, "When Captain Dexter arrives—which I see will be soon— kindly inform him that I have gone to the village."

Charlie Martin squawked, "But you can't do that!"

"Why not, Mr. Martin? Are there snakes?"

She saw him blink, and blankly shake his head. He winced, putting his hand to his forehead again, and mumbled, "I can't say I ever saw one."

"Well, then," she said, "there seems to be no problem." Then she nodded at her audience, took the handles of her

35

valise-like baskets, and set off inland. No one tried to stop her.

By the time Captain Dexter arrived at the top of the cliff, Charlie was about to cry mutiny. His mood and his headache were awful. It was impossible to believe that these were the very same *Gosling* men who'd begun their digging with such exuberant optimism ten days before. Ten days of nothing had rendered them lazy, and when he'd arrived with Dan and Abijah that morning, the men who had camped here overnight were not digging at all. Instead they were still about the breakfast campfire, yarning, and Charlie had had to shout sharp to get them back to their shovels. They had shambled then toward the diggings, but then Dan and Abijah had let out the news of the passenger, and that had been the end of their work.

Instead, they had set to trading dirty stories. Ten days on dry land with nothing but digging and measuring to do had made them as rascally as oat-fed colts, and Dan Kemp and Tib Greene were the worst. They were fond of saying that they had shipped together and would go to hell together, and now their laughter was the loudest, and their questions the rudest. Miss Gray was a decent young female, a lady in distress, Charlie insisted, and he was most heartily ashamed of them all, and their dirty comments and salacious jokes were nothing short of scandalous.

Goddamnit, she was English, he protested, but that made the situation worse, for Tib produced a yarn about an Englishwoman who stowed away on a trader out of New York, having run away from an Australian penal settlement. The captain of that trader certainly *helped* that woman, my God he did, and then when he had finished a-helping her, he had handed her on to the crew. She had been more of a pain than a pleasure, though, or so he ruminated. My God, she had a temper on her, and so the crew of the trader had been glad to get quit of her at the first island they'd touched. The last anyone had heard, the natives had gotten fed-up with her nasty temper, too, and had killed and eaten her, just to get some peace.

It had been at this stage in the yarn that Miss Gray had put in her appearance — which had been doubly unfortunate, as Charlie ruminated, since she had exhibited a touchy temper of her own. When Dexter hove into sight over the top of the cliff, he thought he had never been so glad to see his skipper.

He told Captain Dexter about it, at exasperated length. Dexter listened patiently, remembering rather wryly that Miss Gray had promised that she would be no trouble. "And," said Charlie moodily, "she has a fair old temper."

"You noticed?"

"Aye, sir. In fact, I reckon she might be about crazy."

Never, Dexter mused, had he seen calf-love wilt and die so quickly. He said mildly, "She seems coherent enough."

"But to storm off to the village like that, sir, surely it ain't the act of a balanced temperament?"

"Perhaps she thought she had a good reason."

Dexter sighed then, thinking that Harriet was more melodramatic than crazy, and said, "We'd better sent a man along after her, to fetch her back and keep her out of trouble. She's likely to turn an ankle at the very least. Who can we trust with such a delicate errand?"

"Jonathan?" hazarded Charlie, and Dexter sighed again, for hayseed Jonathan was such an unlikely proposition. However, he agreed, for every choice was a bad one.

Jonathan was summoned, and ordered to get Miss Gray and bring her back, and then he set off muttering rebelliously, trailing a wake of catcalls and whistling and dirty suggestions. Then, when his shambling form had disappeared, Chips, the chairman of the *Gosling* Company, called an extraordinary meeting.

It was no less than Dexter had expected. Ten days of fruitless digging had discouraged them all, and they were ready to give up and make sail. But, the Company being what the Company was, none of them would allow that to happen without a proper meeting and a proper vote.

Bodfish was the secretary, and because of that Dexter had brought him out from the brig. This meant there were only three souls left on board—Bill, because he was too young to be a proper member of the Company, Cookie the Irishman because he had a rooted objection to the English custom of voting, and the nameless ex-slave they all called Davy Jones Locker, because no one had managed to persuade Davy that a black man was allowed to vote in a white man's meeting.

For safety's sake, the meeting should really have been held on the brig, but the problem of Miss Harriet Gray had made that impossible. Dexter sat down on a nearby rock, quenching yet another sigh. Bodfish perched on a second rock with a notebook on his knee and his pencil poised in his hand. Everyone shuffled about, and gradually the muttering died down.

Chips said gruffly, "I declare this meeting in order and open. This matter a-fore us..."

Abijah cried, "But what about the minutes?"

"Is that necessary, for an extraordinary meeting?"

"Of cuss it is, of cuss! How can we do things proper if we don't start proper? If you can't get it right, then we need a new chairman."

Everyone shifted, and Dan and Tib muttered. Chips turned his pipe over and puffed great clouds of offended upside-down smoke. Bodfish rattled papers, radiating martyrdom, and then recited crossly, "Minutes of the meeting of the *Gosling* Company Friday June the eight, 1848, commenced with gales from east nor'east, heading sou'east, steering for Judas Island, called a meeting of the Company at six p.m. to act on various suggestions recommended by the board of directors, namely that we send parties on shore to dig for treasure. After discussion the matter was put to the vote..."

Dexter stopped listening. Instead of paying attention, he wondered what Miss Harriet Gray had made of the Judas Island village.

SIX

HARRIET trudged with her head down, a basket in each hand, her cloak about her. The clouds had left the sun and the sky was full of birds, but she was hot, sweaty, and very apprehensive. Everything was so unreal. It an unsettlingly empty landscape, with no sounds of people ... and why had those seamen been digging those holes? There was something very wrong about it all, she thought, and despite her heavy clothes and the hot sun, she shivered.

Empty, it was all so empty. No sounds, except for the distant shush of the sea and the birds. When a gull screamed directly over her head, she flinched. Trees loomed ahead, though, promising cool shadow. Her step quickened.

Then the trees were all around her. They were fruit trees in rows ... mango, avocado, fig, and grape ... but their branches were neglected and tangled. The mango fruit lay all about, and Harriet could smell the rubbery scent of their spicy running juice. She wondered why Captain Dexter had not sent a party to gather them up. After all, there was no one to stop them from taking the harvest...

And that was what was so uncanny and unsettling. There were no humans in this place. No human voices. The trees had no caretakers, and the village ahead was just as silent. *No human voices.* Harriet was suddenly very afraid. She had to force herself to leave the shelter of the trees and walk into the village.

The village was nothing more than a handful of cracked adobe houses. They were built about a dusty plaza in the old South American style, all crouched in the sun, the shadow of the jagged church spire falling like a broken needle over them. Nothing moved, and no one came out to inquire her business. Even the birds were quiet. The houses waited, empty ruins, populated by ancient ghosts — angry ghosts, for the buildings had been half-destroyed with a ferocity that was human, and not just that of time. Something dreadful had happened here, or so she sensed. The sun shone inside the ruined church, but the sun outside seemed cleaner.

A movement, at the corner of her eye. Harriet's heart leaped into her throat. She stood in the middle of the plaza by a broken-down well, looking around wildly. Another stealthy rustle. She cried out hoarsely, "Who goes there?" and a yellow dog came slinking out from behind a cracked wall. Its chest was furrowed cruelly with prominent ribs. It ran in the other direction, away from her. Harriet's trembling fingers let go of her baskets and grasped the parapet of the well. Shivering, she turned and looked down the well ... down...

Down to a far-off gleam of secret water, and a pale round reflection within. It was like looking down an endless wet tunnel. The effect was eerie, and for a terrible instant she felt as if she were falling. The round pale shape beckoned her. Then, dryly swallowing, she thought it must be the reflection of the sun on the water. A lizard flickered by her hand, and she bit back a frightened yell. Then, behind her, she heard a footstep.

This time she did scream, whirling round as the scream was jerked out of her. There was a young man there, scowling at her. He didn't wear a hat, and his short brown hair stuck up in spikes all over the top of his head.

42

He said, "Did I a-fear you, miss?"

She took a deep, shaky breath. "You most certainly did."

"Ah," he said, and looked gratified at the accuracy of his guess. "I be Jonathan. Cap'n Dexter and Mr. Martin, they told me to fetch you."

She said, "I see," biting down the words *Thank God*, trying to gather some shreds of dignity. When he picked up her baskets and set off, though, her feet betrayed how scared she really was, because they kept pace with him so eagerly.

He seemed very silent, and when she smiled politely, his scowl deepened. He wore overalls, and he shambled as he walked, and his freckled, sun-reddened forehead was heavily furrowed.

Then, as they passed through the trees, he suddenly said, "Say summat, ma'am."

"What?" She almost laughed. "But why?"

"Nobbut, miss, but to hear your voice. You come from the old country, they tell me."

"If *they* mean England, then *they* are right."

"But you been living summat else, they say." He paused, and then went on with mysterious disapproval, "New South Wales, they say."

"What?" She stared, and then said coldly, "I've been living in New Zealand, if that holds interest."

"But they knew it must be summat where they speak true English, and that you been in New South Wales for a long time, too, for we can all understand what you say, ma'am, and they do tell me that be plumb unusual, in folks what hail from old Lunnon. In old Lunnon, they tell me, they hardly speak to one another at all, their speech being so sundered that they be at their wits' end to understand what each other says."

Harriet paused, unsure whether to be insulted or amused, and in the end said, "New Zealand is not in New South Wales, Jonathan."

"No? Wa'al, I guess it makes no mite of difference, for I

be certain sure, ma'am, that New Zealand and New South Wales both be barbaric places. You have to come to America, now, to see some real sights."

"I do?" She snapped, "Then it amazes me that you left America and chose to be a seaman."

"But I ain't no seaman!"

"You're not?"

"I be a Massachusetts man, and right proud to say so. My gran'pappy fought on Bunker Hill, a true-blue son of American liberty, jest like my pappy and myself, and we can say we're true-blue sons without any argument, for true-blue men all fight with guns."

"Well," said Harriet, deciding to be amused, "I must take care to avoid any battle of words with you. I trust, if I ask you what brings you here, it won't lead to a bout of gun-slinging?"

This foxed the boy completely, she saw, for he furrowed his brow in the mighty effort of trying to work it out. Taking pity on him, she said, "So, if you are not a seaman, what is your trade?"

"I be a carpenter, ma'am, and on the brig I be carpenter's mate to Chips, because he be bo'sun as well as carpenter, so needs a mate, seeing as he does double duty."

She blinked, because she thought a carpenter would find plenty of work on land, and said, "Why did you come to sea, then?"

"To make my fortune, of course!"

"What else?" she agreed, still amused. Then, looking thoughtfully about the rolling slopes, she said, "Do the men hope to find a fortune in those holes they are digging?"

"About that, ma'am, I am not at liberty to say."

"You're not? Tell me about Captain Dexter, then. Did you join his brig in Massachusetts?"

"Cap'n Dexter in Massachusetts?" he exclaimed, then snorted pityingly, and said, "Don't they even know in Lunnon that Cap'n Dexter dassent show his face in New

44

England?"

"*What?*"

"He'd be arrested, and probably hanged."

"My God!" Harriet stopped short, remembering her tirade about notorious rogues. "What in God's name has he done?"

"About that, ma'am, I am not at liberty to say, neither."

"Not at liberty?" she cried, at the end of her tether. "You don't seem to be at liberty about much at all, yet four minutes ago you assured me that you are a true-blue son of American liberty! What more liberty do you need, pray?"

If he had had a gun, she saw then, that would have been the end of things, because he was positively snorting with rage. "Ma'am," he said. "You may as well shut your mouth, because I ain't going to tell you what you're so plumb intent on knowing. And you may as well put your mind to that, for I ain't susceptible, I ain't."

She shook her head, puzzled. "You're not susceptible to what?"

"Your wiles, ma'am. They all told me when I were given this job to watch out for your female wiles. They told me you would tease me, ma'am, and told me too that if you tried your tricks, I were to tell you straight I am as good as married."

"They did?" she said dangerously.

"Aye. Mary-Jane at home be my intended, and I promised her faithful to be true."

"And may the best of connubial bliss be yours," she snapped.

"Thankee, ma'am, but that won't alter my disposition."

"And I am not accustomed, sir, to being the subject of salacious talk!" But she was, she mourned furiously, she was, and familiar shame and frustration threatened to rise inside her, bringing angry tears.

Then a volley of shots sounded from ahead, from the diggings, and she cried out in shock, "What's that?"

Jonathan began to run, in great shambling strides. She ran beside him, clutching her cloak with convulsive fingers. "They want us back fast," the boy gasped. Black clouds were gathering over the face of the sun. A sharp gust of wind jerked at her skirts and her cloak, and then they crested the hill. The diggings were before them.

The first man she saw was Jahaziel Dexter. She recognized him instantly by his height and his hat, and unthinkingly ran over to him. He put out a hand to stop her but did not turn. Like the other men he was staring downward into one of the holes they had dug. Then a man cried out from the depths.

Harriet gripped the tossing edges of her cloak. A man came into view, bursting frantically out of the hole, followed closely by another. The men at the top all lurched back, scattering away from the leaking edge of the excavation. More dirt fell and disappeared as the edge collapsed, and Harriet saw the pit that the digging had revealed.

The dark hole was lit to one side by a shaft of light that seeped in from the bottom. It was as if there had been a cliffside entrance to the pit, which at some time in the past had been filled in. One man remained at the bottom of the hole. Harriet saw him bend and then straighten with something long and brown in his fist.

He thrust it upward, and someone took it. It was a bone, a long bone, a human bone, a femur. Thunder rumbled, almost drowning out the babble as the men around all talked at once. They milled about, their faces drawn with ghoulish fascination. Lightning flickered silently on the horizon.

Harriet looked at Captain Dexter. He had his fists propped on his hips and his hat tilted back. Like all of his men, he seemed unaware of her. Lightning pulsed again, and his silhouette was framed with silent blue fire. Then he spoke. She did not hear the words, but a rope was produced, and two men lowered into the hole.

46

Other men took up shovels and began to hack at the edges of the hole to make the gap bigger. The dirt resisted and then flopped out of sight with loud pattering sounds of earth and stones. A fist appeared above the edge of the hole, handing up something round ... and pale. Lightning licked again, and Harriet saw that the object was a human skull.

Someone took it, and it was handed round quickly and nervously. She could hear men trying to make feeble jokes. Some, like the skull, were grinning. Jahaziel Dexter said something again, and a bundle of rope yarn was produced and lit to make a lamp, then lowered into the hole. Abruptly Harriet could see the entire excavation, as the darkness gave way to the flickering light.

The men had dug — on purpose? — into the roof of a cave. She could now clearly see the remains of the passage that had led into this cave from the side of the cliff. The floor of the cavern was heaped with the dirt that the men had disturbed ... and with bones. The cave was filled with dirt and sprawled disjointed skeletons.

Some had arms still outstretched to the passage, while others hugged the floor of the cave, as if in a last frantic struggle for air. When had they been trapped in here? Long ago, she thought, and could picture their horrible ending. It was impossible to look away.

There were four men down in the cave with the bones, walking back and forth, holding the torch high, raking back the dirt, searching. One man straightened and held up a dark object like a snake, and one of the men crouched to take it. Then she saw it was a rotting leather belt. Other objects came up — fragments of black coarse gabardine, a few horn buttons, a rough wooden crucifix. Thunder grumbled, closer.

Then, a louder clap, deafening. Lightning fizzed and the wind gusted, flapping Harriet's loose hair about her face. Her cloak and skirts tossed wildly. She saw Captain Dexter turn and look at her. The sky slammed again as thunder

47

bellowed right above their heads. She saw his mouth move but could hear nothing. Then he took her arm. She flinched, lost in a kind of nightmare.

Men began to run like birds over the edge of the cliff and down the terraces, carrying their shovels. Down in the bay the brig was pitching wildly at her anchors. The men in the cave were scrambling up the rope. Then they were running down the cliff, too.

Jahaziel Dexter shouted, "Come on, Harriet—move!" And numbly, she obeyed.

SEVEN

WITHIN moments Harriet was sitting in the whaleboat. The wind had veered, blowing in whirling gusts so that the sea was becoming rugged. Harriet shut her eyes and gripped the sides as the boat bounced and surged through the breakers. She heard an oarsman curse in a high, frightened voice. Her eyes flew open then, and she was more scared than ever.

Jahaziel Dexter was steering with a long steering oar. He stood just behind her, in the stern of the boat, and she could feel the tension in his braced legs and hear his grunts as he thrust the big sweep into the tumult. Her hair, like the rain, was streaming down her face. The boat pitched—she thought they were lost, and her grip became convulsive. Then the oar seized the wave, bending like a newly cut willow, the five oarsmen heaved at their oars, and the boat was through the surf and safe. Jahaziel was shouting. Harriet could make no sense of his words, but the oarsmen seemed to understand. They set their shoulders into their pulling, and the boat surged smoothly for the brig.

Harriet stayed in the boat while it was hoisted up into the stern davits, and Dexter stopped with her to work the falls. They instant they were level with the deck he bent and scooped her up in his arms, hauling her out of the boat and dumping her on the deck with no ceremony whatsoever. Then he pushed her in a run to the ladder, and jumped down to help her onto the amidships deck, in front of the afterhouse. No sooner had her feet touched the planks than men were hauling at the first of the two halfboats, which were in the water below, waiting their turn, while oarsmen were scrambling up the side of the brig. One at a time, at incredible speed, the boats were swung in and stowed one inside the other on the amidships deck, and all the men were safely on board.

Jahaziel Dexter was roaring orders, which Charlie Martin relayed in even louder shouts. Men jumped on the bulwarks and then sprung up the masts, racing to loose the topsails while others heaved at the windlass in the bow. Two more were at the wheel, on the flat roof of the afterhouse, which she understood was the quarterdeck. Lightning spat and flickered again, and the *Gosling* bucked like a horse, plucking her anchor and beginning to make way. The noise was terrific, of wind and rain and dashing sea, and frantic activity on deck and in the rigging. The rapidly darkening day was a cacophony of shouting, of the thump of canvas and thrumming of rigging, syncopated with the clap of thunder. Harriet stood rock-still, held by the drama of the scene around her. The brig came round, sharp on the wind as the sails fell loose, and men ran to grip the flailing sheets. The great sails billowed and then came taut, and the wind on deck gusted in different directions as the canvas rose against the sky and the racing thick clouds. Harriet stumbled, hitting the wall at the front of the afterhouse, then stumbled again, before crashing into Jahaziel Dexter rather hard.

He steadied her, looking irritated, and shouted in her ear, "Get below!"

Harriet merely stared. The last place she wanted to be was down in the cabin. She was determined to stop right here, where she could check that these variously unpleasant men were doing something to save their brig and her life. Dexter reached past her and slammed the door open, then gave her a shove so that she literally ran down the steps. As she arrived in the passage the door slammed shut, and Harriet was alone.

The noises were even louder in this confined space, so she staggered into the empty mess cabin, then hung onto the edge of the table. When she shrugged her sodden cloak off her shoulders, her equally drenched garments were clinging to her body. Skirts and petticoats and shawls gripped her in a clammy grasp, and the brig rose and rose as a huge wave lifted her and then pitched down with a crash. There was a tremendous thud of something fetching loose on deck.

"Are we wrecked?" shrieked Harriet—and as if the very heavens answered, a monstrous wave pooped the brig.

Countless gallons of salt water came hurtling through the skylight and fell directly on Harriet's head. She tried to scream, her mouth filled, she spluttered and tried again. She managed a shriek at the top of her voice, and the door slammed open and boots clattered down the stairs.

Her eyes were shut. She shook herself violently, sending scatters of water all over the cabin. When she tossed her drenched hair away from her face, Jahaziel Dexter was peering down at her, and to her incredulous rage he was grinning.

"What?" he said. "Afraid of a little squall and a cold bath?" She stared at him, speechless with hatred, and his face creased up with laughter. "Take comfort," he urged. "The wind bears fair for Capricorn."

She shouted, "You!" He stepped back hastily, ducking under her swinging arm. "This?" she shrieked. "A little squall?"

And with a crash like doom a thunderbolt struck.

Jahaziel whirled and ran, and Harriet pursued him up to deck, terrified at the very notion of being left alone below.

On deck it was like a scene from hell, all black and gray

and flickering orange and yellow flames. The top of the foremast was on fire. Captain Dexter had run forward, shouting, but Harriet stopped in the doorway, rigid with fright. The wind gusted and the flames curled and danced and the rain had stopped. Oh, God, she thought, the rain had stopped.

Men were springing up into the rigging, and more men were running with tubs of water. Others ran in small circles on the deck, hauling at clewlines as they tried to save the topsails. The brig was pitching wildly, digging in her bow as she tried to shake free of the water in her scuppers, and another wave came in and crashed through the skylight and landed with a foaming splash below. Harriet watched in dreadful apprehension, unable to move, hanging onto the doorframe as she watched the struggle to save the brig. Thunder growled again, more distant, and the horizon pulsed with eerie blue light, as if mocking the flames that rose from the mast.

Another wave. The brig crashed down her prow and shuddered, creaking in every tortured plank. And then, as Harriet watched in utter uncomprehending horror, the foretopmast backstays parted, and the foretopmast fell forward in a tangle of spars and ropes, collapsing inch by inch over the slackened web of the jib, spluttering flames as it went. First one man who had been aloft there and then another cried out and fell, bouncing down the rigging to the deck with grotesque moment-to-moment slowness.

Only dimly hearing Captain Dexter roaring orders to get the ship on the other tack, Harriet lurched out of her mesmerized state and began to run toward the fallen men. Her skirts flapped wildly, and her wet hair tossed too, blinding her. As she arrived one of the men miraculously stood. His mouth was agape and one of his arms hung like a broken wing.

The other man lay still. Harriet fell to her knees beside the prone form, certain the man was dead, but as she started to turn him over, the man roused and groaned. Then she crammed a shocked hand over her mouth. The man moaned, and each time he shook his head great coins of blood sprung out and spattered in the water on the deck. Then by some strange miracle his face was abruptly washed of blood, and Harriet could see his wound.

She swallowed. His right cheek had been almost entirely severed, caught by some projection as he fell. It flapped grotesquely, revealing shiny white teeth, the blood constantly washed away by a watery stream.

Water. Harriet shook her head in bewilderment. Then at last she realized that the heavens had opened and it was raining again. There was a gap in the sky where the heavy clouds were torn apart, and as she watched a rainbow sprang up in the murk. She listened to the flames hiss angrily in the wreckage. Then they sulkily flickered out.

Having wreaked its damage, the squall moved off as swiftly as it had struck. The rain stopped, the sea moderated, and there were enough blue patches in the sky to dress a whole navy of sailors. The wind gusted fair for Capricorn, but though the brig had been lucky to escape so lightly, she was not going anywhere for some time yet. The foredeck was a mess of rope and spars, and the *Gosling*, in the meantime, had her wings clipped.

Dexter strode about organizing the clearing up of the wreckage, the bracing of the main topmast, and the setting of a main staysail to keep the ship up to the wind. Then, when everything was ready for sending up a new fore-topmast the next day, he left Charlie in charge, and braced himself for the next challenge — down in his transom cabin in the afterhouse.

A tarpaulin had been tossed over the big sofa that was built under the wide gallery of windows in the stern. Abner, the wounded sailor, lay senseless on top of the waterproof, his eyes turned up to show the whites. Harriet Gray knelt beside him, holding a cloth over his dreadful wound, and replacing it with another as it became soaked with blood.

First of all, Dexter noticed that she had stripped down to the usual number of garments, so looked as slender as a reed again. Then he noted that she did the job quite casually, most of her mind apparently taken up with an argument with old Chips, who was whittling away at a splint for the man with the broken arm, Tib Greene. Tib's comrade, Dan Kemp, was there too, and Bodfish was mopping up water and sweeping up broken glass from the skylight. His apartments, Dexter meditated, were too crowded altogether.

Everyone ignored his arrival, including Miss Gray. "I do assure you that I am right," she scolded Chips, as she mopped the severed cheek. "Any medical book—even the captain's famous shipmaster's medical guide, which you quote all the time but has *not* been produced—will confirm that men do *not* smoke by a sickbed."

"But I ain't never heard of such," the boatswain said stubbornly. "My own father, he *died* with a pipe atwixt his jaws, and we was all there a-smoking, too, keeping him company in his extremity." His lower lip stuck out as he whittled, and he blew clouds of offended smoke.

It was time, Dexter thought, to make his presence known. He snapped at Bodfish to take himself and his mop away, snapped at Chips to hurry up with the splint, snapped at Miss Gray to shift along and give him some room, and hunkered down to look at Abner's cheek.

The wound was even more ghastly than he remembered. Every time Harriet mopped, the cheek lifted and then flapped back. Each flap revealed a row of white teeth and a swollen, bitten tongue. Abner's unconscious body threatened to roll off the couch with each pitch of the brig, so Harriet held him in place with the side of one arm as she dabbed.

Dexter said nothing. Instead he stood up and busied himself in fetching out his medical guide, his medical chest, and some instruments for surgery.

One of the instruments was a bottle of potato whiskey, which had been given to him several months before by a Russian beaver-trapper. Dexter poured out four tots. He gave one to Chips, who immediately looked less affronted, gave one to Tib, and a third to Dan Kemp. Both men grinned widely despite the broken arm, and Dexter noticed for the first time that they both had their whiskery gimlet-eyed attention fixed on Harriet's face. He thought, *What the devil did I do to deserve this?* — and drained the fourth tot himself.

Harriet said, "Captain Dexter!" in exactly the tone she'd used to berate old Chips. Dexter ignored her. He hunkered down again by Abner's head and sorted out a new sewing needle and some silk. Then he refilled his glass and soaked both silk and needle in it. A hunk of cotton waste was soaked there too, liberally, before it was popped, dripping, right on top of the wound.

The effect was instantaneous and dramatic. Abner came to his senses with a bloodcurdling shriek. He reared upright like a corpse revived. The cheek flapped down and blood spurted out from around the white teeth, and with a mighty crash Dan Kemp fainted.

Dexter called out to Bodfish to haul Dan's unconscious body out, then turned back to his patient. Abner was thrashing about in fear and pain, so he then told Chips to hold his feet. The carpenter did not move, sitting frozen, instead. Dexter sucked in an infuriated breath, but when he looked at his patient again, Miss Gray was holding him down by the simple means of sitting on his lower legs.

Her expression was as matter-of-fact as ever. Tib Greene said, "Good lord, sir, what d'yer reckon, sir, and her but a scrap of a girl … how old?"

Yes, thought Dexter, and looked at Harriet. She met his stare with hauteur, and said distantly, "Nineteen."

"*Nineteen?*" said Dexter. It was worse than he'd thought.

"Well … almost nineteen."

"*Eighteen?*" Dexter winced, then roused himself, catching Abner's head with one hand, and feeding the boy brandy with the other. The boy choked a bit, but then managed to keep some down. The loud whines of pain became whimpers of terror. Dexter stood and looked at Chips, and this time bid him hold Abner's head.

"Tight," he said. And never did a snail move as slow as Chips did to the head of the couch. However, he was finally there, and holding the head the way Dexter wanted. The boy was sobbing, tears running down from his tightly shut eyes. And this, thought Dexter, was the fine young mariner who boasted the most of his manly prowess. He shut one eye, aimed the needle, and pushed.

Abner exploded with an agonized yell, rearing upright again. Dexter swore, Harriet gasped, and old Chips winced. After more brandy, however, the boy subsided, and Dexter finished the stitch. He worked in a neat herringbone pattern, as in a well-mended sail. Abner, he mused, would have something new to show the girls; it would be a scar to be proud of indeed.

Then, just as he was getting nicely set into the rhythm of the job, he heard the carpenter clear his voice. "Cap'n..."

The sound was so strained that Dexter looked up at him. Chips was pasty-faced and shiny about the forehead. Dexter sighed, wondering how many of his men were prone to feeble nerves, and said, "Yes, Chips, yes. Consider yourself relieved. Send in Bodfish — he should be just outside that door, listening to everything we say."

Bodfish lasted just two stitches. Then he confessed in a shamed mutter that he was not equal to the task. Dexter nodded, watched his hasty withdrawal, and wondered who to send for next.

To his disbelief he heard Harriet say, "Oh, for heaven's sake, Captain Dexter, let me hold the boy's head, or the entire crew will fetch the vapors. All we need is one stout soul to sit on Abner's feet."

That was easily organized, as even with a broken arm Tib could sit on Abner. "Fancy that," he kept saying as he settled. "And naught but eighteen, sir."

Fancy that indeed, thought Dexter. Then he concentrated on his stitching.

EIGHT

DEXTER spent the early evening tidying up his cabin, wiping down his books and replacing them carefully. He whistled as he got his accommodations the way he liked them, and sipped at times from a glass of good French brandy. Above, on the quarter deck, Chips and Jonathan were talking as they replaced broken panes in the skylight. It didn't take long before he heard them pack up their tools and head forward, with yet another job finished. Then eight bells was struck, and the brig was quiet, snugged down for the night as cozily as if she bore no wounds at all.

Dexter poured another drink, then settled in his wooden chair with his back to his chart desk, an old journal on his knee, his stockinged feet propped on the sofa. When there was a knock on the door that led to his transom cabin from the little lobby at the end of the passage, he did not stand, but called out.

He expected it to be Charlie, come to report on the state of repairs. To his surprise and exasperation, it was Harriet Gray who came in. She had not bothered to grace the supper table with her presence — too busy, he'd heard, with settling Abner into the bottom berth in the junior mates' stateroom. And now it was night, he'd thought her safely bedded down in Charlie Martin's old room.

She had changed into a different dress—because some of Abner's blood had got onto the other one, he supposed. Her simple gown was pale blue, and a light shawl was tied about her slender waist and draped about her hips like a kirtle, emphasizing the sweet hollow in the small of her back. Dexter felt little muscles of awareness shift and tug inside him. How could he have guessed when she first came on board that the bulky silhouette hid this graceful and willowy form, that her small breasts would swell so pertly in the low confines of her bodice? If he had known it, he grimly thought, he would have sent her packing before she could open her eloquent mouth.

Dear Jehovah, he meditated on, what would his men say when they heard about this night-time visit to his private quarters? But he supposed she had a good reason, having taken on the job of nurse for the wounded. Putting his glass and the journal on the chart desk, he stood up, and said in a deliberately businesslike tone, "How's our patient?"

Harriet had been studying the narrow length of the lovely cabin, frowning slightly at its mahogany paneling and its graceful gallery of ranked window-panes overlooking the sea. Now she roused herself, and sat down on the sofa without bothering to ask permission.

Instead, she said in reproving tones, "I have hopes that suppuration won't set in."

He said, "I beg your pardon?"

"Despite the unwise use of alcohol in the surgery. Alcohol stimulates the flow of blood, Captain Dexter, particularly in the head. The results could have been disastrous!"

He couldn't believe that a minx of eighteen would lecture him like a dowager. Then he grunted with amusement and said, "I've never known alcohol stimulate anything, particularly the head." Sitting down on the chart desk chair, he went on, "I've seen plenty of evidence of the dulling of the brain by alcohol, believe me. Spirits make an excellent disinfectant, in my opinion. Or would you rather I had used tobacco spit?"

"What?"

"A well-chewed tobacco cud is a favorite with many captains."

"That's disgusting. Surely you don't do all the medicating on this brig? Don't you usually carry a surgeon?"

"It's not American practice to carry a surgeon, Miss Gray."

"It's not?" She frowned even more deeply. "But there was a doctor on the whaleship *Humpback*."

"And did he do any doctoring?"

"Oddly, he was fully engaged with the cooking."

Dexter couldn't help it—he exploded with laughter. "He *was* the cook!"

"I beg your pardon?"

"*Doctor* is a shipboard term of endearment for the ship's cook."

"Oh!" Then, to his surprise, she laughed. It was a warm, lighthearted laugh, and for the first time she seemed as young as eighteen. The giggle was so infectious that he laughed again himself. The light from the lamps gleamed on the disordered thickness of her hair, now dried and gold again ... and he couldn't help but wonder how it would feel in the cupped palms of his hands, so soft and weighty...

Then she said slyly, "I presume that ... graveyard on Judas Island is a memorial to the surgery of American captains?"

So that was why she had barged into his private sitting room, he realized. Inquisitiveness had battled with her sense of propriety, and curiosity had won.

He shook his head, and said, "One of your own countryfolk was responsible for that—a Welshman, to be exact. A pirate by the name of Henry Morgan."

"A pirate!" she exclaimed, and then, as he watched her, she rearranged herself.

It was almost eerie to see the way she disposed herself for listening. Even the lamps seemed to dim as she gazed with complete attention at his face. She leaned a little forward, wide eyes fixed on him, and when she whispered, "Who were those people who were murdered on that island?" it was as if she whispered, *Tell me a story, fascinate and enthrall me…*

It was unsettling how flattered he felt to have a listener who watched and listened with such complete attention — but why not tell her about it? After all, the expedition had been a failure, so he may as well spin his yarn.

Dexter sipped brandy. "You've heard of Henry Morgan, and how he led a gang of desperate men across the Isthmus of Darien, to seize the gold of Panama?"

Gold. Quietness surrounded them, with the chuckle of the sea for music, while the brig rocked as gently as a cradle. On impulse Dexter picked up the old journal that lay on the desk by his elbow. He turned pages, searching for the right place, conscious all the time of Harriet watching him. When he found the page he reached over and gave her the book.

She took it cautiously, saying, "What is this?"

"Never mind. Just read that entry."

He expected her to read it silently, but instead, to his surprise, she read aloud, in her clear English accent. She read it beautifully, every word perfect, ringing like a bell.

> *I saw such things which were brought from Panama.*
> *A sun entirely of gold, a moon entirely of silver,*
> *likewise sundry curiosities, all of which were fairer to*
> *see than many marvels. I have never seen in all my*
> *days what rejoiced my heart as did this gold…*

She stopped, looked back at him, and said, "What *is* this, Captain Dexter?"

"Don't ask. Just read it."

"But it's most ungallant, sir, to tempt and then provoke!" But she studied the book again. "There's a map."

"Yes." He knew the map by heart, so instead of looking at the book he watched her as she deciphered flowing script and curlicues and studied fanciful animal shapes. It was a most elaborate chart, adorned with dragons and whales and sea-serpents, with something circular in the middle. At the top the page was torn and stained, but the letters L, A, S were decipherable, standing over the drawing of a ferocious bear.

She said, "Is this the map of a lake?"

"Perhaps. The Indians had tales of a lake of gold, and a race of women who lived there, who ate off gold, and dressed in gold, and had a queen called Calafia, who named her kingdom California."

Her frown deepened. "But this isn't a map of California."

"Calafia's kingdom must be somewhere in South America," he agreed. "Where the Spanish conquistadors looted unbelievable treasuries of gold … and in the year 1670, much of this gold was in Panama."

"So the pirate Morgan assembled his gang of desperadoes?"

"Aye. They set out from Portobello on the Caribbean coast, and battled across the Isthmus of Darien, paddling up the Chagres River in dugout canoes, and then heading into the jungle and marsh, fighting the Indians as they went. Disease and poisoned arrows killed a lot of them — as the poets say, death ate into their ranks. And it was all for nothing. By the time they knocked on the gates of Panama City, the word had run ahead, and the gold had been hidden, or taken away."

"Hidden?"

"The great gold altar in the cathedral had been painted to look like wood, and Henry Morgan was too angry, or too stupid, to look closely."

"And some had been taken away?"

"Put on a ship, along with the nuns of the cathedral."

There was a glint in her eye, as if she guessed what was coming. "Where did they sail?"

"No one knows. They were never heard of again."

"Judas Island." The words were positive. "That's what you think, anyway."

He lifted his glass in a salute to her intelligence. "How did you guess?"

"I felt something in the village … some past terror. The well, there was something about the well … and the skeletons in the pit. You think the ship arrived at Judas Island, and the nuns were given refuge by the villagers — that Morgan pursued them, and that he tortured them to get the secret of the treasure. When he and his men had finished, they herded them into that cave and filled in the entrance, then left them to die."

"Perhaps. If the gold was gone, or if the nuns had refused to reveal the secret, their rage would have known no bounds."

"Yes," she said. "Yes." Then, to his amazement, she began to recite — from memory, this time, and not from the book.

Methought I saw a thousand fearful wrecks,
Ten thousand men that fishes gnawed upon,
Wedges of gold, great anchors, heaps of pearls,
Inestimable stones, unvalu'd jewels
All scattered in the bottom of the sea
Some lay in dead men's skulls …

She stopped, and it was as if a spell was broken.

Jake said, astonished, "What was that?"

"Shakespeare. Do you think the nuns' ship was wrecked — and the treasure was lost?"

Dexter shook his head, and picked up his glass. He drank brandy, and then said, "Maybe — or maybe not."

"So what do *you* think happened to the treasure?"

He shrugged. It certainly hadn't been in the cave.

"And why are you so sure that the treasure ship sailed to Judas Island?"

"The map."

"The map of California?"

"It's a map of Judas Island. The whales and sea-serpents are put there to conceal that it is an island, not a lake."

She studied the book again. "How ingenious!" she exclaimed. "There are positions hidden in the animals — that's how you knew it was Judas Island. And what are these ones here ... llamas?"

"The sheep of the Andes. Cousins of the much more valuable alpacas."

"Alpacas?"

For some reason her expression had become guarded. Dexter waited, feeling puzzled, but she made no answer to his nod, so in the end he went on, "Schouten wrote down gold yarns as he heard them or read them — like a lot of men, he was obsessed with gold. There is an entry in there about llamas, saying that the Golden Fleece of Greek legend was probably a sheep fleece used to trap particles of gold from streams, and that llama fleeces were possibly used the same way."

"Schouten?"

"An American descendant of the great Dutch navigator — the man who kept that journal. A long time ago, he owned this brig. When he launched her, he named her *Gosling* — because he hoped she would prove to be his golden goose, no doubt, though he died a poor man. When I bought the *Gosling* I changed the accommodations — this room and what is now the mess cabin were one big room. I put up that partition," he said, poking a thumb over his shoulder at the wall where his chart desk was set, "and took over this sternward part as my private transom cabin. There were mahogany bookcases along the starboard bulkhead, and when I had them removed, I found this book in a secret compartment."

"And Captain Schouten was an adventurer, like you?"

"He was a pirate."

"*A pirate?*"

"He was reasonably legal during the war of 1812, having a letter of marque from the American government. Piracy being his vocation, he was very successful, taking quite a few British prizes in the Atlantic. Then one day, off Patagonia, he was surprised by two British men-of-war, and escaped through the Magellan Straits into the Pacific — and the *Gosling* has never left the Pacific since."

Her eyes narrowed. "Captain Schouten never returned to America?"

"Once the war was over, his letter of marque didn't signify any more — he was back to being a pirate."

"*Back* to being a pirate?"

"Who knows how long he had been one, before he got that letter of marque?"

"Dear me," she said. She looked at the map again, and said, "How did he get this?"

"According to the story, he borrowed it from a drunken Spanish seaman in a taberna in Rio, and copied it into his journal — but whether that was the truth or not is beyond me to tell."

"Perhaps he found the Judas Island treasure."

"If so, he didn't mention it. And as I said, he died poor."

"Then I don't believe the quest is over. The gold could still be there — and maybe there are more clues in this book." She turned pages slowly, and then her brows rose, and she began to read in French, which rang as clearly and cleanly as her English.

> *Vers ce beau ciel ou Dieu vous accompagne*
> *Parlez joyeux, ne prenez aucun soin*
> *Dans ce pays, vrai pays de cocagne*
> *L'or du Peron tiendrait un petit coin*

Then she laughed, and said, "A cultured old pirate, this

Captain Schouten. *Quel d'or*, he writes, *such awe*. What a dreadful pun! Here's another—*Could the golden goose have been French, that golden goose that barked like a dog, oeuf, oeuf, oeuf*. Oh dear! No, Jahaziel, though I'm convinced that the treasure is still on the island, we have to accept the fact that the map is our only clue. Tell me, what does *L, A, S* mean?"

"I don't know, but I've often wondered if the *L* is half of a *D*, and it reads Judas, except that the first two letters are missing."

"But why make the island look like a lake, and hide the positions in the animals?" Then she echoed thoughtfully, "*Often* wondered? How long have you been searching for this treasure, Captain Dexter?"

He said wryly, "Two years."

"So you really are an adventurer! Do the owners know you're such a romantic at heart?"

He was instantly furious. "The brig is mine!" he shouted, and dropped his feet to the floor with a thud. "The *Gosling* is mine by right!"

"Captain Dexter…"

"Every plank and knee and strake and spar and every inch of rope-stuff…"

"Captain Dexter, I believe you!"

He subsided, and she went on in a soothing murmur, "You are perfectly justified in your pride of ownership, Captain Dexter. You own and run a most remarkably happy ship. I hear that men line up to ship with you, partly because of the quality of your grub. Furthermore, I gather that you have a most unusual method of managing your crew, that they make up a Company and hold meetings and have a democratic say in the brig's affairs, a pioneering plan indeed. It's most praiseworthy, and any resemblance to the way that pirate ships are managed is a coincidence, I'm sure."

Dexter stared at her, wondering how much soft soap one girl could produce in one short speech, and she smiled coaxingly and said, "And sir, since you are the owner of the brig and founding director of the *Gosling* Company, there's no reason at all why you can't change your mind and steer for Valparaiso."

"I don't need a reason," he snapped, furious at her blatant attempt at manipulation. "Why should I make up for Captain Smith's dishonorable behavior?"

Then he forgot it, because he heard a little rumble from the direction of her waist. He exclaimed, "You're hungry!"

Harriet said haughtily, "I beg your pardon?"

"You didn't arrive at the supper table, yet the grub—as you call it—was exceptional. There was soft bread, butter, ham, cake, coffee, mangoes, bananas ... why, you'd think old Bodfish was putting on a show, just for you. But you were making another melodramatic gesture!"

"Well, how can I accept the grudging hospitality..."

He laughed, and said, "We'll be quite a few hours puddling about fixing the rigging, you know, and it's another thirty-six hours to Capricorn. Do you think your pride will keep its backbone that long?"

"Captain Dexter, you don't understand..."

"And don't call me that—and don't call me Jahaziel, either. My friends call me Jake." Then he stood and threw open the door to the mess cabin.

He nearly felled Bodfish, who hopped back in a hurry, rubbing his ear. "So there you are," he said. "Fix this obstinate female a tray, and tell her the time to turn up for breakfast. And at the same time learn her some manners."

Harriet shouted, "Who the hell do you think you are?"

"A pirate, ma'am, just another pirate," said Dexter, and swept her a bow. But it was a wasted piece of theater, for she swept past him with her head held high.

She didn't believe him, he thought, and grinned.

NINE

NEXT morning the sea and sky were brightly rain-washed, full of promise for a fine brig-mending day. The men looked cheerful as they assembled for ship-repair orders, and when Jake Dexter went below after leaving Charlie Martin in charge, he whistled as he shaved. Even his reflection made him cheerful — that face was all he had and he did not consider it particularly beautiful, but he'd come to terms with his a-kilter expressions long since.

He even broke into song as he strode into the mess cabin. "Has a love of adventure, a promise of gold," he musically inquired —

> E'er tempted ye to roam where wide billows roll
> Where could-crowned coasts and green islands call
> As large as the world and free to ye all..?

He broke off and lifted an eyebrow at Harriet, who sat freshly washed and groomed herself, eating breakfast at the table. She ignored him, talking to Bodfish instead, but this didn't trouble him a whit. He began whistling again as he went to attend to Abner.

Abner was sitting up in Valentine Fish's berth, which was the lower of the two bunks in the junior mates' stateroom, and frowned grumpily at his captain as Dexter came in. Miss Gray, he informed Jake, had already come and tidied his bed. She had fed him beef broth with a spoon. Abner was feeling sorry for himself, as his cheek was swollen and the eye on that side was shut, and he didn't want his captain, he wanted Miss Gray back. A woman's hand at the sickbed, as his manner made plain, was unmatchable.

Jake inspected the wound without comment, and then administered a teaspoon of laudanum, according to his *Ship-Captain's Medical Guide*. The book also recommended a blister plaster on the back of the neck and wetting his bed with vinegar, but Jake decided against that advice, considering that Abner was uncomfortable enough already.

As he opened the door to leave the boy peered one-eyed past his shoulder, in the patent hope that he would see Miss Gray. Charlie Martin might have fallen in and out of love with Harriet with the speed of lightning, Jake mused, but Abner's sheepish devotion had taken his place, and the sooner they arrived at Capricorn Island, the better. The European trader there had been a rogue in his youth, but he was old and creaky, with a native wife and sixteen brats, and the girl would be a damn sight better off there than on his brig, at the mercy of his lusty crew.

But then, when Jake finally arrived on deck, Harriet was standing on the quarterdeck as if she owned the ship.

The men were laboring hard to get that ship back to rights, sending up a new foretopmast and setting up the standing rigging while Charlie Martin ran around shouting, assisted by his subordinates, Valentine Fish and Crotchet. On the surface, the work was as routine as could be expected, but it was apparent to Jake that everything was being done with unusual daring and flamboyance.

He stood in the doorway of the afterquarters, observing it all, and wondering if Harriet knew that his men were showing off for her benefit. Irish Cookie, the ship's "doctor," was chopping kindling as if he were removing English heads, while Crotchet was testing the shrouds he'd just rattled down with the air of an acrobat, and Pablo the Chilean strutted along with his bum stuck out in man-of-war pants whose hems brushed full on the deck.

Whether she knew or not, she was supremely at ease. As Jake watched, Harriet turned and bent over the rail to look at something in the sea with an air of intent curiosity. She'd declared that she was never seasick, he remembered, and he believed her, because she looked so very much at home in this world that properly belonged to men. The brig wallowed uneasily, but this did not seem to trouble her at all. Her posture pulled up the back of her skirt so that narrow feet in ribboned slippers were revealed, and those feet were set as confidently as if she were on land.

Jake moved abruptly. When he arrived beside her she smiled up at him and said, "Why did you give Davy that name?"

Jake blinked, taken aback, and turned involuntarily to look at Davy Jones Locker. The tall silent black man was working quietly at a task his damaged mind could comprehend, which was overhauling some blocks.

Glancing back at Harriet, Jake said, "Why do you want to know?"

"Because your brig interests me so extremely, Captain Dexter! Bodfish has been telling me how your *Gosling* Company works, how the men each buy shares, and then become interested owners, and how they make motions, and second them, and vote, and in that way help run the brig. It's revolutionary — so enlightened and democratic. Truly, it fascinates me!"

"As you mentioned yourself," he said dryly, "it's the way pirate ships are organized."

He regarded her for a moment, every suspicion alert. She was up to something, he knew it. Then he said, "There's not much of a story to Davy's name. He swam on board one night when we were anchored off Tombez, a runaway slave

71

with a cracked head. We found out later that he had run all the way from a plantation in Guyana, so God alone knows how he got to Tombez, but somehow he had done it. Maybe it was as a stowaway, as we found him in the sea. He grabbed the chains as the current took him past us, and so we saved him from the sharks. He can't remember his name, so we gave him the obvious one, instead."

"Because you rescued him from Davy Jones's Locker?"

He did not answer, instead saying in his most businesslike tone, "Miss Gray, I would prefer it if you remained below."

Her eyes widened and her smile faded. "But why?"

The reasons were obvious; he said nothing.

"But—on the ship to the Cape Colony from England, and then on the ship from thence to New Zealand—why, I walked the afterdeck quite freely."

He said involuntarily, "Cape Colony?"

"Yes! And I do assure you, Captain, that the ladies were given complete freedom to take the air on beautiful days like this. Otherwise, how bored we would have been—and how fat! We recited to each other, Captain, and staged small dramas, and the crew put on concerts to entertain us."

Jake's eyebrows were hoisting higher and higher. Then he said with deliberate emphasis, "You said *ladies*. In the plural."

"I did," she agreed. "That, sir, was the reason we steered for the Cape. There were jealousies, you see, and no fewer than four duels had been arranged. The captain himself was one of the principals, because he had challenged one of the passengers in a passion."

Jake ejaculated, "Jehovah!" Then he barked with laughter.

"Yes," she said, looking very animated. "It was dreadfully exciting, for the captain was indubitably mad. He used to mutter and take fearful rages, and once he took all the weapons out of the armory and put them in his stateroom and locked himself in with them for quite five days. My father kept on leading delegations to reason with him, especially when he kept up a press of canvas in most threatening weather. However," she sighed, "my father's counsel did not prevail. Then two of the sails split in a squall, and one of the ladies swooned, and the captain was so delighted with her abject terror that he reduced canvas for the first time in the voyage."

Jake shook his head, perfectly aware of what she was doing — she was entertaining him with her yarn to help him forget his decision to send her below.

He said, "I think I can safely wager, Harriet, that it wasn't you who swooned."

"No," she agreed, and laughed. "I wasn't frightened at all, not then. However, a few nights later the captain ran the ship on a rock, just outside the harbor."

"And ..?"

"And my father organized a contingent of passengers to man the pumps, and so we limped into port. The captain had shut himself up in his room again, but luckily one of the passengers was a mariner himself and he, in the meantime, took command of the ship."

Jake paused, wondering whether to believe her. Then he said firmly, "Harriet, go below." And, casting him an inimical look, she headed for the afterhouse. Jake watched her go, and when he looked back at the men, they were watching her, too.

74

TEN

THE crew got back to work after they caught Captain Dexter's stern eye, and the swaying up of spars and bending on of canvas proceeded with the usual efficiency. However, the deck had lost a certain jaunty air. So, somehow, Jake was not really surprised when Charlie informed him in the late afternoon, after the *Gosling* was back on course and under all sail, that the men had requested a meeting of the Company. It was obvious that they wanted another go at discussing the problem of the passenger.

Jake did not anticipate any trouble. The weather was still calm, so the meeting was held on the afterdeck, and he stood by the helmsman at the wheel watching as the Company assembled.

What a load of ruffians, Jake Dexter thought as they came up the ladder and straggled to their places—all shipped in various ways in the past. Pablo had arrived in Valparaiso in a gloriously embroidered suit with his disappointed bullfight audience hot on his heels, while Jonathan had come on board in Honolulu, attired in a green clawhammer coat and a black chimneypot hat, with his chest of tools on his shoulder. Tib Greene and Dan Kemp had slouched up the gangway in Callao, swearing they had missed their ship, but had been taken on despite Jake's sure conviction that they were deserters, as they were seasoned mariners. And, like everyone else here, they had proved to be an asset. Tib's arm was in a sling, of course, but he had done his full share of work that day, in the manner of seamen the world over.

Harriet was right, he meditated idly, as men did volunteer eagerly for positions in the crew—but she was also wrong, because it was not for the far-famed grub. They applied in their dozens in ports the Pacific over, because they wanted to make a fortune. They were adventurers— fortune hunters. And, because of the way Jake ran his ship, making that fortune was possible.

The inspiration had struck him one night soon after buying this brig with his first ill-gotten gains, and Harriet was right again, because the way the *Gosling*s earned their little fortunes was based on the way buccaneers shared out their prizes. Just as on pirate ships, the bargain was the plain one of no purchase, no pay—if a venture made no money, then all the men missed out, because they weren't paid wages. If there was a profit—and the profit could amount to a sensational sum—then it was shared out according to an age-old system. After the costs of the venture were deducted, Jake took half, and the rest was divided equally between all the *Gosling* Company members, whatever their rank.

Out of his half, Jake paid for the maintenance of the brig and the first-rate provisions that made the *Gosling* famous. This was no insignificant expense, yet he felt very comfortable indeed as he contemplated the large sums he had stowed away in banks in Sydney, Singapore, and Manila. And he'd never known a man complain when he finally cashed up and left the brig, because whoever he was, whether cook, carpenter, or seaman, he went away with a lot more money than he would ever have made out of working for ordinary pay.

So Jake felt complacent and quiet as he watched the

Gosling Company assemble, having no premonitions of a crisis at all. And at the start, everything was just as usual. Once the voting members were all there, either hunkered down on the deck, or leaning against the rail, Chips declared the meeting open, and Bodfish droned the notes of the minutes. But, when the steward said, "Would someone please move that the minutes be accepted as correct?" no one answered, because Miss Harriet Gray had come up the ladder to the deck.

She smiled beautifully at them all as she arrived, and Crotchet gave her his stool before Jake could say a word. Then he said sharply, "What is this, Miss Gray?"

"But I've already told you, Captain Dexter," she said with an innocent air, tilting her head to one side. "I've already declared myself fascinated by your democracy, and I wish to observe it at work."

"I'm sorry," said he, baring his teeth in an unamused grin. "But you will have to declare yourself disappointed. The meetings are open to members only."

"Yes, I know," she said brightly. "That's why I want to join."

"You ... *what?*"

"I want to become a member of the *Gosling* Company — and I've brought the price of a share with me." She held out her hand, palm upwards, and there lay a small velvet bag, which clinked ever so slightly.

As the men all watched, their mouths hanging open, Harriet pulled the tie, and shook the contents into her other hand. Small gold coins fell out. Sovereigns. Harriet counted them aloud, from one to ten, and then held them out to Dexter. "The equivalent, I know, of fifty American dollars," she informed him. "Which I also know is the price of a share in the Company."

Jake couldn't believe her barefaced audacity. When he drew in a breath he didn't know if he was going to snap or laugh. Then, with disbelief, he heard Abijah Roe say in a thoughtful kind of voice, "You can buy more than one, if you wish, Miss Gray."

"One share, Mr. Roe, will be sufficient."

"Even one share is out of the question," Jake snapped. "Joining the *Gosling* Company is not that easy, Miss Gray."

"Really? Is that so? But I'm not sure I believe you, Captain Dexter," she said, very sweetly. "Why not put the idea to the vote?"

Incredulously, Jake saw that all the men were nodding. Then, on thought, he nodded himself. A vote would end this farce, he decided, so he relaxed as Chips put the motion.

"Affirmative?" said the carpenter, and...

Abijah Roe, thought Jake, certainly wouldn't agree. Abijah was a sailmaker, and a very good sailmaker, too, but like all the sailmakers Jake had ever known he was hidebound in his opinions, which in his case included disapproval of females. The sailmaker raised his hand, though, his eyes fixed firmly on the sovereigns on Harriet's palm. Then Valentine and Crotchet put up their hands, too, simply for the sake of devilment. Davy ... Davy never voted, because he didn't think he had the right, but for the first time ever Davy put up his hand, because though Jake had no way of knowing it, in the dim recesses of his wounded mind he remembered his mistress on the Guyana plantation, who had been an elderly white-haired woman, a woman he vastly respected.

Jake's was the only dissenting vote. He couldn't believe it, but perforce, fuming, he had to watch as Harriet was enrolled in the *Gosling* Company.

As usual, Bodfish read her the rules, and all the men watched Harriet avidly as she listened with perfect attention to the droned words "...that shares in the Company shall be each worth fifty dollars, or the equivalent of work done for the brig ... that all decisions be faithfully followed when voted in favor by at least three-fourths of the Company ... that each share of whatever value be entitled to but one vote, and a single portion of the prize money, which is to be apportioned equally without regard to rank, once the captain has taken half for his own share plus the use of the ship … that Captain Dexter has sole discretion in the promotion and demotion of officers … that every man, whatever his rank, has equal title to the ship's provisions…"

At last Bodfish came to a stop. Harriet handed over her coins and neatly signed the document, adding her name to the list of members. All the men leaned forward to watch her. Most of them were smiling.

Even Abijah Roe smiled as he observed, "You won't have a vote, of course, Miss Gray."

Harriet sat up straight and stared at him. Jake felt a grin steal over his face — this, he thought, was where Miss Gray met her nemesis.

She said pertly, "Why ever not, Mr. Roe?" "Wimmenfolk can't vote! It ain't proper, it ain't right, no matter what them wimmen's rightists says. There ain't no country in the world what allows wimmen that unnatural right, and it don't happen in the *Gosling* Company, neither."

Harriet said nothing. Jake watched her with his thumbs tucked into his belt, relishing the moment of her defeat. Then he saw her shrug. She looked about at the men, waved a nonchalant hand, and said, "Very well, then."

Jake blinked, feeling very suspicious, and Abijah looked only grudgingly mollified. Then Harriet said, "But I would like to propose a motion. I wish to propose that we steer for Valparaiso, where I can put a most profitable bit of business our way."

Jake straightened, ready for argument, but Abijah beat him to it, crying, "Business, Miss? But that ain't right! Wimmenfolk can't put men in the way of business, it rates the same as a vote!"

Harriet said, "I must confess I don't understand your logic, Mr. Roe. You were glad enough to sell me a share, so do I have no rights at all?"

"There ain't one legal act what a mere female can perform, and it just ain't right for wimmen to presume in men's business, so that surely is so, Miss—you don't have rights, just face it."

"Women pay taxes, do they not?"

"That don't signify," said he doggedly. "Wimmenfolk just ain't formed to take responsibilities for more than children and the hearth, and that is a Biblical truth. Why, for a start, for one whole fourth of most of their lives they're unclean, that's what, they ain't even in control of their minds—"

And, to Dexter's utter stupefaction, Harriet surged to her feet and shouted, "Throw that man overboard!"

The silence was stunned. Harriet had one arm extended, one doomladen finger pointed straight at Abijah's bulging eyeballs, while the men gawped like spellbound sheep.

Then she cried, "Do you think to condemn me and shackle me on account of my sex? But why, sir, why be so unjust? Are women so weak and despicable—do they not have the same appetites, the same aspirations, the same disappointments as men? If I am a woman, am I not allowed to dream, feel emotion, respond to the search for riches, respond to the promise of gold?"

My God, thought Dexter, utterly benumbed, the minx had the whole crew bewitched—by nothing more than a melodramatic tantrum. "I am a woman!" she cried. "A woman! Is a woman not allowed dimensions, passions, senses, affections, ambitions—is a woman not hurt when wounded, sick when afflicted? The same sun warms her, the same wind chills her—and if she is poisoned, does she not die?"

And at that she stopped—and smiled. And Jake thought he understood exactly why Captain Smith had been so desperate to get rid of her.

But before he could rouse himself to say a word, Chips said gruffly, "She do have rights that go with a share."

"I do," Harriet agreed, and sat down again, smiling as calmly as if the remarkable tirade hadn't happened. "And I promise that once we drop anchor at Valparaiso I shall step aside and let men take over the business entirely, for my brother is in control of the scheme, and the *Gosling* Company can deal with him."

Dexter said suspiciously, "Brother? What brother?"

"My brother, Royal Gray." And again, oddly, she looked at Jake expectantly, as if she thought he would know the name.

Jake had never heard of the man. "And what exactly is your brother doing in South America?"

"Oh, he has been there more than a year, Captain Dexter, on a secret mission, working on behalf of the British Government and the merchants who own the mills at Bradford."

Another rapt silence. Then Jake could hear the whisper *secret mission* running round the young bloods in the group.

He said, "And what exactly does this business involve?"

"Alpacas," she said, and then, to the men, "A kind of South American camel, with very fine and luxurious wool."

Looking back at Dexter, she went on, "My brother has accumulated a flock of three hundred alpacas, Captain, and his brief from the British Government is to smuggle them out. Look at your record, sir — the mission is perfect for you! My instructions were to find a vessel that could be fitted out to carry the flock to New South Wales in Australia — and if we get them there, and break the South American monopoly by establishing a breeding stock, why then the British Government, through the generosity of the Bradford merchants, will give us a hundred thousand pounds. In gold. The equal to half a million dollars."

Half a million dollars. Before the men even started to shout out their questions, Jake knew he had lost the battle.

ELEVEN

THE passage to Valparaiso was swift—but at times, to Jake, it seemed as if it would never end, simply because Harriet annoyed him so, because she was always there, because she was just too much at home on his brig. Even more irritatingly, the men, all save his sour-natured sailmaker and the disillusioned Charlie Martin, were as enraptured as ever.

When, by the end of the second day, he felt as if she was going to be on board for ever, he ordered Jonathan, in his capacity as carpenter's mate, to put a latch string on her stateroom door. There was a latch already on the door, and Jonathan bored a hole next to it. Then he took away the half of the latch that was on the outside of the door, and fed a string from the inside latch through the hole. This meant that the door could only be opened from the outside by pulling on the string. When the string was drawn inside, no one could open the door from the outside, which meant that Harriet was safe from unseemly intrusion.

"What intrusion?" she demanded when she was shown how this worked. Irritatingly, she was very amused. "Who would want to sneak up on me?" she demanded.

And, though he didn't want to admit it, Jake knew he was acting like a prim old Puritan, because she was safe from intrusive men already. Charlie Martin was still smarting from being gulled by the Smiths—he might have voted for her, but, as he righteously declared, it was only to make her position on the brig more regular, and the thought of Bodfish barging in on her was equally ridiculous. Abner might have been a problem, but his scar was healing nicely, and so he was back in the forecastle, and the junior mates, Valentine and Crotchet, were unfailingly courtly in her presence.

On deck it was different. The men watched her as avidly as ever, and so Jake conducted a running battle with her, sending her below whenever he saw her out in the open.

"But I must take the air," she insisted. "It's not healthy to have no fresh air, and it's bad for the complexion, too. And the exercise is doing me good."

Her complexion was radiant, and Jake thought it always had been. He was forced to admit, though, that she was right again, because it was obvious that the voyage was doing her good. The *Gosling*'s good grub was smoothing out the hollows in her cheeks, so that each day she looked less waif-like. She had not lived well in New Zealand, he thought, which was a thought that made him feel uncomfortable.

"Anyway," she argued another time, "I have to hang out my washing." Her petticoats were flapping in the after rigging, and were getting a great deal of attention from the crew, as well. "On the ship to the Cape Colony," she said, in the start to a sentence that Jake knew by heart, "we ladies…"

"…hung out the washing," he said for her, in his sardonic fashion, but she merely smiled brilliantly.

"Yes!" she exclaimed. "Once a flock of unmentionables lost their stops and took flight, and the men hauled back the mainyard and lowered a boat, and rescued them all."

"And how did the captain feel about that?"

"Oh, that was the source of one of his rages. He fired the first mate, who had been in charge of the deck, and threatened to make spread-eagles of the men. When the first mate ignored him, which was nothing more than usual, he took out a musket and fired it, but all he did was shoot off a rope, so then he went into his cabin and muttered, and refused to come out and take care of his ship. So," she said with an elaborate sigh, "my father had to form another delegation."

"And what else did your father do, while you and the ladies were reciting and playacting and hanging out the washing?"

"But he was reciting and playacting as well! And he taught himself to play the clarinet. And then, on the passage to New Zealand from the Cape, there were the horses."

Jake knew she was up to her trick of distracting him from ordering her to go below, but he couldn't help himself, saying blankly, "Horses? What horses?"

"The horses my father bought at the Cape. We spent quite four months in the Colony, because the captain of the ship that brought us there refused to let us on board again, and so we set ourselves to work. The Cape Colonists thought we were rather wonderful, and my father made a lot of money. So he invested much of it in two stallions and four mares. Such beautiful thoroughbreds, you have not a notion how beautiful! My father had heard that thoroughbred horses fetch great prices in New Zealand, for the colonists there are so very fond of the sport of horse-racing, so he decided to make a fortune that way."

So the Grays had a history of carting animals about on ships, Jake brooded. "And did the ship have stables?"

"Of course it didn't! But my father, remember, was rich. Money makes such a difference, you know. He simply bought the tickets for the deck cabins from the people who had them, and he installed the horses in the cabins."

Jake winced. "So you're going to keep alpacas in your stateroom?"

She laughed, her eyes dancing in the speckled shade of the straw hat one of the men had made her. "We'll build stalls, of course. You told me yourself you have timber on board, Jahaziel. And I volunteer to be one groom, and Royal can be the other. We're used to it—not that it is pleasant. Have you ever seen a seasick stallion?"

Jake had not. He snapped, "Why don't the Bradford merchants buy their wool directly from the Indians, if it is so very valuable?"

"Because of its length. The Indians refuse to shear the alpacas more often than every second year, it's a religion with them. And because of that the wool grows too long for the mill machines. They've tried to talk the Indians out of their ideas, but without result. So the only alternative is to grow alpacas of their own—and New South Wales is ideal, apparently. The problem is that the Indians worship the animals, and refuse to let them out of the country, so the British are forced to hire men who are willing to smuggle them to Australia."

Put like that, it was logical, Jake thought. English merchants were advertising openly for men to smuggle rubber-tree seeds out of Brazil, and as a free trader he flouted local laws without a qualm, but still...

Feeling uneasy, he said, "Where is your father in all this, Harriet?"

She silenced, and her eyelids dropped. Looking at the deck, she said quietly, "He's dead."

"He died in New Zealand?"

She nodded.

"Does your brother know?"

"Probably not. He was on his way to South America when it happened."

Jake frowned, thinking that she had been alone after her father died—a girl, alone in a foreign land.

He said, "Was it sudden?"

"Very sudden," she said, and turned and quietly left him. For the first time she left the deck without being told.

TWELVE

TWO days later the lookouts raised land. It was dawn. Harriet came on deck to see a ghostly streak of mountaintops in the eastern sky, a pattern of disembodied brush strokes with no apparent connection to land. After breakfast the brown hills of Chile were visible on the horizon, a shadowy fringe of crags and peaks where fragile mists wafted out to sea. At noon the yards were braced about and a land breeze seized them. And, four hours later, there was Valparaiso, surrounded by lofty, shadowy hills, a romantic clutter of houses and towers on up-and-down streets. Pastel colors, red brick and whitewash were brilliant in the late afternoon sun, along with the terracotta domes of ancient churches and monasteries. More than seventy vessels lay at anchor in the bay—schooners, whalers, local sloops all brightly painted, barges, scows and guano-ships. Among this exotic crush of shipping, a British steambark-of-war and an American frigate bobbed ponderously at their anchors, flying many flags.

Harriet leaned her forearms on the warm wood of the port rail of the poop deck, gazing entranced at the scene. She had never visited Valparaiso before, and found it perfectly charming. The houses were built in the unlikeliest places, in rows along crags and up and down terraces. The foreshore, too, was picturesque, being a broad strand where strings of donkeys and mules moved slowly in laden procession. Men rode about at a much faster pace, calling out and waving wide hats. Others pushed little painted wagons, from which they appeared to sell grog, which they propelled into the water's edge in a race to meet the boatloads of sailors pulling out from the ships.

Jake's voice said, "I see no alpacas."

"No," Harriet admitted. She looked at the horses and donkeys and mules and wondered what alpacas looked like. She had seen pictures of them, but was not sure of the scale. Were they big, or small? And were their long-necked heads always stuck up in the air, like the drawings in Captain Schouten's map?

"And now that we have arrived, how do you expect to find your brother?"

"I thought I would ask at the Customs House, and leave a letter there." Then she reflected uneasily that the Customs House boat hadn't called to clear the brig yet, though a signal had been flown.

There were plenty of other small craft, gaily colored little boats plying the bay like waterbugs. Many of them were heading purposefully for the brig, paddled Indian style, and as they neared the paddlers stood up precariously, calling out inducements in a gabbled mixture of English and Spanish. These entrepreneurs wore big straw hats, and their clothes were brightly colored. They hung onto the straking of the brig, shouting out offers of wine and *aguardiente*, beans and potatoes, bananas, plantains, watermelons, cakes, cheese, cigars, sardines, tortillas and women. Then three boatmen sighted Harriet, and paddled to where she leaned over the rail, vying with each other to sell her ribbons and laces.

To her surprise, Jake haggled with one of them, and bought her some light-blue and dark-blue ribbons. "For your hat," he said, and she sparkled with pleasure, taking off her hat at once to tie the ribbons about the crown.

Then suddenly there was a hush. When Harriet looked up the boats were rowing off in a hurry. Even the *Gosling* men were quiet. Then she realized that the British bark-of-war had lowered a boat, and that boat was pulling towards them. Jake was frowning, his hat pulled low over his eyes, and she abruptly remembered that he was rumored to be a fugitive from justice.

However, the two young officers who arrived on the deck were full of smiles and empty of suspicions. One was a second lieutenant, the other a midshipman, and their vessel, they said, was the British steambark-of-war *Nympha*, in the Pacific and Indian Oceans on a three-year mission.

They had come, they said in their clear young English voices, because there had been a report of a *lady* on the brig *Gosling*. And they executed gallant little bows over Harriet's extended hand.

"Captain Mara sends his compliments," said the second lieutenant. "He feels some concern that you might be alarmed. A brig-of-war of the Peruvian fleet is expected hourly, and there will be the usual salute of guns. So he bade us come with a word to the wise."

"There will be nine guns to each man-of-war, including the American frigate *Savannah*," said the very young midshipman, sounding excited, "and then twenty-one guns each in respect of the Chilean fort. The good Lord alone knows," he added candidly, "how many guns the fort will fire in return. There will be much noise and a little smoke. Hence Captain Mara's concern."

"A true English gentleman," Harriet murmured, and there was an embarrassed clearing of throats.

"Captain Mara," said the midshipman, "is—h'm!—an Irishman, ma'am."

"Oh dear!" Then Harriet realized that that didn't sound quite right, as there was more throat-clearing.

"He also," said the second lieutenant after a tactful

pause, "requests the pleasure of the company of you and Captain Dexter to dinner tonight, ma'am, with a party of your officers and crew. Dinner on English vessels," he added tactfully, with only the slightest glance in Jake's direction, "is a meal that is served at eight. In the evening."

Jake merely said, "We would be delighted," but Harriet was very aware of his ill-hidden amusement. Then, while she was still getting over her surprise that he had accepted the invitation, the two young officers took their leave.

Captain Mara sent a boat, which arrived an hour after sunset. Harriet was waiting at the rail, and those men of the crew who had been selected to go on board the *Nympha* were milling about forward. She wore a watered silk taffeta gown in the palest blue, with a darker blue silk shawl about her hips in the Spanish style she enjoyed, and she had bound the blue ribbons Jake had given her into her piled hair.

As the *Nympha* boat touched the side, she heard a step behind her, and turning, she saw Jake. He was wearing black broadcloth with a snowy white stock, and had left the jacket unbuttoned, so that it only half-hid an exotically gold-embroidered waistcoat. He looked most unexpectedly splendid — like a picturebook pirate, she suddenly thought.

The boat, an eight-oared gig, was lined with pleated red satin. Never had Harriet seen anything so elaborately ridiculous. Like a coffin, she thought, and when Jake turned after issuing directions to Mr. Martin, who was in charge of the brig while they were gone, his expression was a study. However, he was grave enough when he helped her down into it.

Once she was settled, Jake seated himself beside her, as fastidious as any cat, and the men dipped their oars in well-drilled unison. The *Gosling* boat followed, with six chosen men at the oars, and Crotchet and Valentine in the sheets. At night, the bay looked magical. The darkness glowed with yellow spots of light from the multitude of lamps set on all the ships, and water dripped phosphorescently from the blades of the oars as they were lifted from the shimmering water. The *Gosling* boat was off to Harriet's left, and she watched it dreamily. Then she had to shift her gaze … the *Gosling* boat was drawing ahead.

Dear lord, she thought, the *Gosling*s had decided to turn it into a surreptitious race. Valentine Fish was urging on the oarsmen, his whispers echoing clearly over the water. Then all at once the gig's oarsmen saw what was happening, and with a lurch that forced Harriet to grab Jake's elbow, they set up a sudden spurt. Captain Dexter's arm was trembling with silent mirth, and she didn't dare meet his eyes, in case she exploded into giggles.

Neck and neck the two boats raced, while the huge stern of the bark-of-war loomed near. With a last spurt, the gig arrived at the gangway, hitting the side of the bark with a reverberating clunk that unbalanced Harriet yet again, but the *Gosling* boat was already there, and the grins on the *Gosling*s' faces were victorious. Captain Dexter's face was as inscrutable as ever, but when he helped Harriet stand and climb up the ladder she could feel him still shaking with laughter.

Marines saluted as Harriet stepped onto the deck, and a whistle piped as Jake came over the gangway to join her. The *Gosling*s who were following him shied like nervous colts at the unexpected sound, but recovered in an instant, however, and swaggered off in the wake of Valentine and Crotchet, as a couple of petty officers ushered them all forward to whatever food and entertainment awaited them in the more lowly parts of the ship.

As the captain's guests, Harriet and Captain Dexter were ushered aft, to the more grand and lofty officers' territory, their escorts being the second lieutenant and midshipman who had come to the brig with the invitation. Two Americans were already on board, they gossiped as they walked along the vast deck. One was Captain Mervine, and the other was Lieutenant Bartlett, and they had come from the frigate *Savannah.*

Captain Dexter said, "But the Peruvian brig has not arrived?"

"Perhaps tonight, sir," said the young midshipman. "It won't be long, their mission being so urgent."

Jake echoed, "Urgent?"

"It's on account of a desperado, sir, a villain of the most audacious kind, a man who has managed to evade Peruvian justice. He has offended the Indians in some drastic way, sir, and is reported to be in flight to this port. Hence the brig-of-war. Our assistance has been requested," he added importantly.

"And, of course, will be given," contributed the lieutenant. "One foot in Valparaiso, and the rogue will be brought to justice! Undoubtedly, he will be hanged." And with that, he stopped and knocked on a door, which was opened at once by a portly man in a blue swallowtail coat and blue trousers, with glittering brass buttons and a lot of gold about his large presence.

This, Harriet deduced at once, was no less than Captain Mara. His Irish aura was unmistakable, along with his whiskey breath. "Welcome," he boomed. "Come right in, Mrs. Dexter!"

She should have expected it, Harriet thought confusedly, but her cheeks were as hot as fire. She glanced at Jake, and then just as quickly away again, before she could see his expression. His voice was even, though, as he said, "Please allow me to introduce our passenger, a part-owner of our brig. This lady, sir, is Miss Harriet Gray."

"Not Mrs. Dexter?" Captain Mara appeared thunderstruck, and not very intelligent, either. "A super-cargo, you say?"

"Miss Gray is from London, England," said Jake.

"London?" echoed Captain Mara, thrown off balance even further by the *non sequitur*. "Well, well," he rumbled, and then roused himself to introduce the two officers from the *Savannah*. They were large and noble men, too, wearing just as much gold and lace, though their trousers were white, not blue. Harriet shook their hands, gathering her composure.

Captain Mara boomed, "You say from London, Captain Dexter?"

"Miss Gray has been living in New Zealand—and the Cape Colony."

"Ah, then she can't be that actress gal, the one that I did hear of, the daughter of that Charles Gray that all Britain do revere."

"But I am," said Harriet rather tartly, tired of being spoken of as if she wasn't there. "My father is—was—Charles Gray, and my mother was Mary Sissons, sir."

The effect was all she could have wished for—all her listeners looked equally thunderstruck. "You're from that playacting lot?" Captain Mara demanded.

"I am, sir."

"The family of the London stage?"

"And the provinces, yes."

"By thunder," said Captain Mara. He shook his head, drained his glass, and looked around for another. "But confound it," he said to Jake, "this be a true compliment. I do swear I saw her father thrice—no, stump it, four times at least! It was a while back—it don't really matter when, but by God, the experience was tremendous inspiring, and her mother, sir, her mother..." His voice faded away, and then, clapping himself on his bright red forehead, he cried, "But I must beg a favor of Miss Gray!"

"You must?" Jake murmured.

"But of course! In the matter of play-acting, sir!"

"Play-acting?" Jake's sideways glance at Harriet was wicked. "I'm certain Miss Gray will be glad to oblige—for on the ship to the Cape Colony, she tells me, she and the other lady passengers often play-acted for the edification of both passengers and crew."

"But I mean more than that, sir!" Captain Mara cried. "We have a band of Thespians on board this very ship, a play-acting group that this very night is to stage a portion of Shakespeare for the entertainment of our guests! Tell me, Miss Gray, are you amazed?"

Harriet wasn't amazed at all, but didn't have a chance to tell him so, because the door opened and more guests were announced. A babble of dignitaries from shore had arrived, the women like flowers and the men like peacocks, and Harriet found herself alone with Jake.

She sipped champagne to fill the silence. He had a glass in his hand, but was not drinking. Instead, he was studying her with a quizzical expression.

He said thoughtfully, "And are you amazed?"

"No, of course I'm not. Wherever British troops are stationed in a far-off place, they immediately set to and form a play-acting group—and it's usual, too, for them to play Shakespeare."

"I strongly suspect that the favor our host has in mind is for you to act with the *Nympha* troupe."

"I'm sure you're right."

"You sound resigned."

"Well, it's happened often enough before. There was a British man-of-war at the Cape, and my father and my brother and I were all invited on board, and then asked to take part in the shipboard production. I," she added, "was the Shrew."

"How very well cast," he observed with a malicious chuckle.

"Well, I did better than the resident player, who made the gruffest Shrew I've ever heard."

"And the play was a great success?"

"Not really. The ship, you see, was due to return to England, after a tour of duty in the Indian Ocean, and various sultans had sent presents by her for the Queen—and a lot of those presents were animals. The production was going quite well, but then the lions escaped. Royal showed more agility than I'd ever seen before—he was the first in the rigging, but the whole of our audience was hot on his heels."

Jake shouted with laughter, and everyone looked at them.

Harriet smiled graciously at them all, and then turned back to Jake and said, "And were *you* amazed?"

"To find you are an actress? Not in the slightest—for it explained why you expected me to know your name. I presume you and your brother are famous?"

"That depends on who you're talking to."

"Ah," he said, and grinned.

The others were coming their way, herded by their affable host, who was still going on loudly about the unexpected honor of having a member of the acting Grays on board. Dexter cast a glance their way, looked back at Harriet, and said, "And it explained something else, too."

"Yes?"

"The melodramatic tantrums."

While she was still delivering him a simmering look, the other guests joined them. A uniformed steward poured more champagne, while the second lieutenant recited the names of all those present, names that Harriet instantly forgot.

One of the ladies was a large toothy Frenchwoman, who shrieked, "You, an actress? You, a woman of the stage?"

That, thought Harriet, was rather   unfortunately phrased. Jake merely smiled, and said, "The Gray family is famous."

"Aha," said the Frenchwoman.

"I hope," said Captain Mara roguishly, "to prevail on Miss Gray to take part in the interlude from Shakespeare that our troupe is staging for our entertainment tonight. Do you think she'll do it, Captain Dexter?"

"Of course she will," said Jake.

"It's the part of the beautiful Faerie Queen, Titania."

"Excellent!" said Jake.

"Do you think" —anxiously, lowering his voice a little— "she knows the lines?"

"Of course she does," said Jake.

Captain Dexter, Harriet mused heatedly, was having the time of his life. Undoubtedly, she meditated, he considered it a neat revenge for all her mutinies and her deviousness.

Dinner was set at a long table in the wardroom, in a sparkling display of white linen, silver and crystal, with half a dozen different wine glasses to each setting. It was more luxury than Harriet had seen in almost two years.

She was seated between Captain Mara and Captain Mervine of the *Savannah*, while Jake Dexter and the toothy Frenchwoman sat opposite. The courses of fancy food seemed endless, each accompanied by a different wine, which triggered equally endless toasting. The men bobbed up and down with the regularity of corks in a rugged sea. They toasted Queen Victoria, President Polk, and Shakespeare. Then, by process of logic, they toasted Miss Gray. Then they toasted Captain Dexter for possessing the perspicacity to bring Miss Gray to the bark-of-war, and then, with further logic, they toasted the American flag.

After the toasts had finally drifted to a halt, the Frenchwoman cried out, "Tell me, Captain Mara, tell me, what do these tales of the gold?"

Gold? Harriet saw Jake frown as he turned to look at the woman.

He didn't speak, so Harriet said, "Gold? What gold, madame?"

"The gold in California!" Captain Mara boomed, while the Frenchwoman was still opening her mouth. "There be fanciful tales a-running about this coast, right disbelievable tales of gold up the Sacramento Valley!"

96

"It's naught but a hoax." This statement was flat, and came with a Yankee accent. It was Captain Mervine of the *Savannah*, silent as an obelisk till then. "There was a fuss about in Monterey in March. A feller rode into the barracks shouting about some gold he reckoned he'd seen, collected up a fork of what used to be called the Rio de los Americanos, but now is properly named the American River. There be another feller up the Sacramento, too, a Mormon trader and newspaperman called Brannan, he hollers the same hoax. It's just a ploy to hustle up business, so he can sell all the goods he's got in his store at Sutter's Fort, a store full of picks and pans and shovels. He's a notorious rogue — sane men don't heed him. California has a future, glowing, California has riches, true. But they ain't in the form of nuggets or gold dust, they can only be found in the sweat of honest men." Mervine nodded at Dexter then, and said, "Have you ever dropped anchor at San Francisco?"

Harriet watched Jake shake his head. He was frowning, and seemed very thoughtful.

"Well, Captain Dexter," Mervine said, "I prophesy it right now, and I mean it, San Francisco is destined to be the premier port of the whole Pacific. The poor little town of just two hundred souls that I laid eyes on first in 1846 has grown by ten times, and the most of that growth is American. The original houses might have been built of sunburnt bricks, but wooden houses are being shipped over there — by Americans! And, the climate and soil! — suffice it to say because of the climate and soil of California, any enterprising Yankee agriculturalist is sure to make a fast fortune. California is now blessed with American drive and enterprise, and its golden future is inevitable."

Harriet said, feeling puzzled, "But I thought California was Mexican."

"No longer!" Captain Mervine hollered, scowling at her. "The Mexican War — if it deserved to be called a war — is now at an end. It is over, ma'am, American force has prevailed!"

"Oh dear," she said, realizing she had made a political mistake. "I am so very sorry."

Then she winced, because the words had not come out as intended. Captain Mervine gave her a brooding look, and she could hear his heavy breathing. She explained rather lamely, "I have been traveling, Captain Mervine, sir, and — and subsisting in the colonies. The War must have ended while I wasn't paying attention."

"H'm!" he said, only slightly mollified. "The territory will flourish now, and California, under American management, will prove rich indeed."

"I'm sure you're right, Captain Mervine."

"But it will not grow rich with this problematical gold!"

"I believe you, sir."

"A few fools have rushed off to the reputed gold mines. The United States frigate *Ohio* lost a number of marines, and the general suspicion is that they are following the fables, too. One devious fellow picked a quarrel with the first Spaniard he met on shore — knocked him down, was incarcerated in the fort, and escaped — escaped from that notorious black hole! How he did it, no one knows, as no one has seen him since. Others followed his example by bribing a boatman to carry them off from the ship — in the broad of day! Their escape was soon discovered, but when the lieutenant on watch roared out most lustily, the boatman had the sauce to stand up with folded arms, and whistle *Yankee Doodle*. Then, no sooner had a boat been hastily lowered, then he sat down again and paddled fast for shore. Half a dozen men were ordered to the side of the ship, and the orders to *Make ready* and *Present arms* were hollered out loud, but the boat merely quickened its pace. *Fire!* — roared the lieutenant, and fire the squad did, but at some imaginary object about a mile above the heads of the fugitives, the rascals, and when the smoke cleared the whole confounded lot in the fleeing boat were thumbing their noises and whistling *Yankee Doodle*. But if indeed they heard these wild tales of gold, and manage to get as far as the Californian hills, and if indeed they do find gold, the garrison will claim it. Colonel Mason will send out a force to take possession, in the name of the United States government."

"But there is no gold," said Harriet into the silence that followed this remarkable anecdote.

Captain Mervine blinked. "You seem certain, ma'am."

"There can't be, because if the Mexicans had thought there was some, they would have fought much harder, and made sure the Americans didn't win."

She looked about the table, delighted with her logic — and met Jake's highly entertained expression. Then she heard Captain Mara clear his throat, and realized she had blundered again.

"A toast," boomed the Irishman. "Another toast — to er, ah, the Chilean flag."

And the toast was held, giving Harriet a chance to gather her wits. Then the talk turned to the desperate villain that the Chilean forces were hunting down in town, and the Peruvian man-of-war that was due to arrive in pursuit of the same desperado, the same man who had gravely offended the Indians, and had created a riot. But Harriet paid little attention. She was mentally rehearsing her lines, certain that if she missed a single cue, Jake Dexter would tease her unmercifully.

THIRTEEN

THE stage was the afterdeck, and Titania's grassy mound was a *chaise-longue* with a green billiard-table cover thrown over it. Harriet reclined gracefully, listening to the commotion. Captain Mara's party was going full-fizz, having turned into a tremendous success. Particularly, she thought wryly, since she had stopped blundering into the conversation.

The dinner finally over, the guests had come up on deck to waltz to the music of a musical box with drum and bell accompaniment. Then, after Harriet had been danced practically off her feet, the musical box had been set aside, and the *chaise-longue* had been put out, along with chairs for the guests. The seamen and petty officers, who had been having their own fun forward, watched from the bulwarks and the rigging.

Harriet lay with her eyes shut, draped with her silken shawl. She heard a little bell, and the officers shushing the audience until Captain Mara could be heard.

Then, through a speaking trumpet, the Irishman announced that they were about to be greatly favored with a dramatic recital by the *Nympha*'s Thespians. "A famous recital from the Immortal Bard's *A Midsummer Night's Dream*, which will be flattered with the unexpected presence

101

of none other than Miss Harriet Gray, of the famous Gray family of the Royal Opera House, London! She has graciously consented to play the part of the beautiful fairy queen, Titania."

The ensuing silence was stunned, most of the astonishment, Harriet was certain, emanating from the *Goslings*. Then there was a polite round of applause from Captain Mara's officers and guests, after which she heard the actors make their entrance and gather about.

And then: "If I were fair, Thisby, if I were only thine!" the actor playing Bottom brayed. His tone was muffled, and when Harriet opened one eye it was to see he was wearing a most magnificent mask, a very hairy donkey face, made of rope ends fixed to wire and canvas.

"Help, we are haunted!" cried the other actor-yokels, reacting melodramatically to the sight of their comrade magicked into an ass. "O monstrous! O strange!" they cried.

And Harriet listened to the retreating thunder of their boots, as they yelled, "Pray masters, fly masters! Help—help—help!"

"Why do they run away?" asked Bottom plaintively. "Is this a knavery of them to make me afeared?"

"Bless thee, Bottom," cried an actor-yokel, briefly reappearing. "Thou art translated!"—and away he went again.

"I see their knavery," Bottom mumbled to himself. "They hope to make an ass of me—to fright me, if they could. But I will not stir from this place, do what they can: I will walk up and down here, and will sing, that they shall hear I am not afraid—

The ousel cock, so black of hue
With orange-tawny bill
The throstle, with his note so true
The wren, with little quill—

His singing was more loud than tuneful, but not as loud

as the tramp of his navy boots. Then the stamping came to an abrupt halt by Titania's couch, which was Harriet's cue. She sighed and stretched, and inquired in ringing tones, "What angel wakes me from my flowery bed?"

And when she opened her eyes she looked straight into Jahaziel Dexter's face. He had apparently declined to sit on a chair, for he was leaning on the side of a deckhouse, most disconcertingly near. If she was about to fumble her lines he was not going to miss a word of it, she deduced—and never had she seen his eloquent face so wickedly amused.

She delivered him a black scowl, and then looked away, to smile ravishingly at Bottom. "On first view, I say," she exclaimed, "I swear I love thee."

"Methinks, mistress, you should have little reason for that," Bottom objected, and all the *Gosling* men came out of their daze to hoot in agreement. "And yet, to say the truth," the actor philosophized, "reason and love keep little company together nowadays."

"Ain't that the truth," said Valentine Fish—a feeble joke, Harriet thought, but one that was greeted with roars of laughter from all about the rigging.

Harriet waited out the ruckus. Then: "Thou art as wise as thou art beautiful," she breathed. Her fingers brushed the air, hovering over the donkey mask, dared then to caress the hairy hide, while the *Gosling* men whistled and cheered.

"Not so neither," objected Bottom to shouts of agreement, then went on to convey that if he did have wits, he would be well out of this wood.

"Out of this wood do not desire to go," Harriet commanded—

Thou shalt remain here, whether thou wilt or no,
I am a spirit of no common rate
The summer still doth tend upon my state
And I do love thee, therefore go with me
I'll give thee fairies to tend thee—

103

—and four fairies arrived, right on cue, clumping out of the darkness with a dutiful clicking of boot heels. She cried out their names—"Pease-blossom, Cobweb, Moth and Mustardseed!" and, "Ready!—And aye, aye, aye!" four heavily bearded and tattooed fairies chorused.

"Where shall we go?" they asked.

"To have my love to bed!" cried Harriet, and waited out the whistles and bawdy comments until she could make herself heard again.

> And pluck the wings from painted butterflies
> To fan the moonbeams from his sleeping eyes,
> Nod to him, elves, and do him courtesies!

"Hail, mortal!" cried the fairies, each in turn, and, "Lead him to my bower!" commanded Harriet, rising from her couch. "Tie up my lover's tongue, bring him silently."

And off the extempore stage she wafted, while the audience stamped with delirious approval.

The applause lasted quite five minutes, and it took a lot of shouting from the mates to hassle the foremast men back to their own quarters. Never, Harriet meditated, had she taken part in such a runaway farce.

Then at last the afterdeck was again the domain of the captains, officers, and guests. The chaise was taken away and the musical box was brought out and wound up, but the male guests were more interested in the tray of drinks, which meant that Harriet was able to retreat to the shadows by the rail, to rest her battered spirits and her overworked feet. But, just as she began to relax, Jake Dexter materialized beside her.

She gave him a simmering look, but he merely said, "My dance, I think."

With no warning at all, she found herself in his arms. He held her loosely. The musical box was playing a waltz at the rate of a feverish gallop, but he made no move to dance.

She said heatedly up into his face, "Jahaziel Dexter, you are the most exasperating person I have ever met."

"The feeling is mutual," he said, and chuckled.

"And I suppose you're about to taunt me with all the blunders I've made."

"Well, it was worth it to see Mervine's expression, which was really very funny. Did you see him go puce? I doubt he will ever forgive you, but I certainly will. And that must be the rowdiest audience of your experience, surely."

"I wouldn't be so certain of that," she said moodily.

"And your fellow actors knew their lines! I didn't believe you when you said that soldiers stage Shakespeare."

"Oh, but they do. The soldiers in the Albert barracks outside Auckland have their own little theater, with a stage and a drop curtain, believe it or not. They put on shows for anyone who cares to come — not that the people of Auckland seem conscious of the privilege. It's rather beneath them, really — or that's the way they behave."

Jake paused, leaning back to study her face. "You make it sound as if the settlers in New Zealand don't approve of the stage."

"They don't approve of anything! Well, they certainly don't approve of actors. According to the newspapers, actors and actresses do little more than annoy the neighbors. And the citizens usually had to be drunk before they'd condescend to attend the theater. Actors are not considered respectable anywhere, really, being such a loose and flamboyant lot, but they're looked down on with emphasis in New Zealand."

In her mind she could hear again the clatter of the wooden-soled shoes the New Zealand colonists wore in town because of the mud, and the rattle as they scuttled along the wooden sidewalks. She remembered the sudden silences when she entered a room, and the hushed whispers as people hurried past. Then Jake's voice brought her out of dark memories, saying, "And your brother, Royal?"

105

She blinked and frowned, puzzled. "What do you mean?"

"What kind of person is he?"

"He's an actor, but you know that. He likes playing Hamlet best, but he makes a very passable Falstaff. You will see what I mean when you meet him."

"We'll have to find him, first."

The words were flat, and she said again, "What do you mean?"

Jake Dexter said nothing for the moment, but began to dance in slow out-of-rhythm circles. She went with him unwillingly, very conscious of his warmth and his scent of brandy and shaving lather, and the way his fingers curled round her waist.

Then he said abruptly, "My pack of rogues will find your brother, never fret about that, but you had better tell me what he looks like."

She stood still, and he stopped too. "Oh my God," she said, her brain working at last. "You think he's the desperado that the Peruvian brig is coming to arrest. Oh dear God, I've involved you in something criminal."

"You've certainly complicated my life." The grim words were matched by his sardonic expression.

"You're used to complications!" she snapped, offended.

He said coldly, "I beg your pardon?"

Harriet shut her eyes. She could have bitten out her tongue the instant the words had left her mouth, but like all her other conversational gaffes that night, it was impossible to take them back.

She looked up at him appealingly, and said, "It was nothing. I'm sorry I said that—please forget it. And Royal is easily recognized, for he looks the image of a strolling player. He's tall and thin, and walks in long strides, like this, see..." She broke away from him, and took long steps, holding up her skirts past her knees, and looking at him over her shoulder. "See how his toes are pointed out to the sides? And how he leans forward as he walks, like this … as if a wind blows hard behind him. His hair is like straw, the same color as mine, but much coarser in texture, and he has a long nose and a pointed beard…"

Jake said in the same icy tone, "You've been gossiping with my men."

"I have not! You told me yourself that you are a pirate!" Then she said more softly, "Please Jake, my tongue slips so tonight, and I am very tired. I honestly think that the way you run your brig is admirably democratic, and I know I took advantage of it, but I was truly desperate — and whatever lies in your past means nothing to me."

"You mean you don't know how I acquired the brig?"

"I don't think I want to know, Jahaziel."

"Yes, you do." And he started to dance again, drawing her with him, moving slowly as he stared down into her eyes.

"Three years ago, Harriet, I was given the command of a fine ship, with a box of bullion and a cargo of Yankee notions, with which I was supposed to buy a profitable freight of Chinese goods. I was twenty-three, and I was just married. I'd built a neat little house with the proceeds from my last voyage, and I had married my childhood sweetheart and sailed away. But what I didn't know was that the owner fancied my sweetheart, and my cottage, too, and had sent me away on a good long voyage so he could take advantage of my absence."

"Please, Jake, I really don't want to hear this."

"Yes, you do," he said again, and his hold on her tightened. "Eight months later, I made the port of Talcahuano, and began to hear gossip. Oh, I didn't believe it at first, but then I dropped anchor in Valparaiso... Then, Callao, then Tombez — and in each port I heard the same story, from men whose word I believed. And then I was given a newspaper from home that told me that the owner of the bark owned not just my wife and my house, but an infant son, too, a boy who could not possibly be mine. So…"

She stopped, and drew back to gaze up into his face. "So you stole the ship?"

"Yes, Harriet, I truly am a pirate," he said. "I stole the ship and kept the cargo, and sold the ship to a trader in Tahiti who gave me an excellent price, and with the proceeds I bought the *Gosling* and founded the *Gosling* Company. And the *Gosling* is mine by right, even if the law doesn't say so!"

She said softly, "Of course it is, and I am so sorry I intruded on your private affairs." And she reached over and up to kiss him on the cheek.

It was meant to be simply an apologetic gesture, but … perhaps she stumbled, perhaps the ship pitched, perhaps… All she knew that somehow she was tight against him as he kissed her mouth. The voices and laughter in the distance all faded as her world diminished to the perfect fit of their bodies, his warmth and taste and her hand in the curve at the back of his head, the feel of his skin under her palm, and her hair loosening so it fell into his hand and over his shoulder, his intensity and her trembling … and then the ship trembled, too, as the night exploded.

Harriet gasped in fright. His mouth left hers. Jahaziel said something but she couldn't hear the words, because the night was thundering again. "My God!" she cried. "Is is the end of the world?"

But then she knew the answer. The thunder was a salute of guns that went on … and on … and on. The Peruvian bark-of-war had arrived.

FOURTEEN

EARLY next morning Jake Dexter stood at the taffrail on the poop deck of his brig *Gosling*, and watched the frenzy of activity that was developing on the harbor.

The Peruvian brig-of-war was anchored to the north of the steambark *Nympha*, and   all three men-of-war in port were flying bunting, as well as flaunting flags. It was as if, he thought, the hunting down of one solitary desperado was an excuse for a holiday. Marines lined up on all three vessels in smart and businesslike rows. Those on the Peruvian brig were wearing white and red regimentals that looked almost spick and span from this distance. Loud shouting drifted over the water, and the smart lines of Peruvian marines stamped in unison and fired their muskets in the air. Then the steambark *Nympha* hooted in a screech of steam and weighed anchor.

The bark puffed out to the perimeter of the bay, fired at a target, missed, puffed back and forth and fired again with equal lack of success, steamed this way and that and then at last dropped anchor, in the very same spot that she'd left. The Peruvians fired six cannon in reply, and the *Gosling*s cheered a round of derisive huzzahs.

The cheerleader was, of course, Valentine Fish. The junior officer was dressed up in honor of the occasion in his best liberty rig, which comprised buckskin trousers with a mountainman fringe down each outside seam, and a bright red drilling shirt. Crotchet, looking equally dashing in black trousers and frilled white shirt, was with him, and Dan Kemp and Tib Greene, too, despite Tib's broken arm. The handsome brown man from the Azores they all called Joseph Fayal was there, in case his Portuguese was needed, and Pablo the ex-Chilean bullfighter, because of his Spanish.

Jake nodded to the boys to get the whaleboat down onto the water. Valentine went down in it to work the falls, with Tib lounging in the sheets, and after it had splashed to a bobbing stop, the other four men tumbled down the side and took their places. Then, just as Jake braced his arm to swing over the side and join them, Harriet arrived in shore-going dress, too.

Jake studied her carefully, remembering their mutual silence as they had been rowed back to the brig, and thinking that she, too, had been dazed by the unexpected passion of that inadvertent kiss. During the night, he had tossed and turned, unable to stop himself from picturing what would have happened if he had followed up on that ardent embrace, and carried her off to his bed. Intellectually, he knew it would have been a foolish move, considering that her position on board was so ambiguous already. But his hungry manhood had remembered the feel of the slim, lithe body in his arms...

He said in a deliberately businesslike tone, "And where, Miss Gray, do you think you are going?"

"On shore, of course," she retorted. "How else will I find my brother? I have to go to—to the Customs House, and—and report my arrival, or how else will Royal know that I am here?"

Jake paused, looking past her shoulder. Behind Harriet, the harbor was busier than ever. The marines on the Peruvian brig had lined up, and as he watched they filed into boats, which began to pull for shore. The American marines on the frigate *Savannah* were lined up likewise, ready to embark when their boats arrived. He had every reason to call the mission off and weigh anchor … but he couldn't. Somehow, he had become inextricably involved in Harriet's affairs. Why? Because she was now a member of the *Gosling* company, with a claim on the mutual loyalties that being a member involved? Or because of that moment of inadvertent passion? He didn't want to think about it, because it made him feel vulnerable.

He looked back at her, and said, "Miss Gray, you have to stop on board, or we'll be in worse trouble than we are in right now. If you call at the Customs House all you will manage to do is alert them to his identity — and even if they know that already, you will be confirming that he is definitely expected in this port. They will use you to trap him."

"But he's my brother — and I have to go on shore with you, or how else can you find him? I'm the only one who knows what he looks like."

"Harriet, you underestimate yourself," he dryly informed her. "Your description was vivid enough, believe me."

Then, before she could say another word, he turned to Charlie and said, "Please make sure that Miss Gray stays on board. Tie her up, if necessary." And without waiting for Harriet to get over her outrage, and Charlie to recover from astonishment, he vaulted over the side and into the stern of the boat.

As the boat was rowed to shore, he turned his mind to the difficult challenge that awaited, thoughtfully studying the men in his boat. Valentine, Crotchet, Dan, and Pablo pulled at the amidship oars, with Joseph Fayal right in the front, at bow oar. Tib Greene, because of his broken arm, lounged at his ease. They didn't look reliable in the slightest, he thought grimly. The forces of four nations searched Valparaiso for one lone fugitive, and somehow he expected this unhandsome group to succeed where all the soldiers and marines would fail. The most he could hope for, most probably, was that they would somehow avoid incarceration in the fort.

But who else could he have possibly used? Abner was wounded, and Jonathan too slow-witted, and Abijah and Chips and Cookie and Bodfish were all too staid and middle-aged to be involved in such a chase. Importantly, too, Valentine, Crotchet, Tib, Dan, Pablo and Joseph knew Valparaiso well. Because of past visits, they were intimately familiar with the terraced streets and the characters who inhabited the back alleys; they knew where the cockfights were held, and they knew the owners of the taps, and the proprietors of the *pulperías*. They also knew the two brothels, which sailors the Pacific over knew as the Maintop and the Foretop, because of the two hills they stood on, and Jake hoped they wouldn't waste too much time there.

"Sunset," he instructed as the boat grated on black sand. "Be here. I'll wait one hour, no more."

Without waiting for a reply, he threw some coins to the urchins who ran up to look after the boat, and strode up the beach to the promenade. His first goal was the Customs House, to post his papers and collect any mail, and after that he would explore the more respectable *tabernas* and billiard rooms, where he would conduct his own discreet inquiries.

He would send fresh provisions out to the brig as well, he decided as he stepped onto pavement. If they did find the fugitive and somehow managed to smuggle him on board, they would be forced to make a quick flight out to the open sea, and it probably wouldn't be wise to venture into any South American port for quite a little while.

Valentine, Crotchet, Tib, Dan, Pablo and Joseph stood in a group watching Captain Dexter go, and then they held a council of war. They did not share Jake's inner doubts, and would have been highly insulted if they had guessed his thoughts. For, by thunder, they surely did know Valparaiso! And they had a good description of their quarry.

"Tall and thin," said Valentine. "Straw-colored hair. Walks with the wind blowing rugged behind him, with toes stuck out to the side." They all nodded. Now, all they needed was a rendezvous. "Maria's fandango," said Valentine. "An hour before sunset." They nodded again, shook hands with great ceremony, and then dispersed in pairs.

Valentine and Crotchet were assigned the upper reaches of the city, where they were familiar figures to the inhabitants. They strolled arm-in-arm along the steep alleys while doe-eyed señoritas leaned over flower-strung balconies and hailed them with joy, singing out their names. Men massaging roosters greeted them by name as well, and nodded and grinned knowledgeably when words were muttered in their ears. It was just that easy—everyone in Valparaiso had heard about the desperado, so knew exactly who they meant when the boys asked them to pass on a message. No one knew where the fugitive might be, unfortunately, but the hours stretched ahead, with plenty of time to spread the word that if located, he should be directed to Maria's fandango.

Tib and Dan covered the northward stretches of the waterfront town, while Pablo and Joseph Fayal carried out their own search in the cafés of the southern end of the lower city. Unfortunately, they were waylaid by the blandishments of Valparaiso, so that by late afternoon, only the quiet, reliable Joseph Fayal had his mind on the job. Tib and Dan had been distracted by the wiles of the raven-haired girls, and Pablo had lost all his money on the roosters.

At the door of almost every house there was a fighting rooster tied to a stick sunk in the ground, each one sending out a shrill challenge to all the other roosters, and Joseph had not been able to stop Pablo from trailing along to one of the cock-fighting pits. At first Joseph, an unsophisticated young man from Fayal, in the Azores, had found this interesting, as the pit was as big as a circus, surrounded by benches on which serried rows of Valparaiso citizens perched, examining the scene with the air of world-weary connoisseurs. But, despite many warnings, Pablo had insisted on laying bets on some of the more spectacular specimens. Unfortunately, good looks did not necessarily equate with fighting ability, and when Pablo finally had the sense to see it was high time he was gone, he was stopped from leaving the ring by an angry man with a long, sharp knife, who swore that he would have Pablo's heart's blood as a forfeit if Pablo didn't produce what was owed to him. They escaped only because Joseph Fayal had the presence of mind to throw the handful of coins he had left into the midst of the crowd. In the confusion of the fight that promptly followed, he grabbed Pablo by the arm, and propelled him away.

In the upper terraces, Crotchet and Valentine were getting into strife by gambling, too, though at another kind of hazard. This was nine-pin billiards, a game that had just been invented by the sharks, and was the latest rage in the taps of the Pacific coast of South America. Nine pins were set up at one end of a billiard table, while the players lined up at the other end. Then, one by one, they competed to knock the nine pins down with just three balls, the white, the spot, and the red. If a man knocked down a pin, or holed the ball he had struck, two points were added to his score. If at one stroke he knocked down all nine pins, it was considered a *coup de main*, and fifty was added to his tally. Whoever reached one hundred points first was the winner.

When the boys had first come into the gaming saloon, it was just in time to see a rangy Yankee challenge one of the local señors to a game, with a stake of twenty-five dollars. The money had been promptly lost, and the rueful visitor had vowed that he wanted revenge, and had slapped the enormous sum of five hundred dollars on the table. As the news of the crazy wager had filtered out into the street, the room had abruptly filled up, and after that, for quite some moments, it had looked as if the brash American was going to lose his cash. But then — then he had taken his cigar out of his mouth, and bowled down all nine pins with one pitch, a feat that he promptly followed with a second.

"I can do that, suh," declared Crotchet, abrim with confidence, and elbowed his way to the table. Hands were shaken all around, and Crotchet was welcomed with such enthusiasm that no one really noticed the Yankee quietly disappear … after handing over his winnings to the owner of the saloon, and receiving a generous commission in return.

Crotchet played with flair and flamboyance, sending off each ball with a loud, "See that, suh!" Unfortunately, the last strike was off, which was when Crotchet found he had none of the ready to cover his bet. He was embarrassed, as he readily confessed, and the proprietor of the establishment gave vent to furious screeches of rage. Valentine had no money either, so a boisterous battle commenced, as the proprietor's large family rushed to his aid.

That was about the exact same moment that Dan at the other end of the waterfront, was battling a huge Peruvian who had cast aspersions on his virility. The Peruvian was one of the marines from the brig-of-war, and, like most of his comrades, had succumbed long since to the blandishments of sophisticated Valparaiso, so was as drunk and penniless as Dan. The port police and the mates of the brig pounded onto the scene with much shouting and blasting of whistles. The Peruvian was arrested on the spot, but Dan escaped in the skirmish, followed closely by Tib.

Valentine and Crotchet were equally fortunate. Just when it seemed that the nine-pin billiards man and his host of brothers and cousins would pound them into the cobbles, a man driving cattle on the street above lost control of his herd. Cows plunged about in every direction, harried by yapping dogs and half the town urchins, who yelled and flapped serapes, driving the poor animals to desperation, and the two *Goslings* escaped in the commotion.

By ways and means, then, they all found their way to Maria's fandango. This was a discreet affair, a long hall, whitewashed inside and out, with only two doors, one at the front, and one at the back. Within its cool interior, dancers and harlots strolled about with little cigars betwixt their red lips, and pimps and gentlemen watched them from the walls, dressed in spurs and showy brocades. All the men were Spanish, and everyone's hair was black. Even Tib and Dan had dark-brown hair, and Crotchet's ringlets surpassed the locals for inkiness. The only tow-colored head in sight belonged to Valentine Fish. The sun, outside, was nudging the western horizon, and as the *Goslings* assembled, they looked at each other uneasily.

Out in the narrow street the air grew cooler. A smoky quiet settled over the town as the populace thought about supper. Echoes of marching boots and barked-out orders resounded from the terraces, and it was painfully evident that though the troops of the day had been drunk and disorganized, replacements were arriving.

A squad of American marines marched by in the alley outside, and when they had finally gone, Tib said, "Why ain't you found the desperado?"

Crotchet shrugged. The conference paused while sailors from the various merchant ships came in and studied the strolling women. Then Maria, the proprietress of the fandango, came in from the back, smiling at the influx of custom — and sighting Valentine, she let out a shriek.

"The boy, yes!" she cried. "The boy who strums, the boy who sings!"

A man who had been playing a doleful guitar was summarily dismissed, and a chair was shoved up to a dilapidated pianoforte, and Valentine was urged into it. "Yankee doodle went to town," he sang, keeping accompaniment, and the sailors all joined in.

Yankee doodle dandy!
And there he met a winsome lass
And sweetened her with ... candy
He put his fingers on her breast
A'cause he felt so ... handy
And put his fingers summat else
A'cause he felt so randy!

"Hooray, fine fellow!" someone exclaimed in obvious delight, and Valentine glanced over his shoulder — and his lifted piano-playing hands stopped dead in the air.

For there stood a tall thin fellow, a man with a pointed straw beard and a long pointed nose with a drop on its reddened end. He was dressed in a shabby collection of South American clothes, and he stank most horribly. Indeed, his stench was so strong it was almost visible.

And he smiled and said in a clear, ringing English accent that reminded Valentine at once of Miss Gray, "Would your name be *Valentine*, my good sir?"

118

FIFTEEN

"TARNATION," said Valentine, astonished that their day's endeavors had actually resulted in the accomplishment of their mission. "You must be Royal Gray."

"I've been receiving messages the whole blessed afternoon, running from tap to tap, messages that told me that if I came to Maria's fandango an hour before sunset and asked for a gallant young fellow named Valentine, then that said Valentine would set me right. Is that so, sir?"

Tib Greene arrived at that moment, took one look, and said, "Wa'al, good lord, this must be the bastard himself." He put out his hand but then froze, as Royal Gray's stench got through to him. "Good lord," he said again, this time rather faintly, but didn't have a chance to say any more, because the door to the alley crashed open, and a squad of Chilean soldiers charged in.

Women screamed, and sailors fought to get to the door at the back, the Goslings and the smelly desperado fighting as hard as the rest. The mass of men struggled and then all at once the whole lot popped out of the fandango, and into the cobbled yard behind.

The yard was as black as a witch's cat, full of men who were fighting to disperse in different directions. Soldiers ran out of the back door too, but then milled around half-blind,

119

lost in the confusion. Whistles were blown, and shots fired into the air, while the women in the fandango screamed even more deafeningly. Then even that din was outdone by the clamor of some vehicle, which was arriving from the bottom of the street in a crash and screech of iron wheels and hooves. Seizing the distraction, the *Goslings* fought their way into the alley, dragging the desperado with them. No sooner had they burst out of the back yard of the fandango, than a huge old carriage jolted into sight.

It was one of the battered coaches that the Valparaiso citizens used as omnibuses, and which drunken sailors regularly commandeered and raced about at suicidal speed. This seemed to be the case here, and the Chilean soldiers simply scattered to get out of the way, shaking their heads and laughing. The man on the driving bench, though, was not drunk in the slightest. Jake Dexter was merely furious.

For good Jehovah's sake, he fumed, he'd relied on his men to ask about discreetly, not let the whole of Valparaiso know that they wanted to meet the desperado at Maria's fandango! The whole town had been laughing about it, including all the captains in the more respectable saloons, and then, to Jake's dismay, he had found that the news had got not just to the Chilean garrison, but to the Peruvian brig-of-war, too. This pirating of a public coach had been an inspiration born of crisis. He cracked the whip, urging the horses on, even though the alley was narrowing rapidly, becoming too constricted to accommodate the carriage. Varnished wood scraped with a scream along old stonework, then Jake sharply hauled back on the reins.

He'd just sighted Valentine, who was cowering in a doorway. "You damn fool," he roared. "Why didn't you just paint your message on the Customs House walls?" Then, sighting the rest of the *Goslings*, he shouted, "For God's sake, tumble aboard!"

He slapped the reins impatiently as his men merely gawped, but then to his surprised relief the tall, skinny fellow with them hollered, "The cavalry, by God!" and made a headlong dive for the coach door. The latch gave, the door slammed open, and in he crashed, followed by the six *Goslings* and an indeterminate number of drunken sailors, one of whom landed on the bench by Jake, evidently because the inside of the coach was too crowded.

Then, to the sound of an exultant shout of, "Cry God for Harry, England and Saint George!" from inside the carriage, they were off. Chilean soldiers came to their senses and fired madly down the street, and shots whined and clunked from wall to wall. Jake hauled the coach round a corner with a shuddering crash, the shooting stopped, and off into the darkness they thundered.

The shouting was lost, too, in the rumble of iron wheels on cobbles as the coach picked up speed, the street widening as it ran downhill. Jake steered surely, knowing every inch of Valparaiso as thoroughly as any of his idiot seamen. The anonymous sailor on the bench beside him was cheering, and Crotchet leaned out of the coach window shouting, "*Alors, alors,* suh!" Down the hill they thundered, heading through the darkness to the water's edge, and then with a lurch they were there, right on the edge of the embarcadero.

The beach was almost deserted, as the Peruvians had asked for a curfew, but the boat still lay where Jake had left it, still guarded by the urchins. Jake thrust the rein's into the sailor's hands, and vaulted onto the sand so fast that he nearly fell. Then he recovered, yanked open the coach door, and shouted, "Tumble for your lives!"

The *Goslings* and Royal Gray fell out in a mass, while the drunken sailors still inside grinned happily. "Drive on!" Jake roared, and heard the seaman on the bench cheer and whistle the whip. The coach was taking pace while they were all still getting out of the way. The door, still open, crashed back and forth, adding to the commotion.

The echoes of pursuit still wafted down from the terraces. Yellow lights were going on all over town, but the bay was black and serene. The limpid water lapped at Jake's knees as they hauled at the boat. The craft seemed impossibly heavy and reluctant, grating rebelliously, but then it was light and alive, floating in the ripples, and they all piled in.

The boys at the oars seemed to take forever to get their rhythm. Jake could hear them swearing and panting. The oarlocks squeaked deafeningly. Then at last they were surely on their way to the *Gosling*.

Tib Greene shoveled himself into some kind of sitting position, pushed his good hand over his stubbled face, and said complacently, "We found him, sir."

"So you did," agreed Jake with heavy sarcasm.

"*Sir?*" echoed the stranger, registering the word of respect. "Does that mean I may infer that I speak to the master of the rescuing brig himself?"

So the whole town knew that it was a brig that had come to pick up the desperado. Dear God, Jake thought, this was going to be the narrowest escape of his whole career — if he managed to bring off the miracle. The tide was on the turn, and he damn-well couldn't afford to waste a moment if he was to make a getaway. Then, with another jerk of apprehension, he saw that the steambark *Nympha* was lowering a boat — a boat with officers in it.

He swore under his breath and then hissed, "Stern two — gently, gently — and for God's sake keep your voices down."

Two of the oarsmen trailed their oars, and Jake leaned on the steering sweep to bring the boat into the shadow of some anonymous ship's stern. For the moment, they were hidden. Jake listened tensely, but the only shouts were distant echoes on shore.

Then, after drifting round the ship's quarter, they set off stealthily for the brig, heading for the starboard side, the side away from the *Nympha*. The boys at the oars were pulling faster, with no need for urging. The boat lurched a bit, and water splashed over the gunwales. The English stranger flinched as the spray hit him.

"And, what's more, sir," Tib Greene mused aloud, lost in an alcoholic haze, "he sure do talk strange."

"Like Falstaff?" Jake suggested grimly.

"And, what's more, my lord how he do stink, sir."

"Like a skunk," Valentine Fish muttered.

"'Tis not my fault," the actor said, his tone defensive. "The odor is not mine, sirs. 'Tis llama spit."

The silence was stunned. They had arrived at the sheltered side of the *Gosling*, but no one put out a hand to hold the boat still. Instead, they all stared at Royal Gray, his skinny form silhouetted by the glow from the cressets in the rigging and the shimmer on the water.

Jake said cautiously, "You did say *spit?*"

"Llamas, like all of the camel species, spit when annoyed — and llamas get annoyed very easily."

Jake put out his hand and laid it on the brig's straking, sensing the liveliness of his vessel as the tide turned on the ebb. The *Gosling*, like her owner, was eager to be free and away from this utter mess. Then he heard a loud, polite English voice hailing the brig. The sound came from the other side, the port side. Everyone in the boat froze.

The officer from the *Nympha* called out again, "Brig *Gosling*, ahoy!"

A long pause. Where the hell, thought Jake, was Charlie Martin?

Then he heard the clear reply, "Who goes there?"

It was Harriet. Royal Gray moved abruptly and the boat bounced. Someone hushed him. Jake, gripping the edge of one of the brig's planks, waited tensely.

"Good evening to you, Miss Gray," the voice returned. "And how d'you do, ma'am?"

"Very well, thank you." For heaven's sake, Jake thought incredulously, in another moment she would be inviting them to tea. Instead, however, she merely said, "Did you

123

wish to speak with Captain Dexter?"

"There is a commotion in the port, Miss Gray. The desperado is on the loose, and they do say he is keeping the company of a crowd of rebellious sailors, and leading them on a looting of the town."

"Merciful heavens!"

"Indeed, ma'am. They say it is the story of the Fish-market Gang all over again—the gang that ravaged the country about Callao just a dozen years ago."

Jake's arm was growing numb as he held the boat steady with his hand on the brig. He could see the whites of Joseph Fayal's eyes.

"Well," said Harriet, her tone judicious, "there has been no commotion here."

"But a word of warning, ma'am—"

"And I thank you kindly. If any desperado so much as puts a foot on this brig, we will fire a cannon, I assure you!"

"But, ma'am, our instructions…"

"Instructions? But you've delivered your warning, sir."

And the officer silenced. Jake could hear him conferring in whispers with his companions. The echoes of shots and shouts drifted from the shore. The tide rippled under the boat and despite his grip on the side of the brig, the boat kept on clicking against the hull.

Then the officer raised his voice again. "If we came on board to ascertain…?"

"Ascertain what?" said Harriet. There was a mocking note in her voice, a note that Jake knew all too well. "Surely it is a dreadful waste of time, when that villain and his gang could be wreaking dreadful devastation in the town?"

"But to set your sensibilities at rest, ma'am…"

"Sensibilities, fiddlesticks," said she in forthright fashion. "Thank Captain Mara most kindly for his concern, sirs, but I assure you that all on board is as quiet as the grave."

Lights were glowing on the foreshore, and Jake could

hear shouting as more boatloads of troops were launched from the ships of war. He was holding onto his brig so tightly he wondered if he would ever let go. He damned the day that Harriet had boarded the brig, he…

The officers had gone. Belatedly, he heard the boat row away. He'd missed the last exchange of stiff courtesies. Harriet looked over the side, and said, "Shouldn't you come up quickly?"

Royal said in a high, incredulous voice, "'Tis Hat, it really is Hat."

Jake said nothing. He shoved Royal Gray up the side and scrambled up on deck himself, followed by Tib, who was as agile as ever with just one arm, while the others swiftly sculled the boat to the stern davits, where men were ready to haul it up.

Charlie Martin came aft, and Jake snapped, "Prepare to heave short and weigh."

Men hurried stealthily about the deck, manning the windlass and sheets, tumbling up the shrouds and along the yards, surefooted in the dark. Boats were swarming more thickly on the water, heading out at random to the ships and boarding them one by one.

On the *Gosling* canvas rustled and snapped as sails were set, hiding the stars. Jake turned to Royal Gray, and snapped, "Lay aloft."

"I beg your…"

"You heard me. Get up the mainmast and keep on going until you're in the topgallant crosstrees."

"But—"

The man's fright was obvious. Jake said mercilessly, "If you want to save us from embarrassment and yourself from arrest and worse, get up there and pretend to be a seaman. We could well be boarded before we can get underway, but they won't hold us back—unless they find their fugitive. I know you can do it—just pretend there's a passel of lions at your heels."

125

The look Royal Gray cast him was full of loathing, but the man obeyed.

Then, without waiting to watch the actor mince his way up the shrouds, Jake strode swiftly forward. He had questions in abundance, but they could wait until he had found his offing.

SIXTEEN

HARRIET scarcely slept a wink. The mess cabin was empty when she came out of her room at dawn, and Jake Dexter, she knew had been on deck the whole night. He had stood watch while the brig cleared the bay and got well away from the treacherous Chilean coast.

Nevertheless, it was a shock to find when she arrived on deck that land was entirely lost to view. The sea was rugged, and the wind tossed the crests of the waves, but even when the *Gosling* lifted to top each billow, there was no sign of the mountains of Chile. The wind was cold and sharp with salt, and the men about decks looked chilled, and yet it had been so warm in the harbor of Valparaiso. The change was almost unbelievable.

There was no sign of Royal. Harriet went to the amidships rail, trying to look matter-of-fact, avoiding the inquiring looks of the crew. She felt apprehensive, fraught with misgiving. She had lived such a long time with the certainty that everything would come right when she found Royal, yet now she had the strong feeling that nothing was right at all.

When she was on the verge of losing hope and trudging down to breakfast, Royal stumbled out of the forecastle. Most of his rags had gone and he had a gray blanket clutched around him. He peered about blearily, stumbling every time the brig rolled.

He saw her, and wavered towards her. The *Gosling* pitched and waggled her stern, and he arrived in a little clumsy rush. Then he stopped, and they stood and looked at each other.

During the past year Harriet had imagined over and over again what she would say when she found him, but all she could say now was, "Oh, Royal." He had seemed shabby enough in the rushed encounter the night before, but the daylight proved even more cruel. His skin was patched and scabbed, nut-brown in parts, pink in others, as if the sun had burned him and then burned him again. His hair was bleached almost white, stiff and sticking out all over his head. He was dirty, and terribly thin, his eyes haggard, and his cheeks hollow.

Royal was twenty-two years old, but he looked fifty. She said again, in distress, "Oh, Royal." Then, "Where are your clothes?"

Instead of answering he gulped, swerved round, and leaned over the rail. She watched his misery as he heaved, feeling helpless, unable to do anything but pat his back every now and then. She could feel the vertebrae, like stones sticking out.

When he at last stopped retching she went to the galley and fetched a mug of fresh water. Cookie said nothing, but rolled his eyes. Harriet smiled distractedly, and went back to her brother. She found him sitting in a hunched, miserable heap by the rail, one long arm hooked over the lash-rail to keep himself still. He swiped at the mucus smeared on his beard and took the mug.

Harriet listened to his thirsty gulping. Then at last he spoke. "Hat, what the hell are you doing here? And where the devil is Sefton?"

She said evenly, "I was the one who got your letter, not Sefton, and I was the one who followed your instructions. I bought passage on a whaleship to meet you in Valparaiso, and ... and the captain of the whaleship let me down while we were still in middle of the eastern Pacific. So I boarded this brig at Judas Island, and ... negotiated with Captain Dexter and his crew to help me find you and then carry the alpacas to Australia."

He gaped at her, and then said blankly, "I don't believe you. You're a married woman, you couldn't do any of that."

She said bitterly, "Married?"

"Yes! You're married, and your husband should be taking care of that kind of business."

"Is that so, Royal? Then where, pray, is my husband?"

Sefton, the man she had so stupidly married. It was like ancient, meaningless history, the scenario of a play where no woman in her right mind would want to play a role—but she'd had no way of knowing that she was acting like a foolhardy child, at the time. Colonel Frank Sefton, urbane, rich, elegant, American, had been the most eligible bachelor in the country, and she had been the envy of every single woman in town ... but now she could scarcely remember what he looked like.

Harriet said in a low, bitter voice, "Sefton left me. He left me two days after you sailed to South America—two days after we were married. He left the country without a word of warning, let alone a reason."

"I don't believe you! Frank Sefton wouldn't behave like that! He's a respectable man—highly respected in America. Everyone told us that he came from a prominent Philadelphia family!"

"Royal, I have been alone for over a year."

"But that ain't possible! He couldn't do it, even if he regretted the marriage bargain, Hat—and that's impossible to imagine, too. Damn it, the man signed a marriage contract—he signed it the day before you were married, and Father witnessed it. I know, because I was there, and I witnessed it, too! Frank Sefton gave you all his worldly

129

goods, Harriet—surely he wouldn't abandon you with everything he owned?"

"But he did. He left me. Despite that contract and the scheme you and he and Father cooked up, Frank Sefton left me."

Furious with herself, Harriet realized she was on the verge of self-pitying tears. Turning her back on her brother, she stared at the sea, so determined not to blink that she didn't even see the waves. Instead, she gazed unseeingly at a world like rain-smeared glass.

Then, when she had calmed down, she went on without turning, "I should have expected it, I suppose. Frank talked all the time of making a fortune in other lands. He talked about New South Wales, and planned aloud to go there and set up a station ready for the alpacas ... and Father thought it was a good idea."

"Well, Father is right."

"Then Frank changed his mind, and talked instead of California, or the northwest coast of America. He told Father he was reluctant to invest in British lands again. He had been stung too badly in New Zealand, he said. When he'd arrived, the British administrators had been glad enough to see his money, he said, but when he wanted to sell out and take his profit, they changed their minds and said he could only sell at the same price that he had paid when he bought the land. Only those of English nationality were allowed to make a profit from New Zealand."

"Well, we knew all that," Royal's voice objected. "That's why the man gave you all his property before you were married, to put his lands in English hands."

Harriet said, "Exactly."

Staring unseeingly at the waves, she remembered how the affable, urbane man who had married her had paced the bedroom floor on the second night of their marriage, shouting for hours on end about the iniquities of English law. When Sefton was angry his blue eyes flushed red, blood vessels standing out in the whites. His rage had terrified her.

She pushed the horrid memory away, and swung around, saying passionately, "He hated me, Royal. After we were married, I found he didn't love me at all, that he hated me—because of my English nationality. He had taken advantage of it to avoid the punitive English laws, but I learned before he left that he had hated me always."

"Nonsense, Hat—he worshipped you! The whole town knew it! Father would never have gone along with the scheme if it hadn't been for that. You know how he feels about Americans."

"Oh, Frank Sefton was a great persuader," she said bitterly.

Colonel Frank Sefton, urbane and handsome man about town, had begun to pay court to her the day after the Gray family had staged their first drama in Auckland. It had been Sheridan, she remembered—and his flattering pursuit had been like a court scene from Sheridan, too. He had been constantly in attendance at the stage door, and had showered her with flowers and gifts. At first, he had seemed too old for her, and too aristocratic, but as time had gone by he had flattered her out of her senses. He, Colonel Frank Sefton, had been a man of the world, as old as her father, and she—

She had been a silly goose-brained girl of sixteen.

Royal argued, "But his reasons for juggling the ownership of his properties were logical, Hat. I agree that it's true that Sefton signed over his lands to you for a devious reason, but it made perfect sense for him to sell at a profit if he could. He discussed it fully and honestly with Father and me, and we understood him perfectly. For God's sake, Hat, I helped draw up the document, and that lawyer fellow made sure it was legal. And he trusted us, remember. We could have disappeared before the wedding, sold the lands and made off with the money, and he couldn't have done a thing about it."

131

"Then how come I was the one who was betrayed?" she cried. The low, shaking words burst out of her. "You've no idea what it was like in New Zealand, Royal, to be left alone, a deserted wife, an object to be despised!"

"Alone?" He frowned.

Harriet shut her eyes a moment, in pain. Father ... she still had to tell him about their father.

She opened them, and said as steadily as she could, "Royal, I—I have to tell you something dreadful. About Father. You need to brace yourself. He..."

She had to stop and try again. "Like you, I thought Frank Sefton loved me. The first night, I was shocked at his—coldness, but I thought it might have been my inexperience that made everything seem so wrong. After the second night, I knew without doubt that he didn't love me at all. He shouted at me, raged at me ... and then he used me, like property, Royal, with nothing in the slightest like tenderness, or even affection, just bitter contempt. In the morning, when I woke up, he was gone. I didn't know what to do, Royal—all I knew was that I couldn't live like that. So I went to Father's hotel. I had to see Father, to ask, to... But he wasn't there. Then, as I stood there waiting for him to come back, I heard screams in the street, right outside the hotel. Father..."

She took a deep, shaking breath, and turned again to stare at the sea. "I f-found him. In the street. He had been run over by a carriage. There were ... people. They said — they said a horseman had shoved past him, and he had fallen under the carriage wheels ... that the coachman hadn't been able to stop in time, and the wheels ... the wheels..."

She stopped again, utterly unable to go on. The silence drummed in her head. She turned slowly, and her brother was staring up at her, his face so pale it was greenish. When he shut his eyes she could see scabs on his eyelids. Then he said, "Oh God, dear God. He was dead?"

"Yes."

"Killed?"

"Crushed. People were kind ... then. The horseman hadn't come back to see what had happened to the man he had pushed out of his way, and because of that they were very shocked ... sympathetic. Kind. And all the time I waited for Frank, desperate to know what to do—about him, about Father's poor body. But he didn't come. He wasn't in town, even. He'd gone. He'd sailed that same day."

"*Where?*"

"To China, or so his lawyer said, on God alone knows what business. The next day was Father's funeral, and when I returned to Frank's house the lawyer was there."

"The lawyer?" Royal's drawn face brightened. "Then you had the law on your side."

"Did I?" she said, more bitterly than ever. "You spoke of that lawyer, Royal, the man who checked that contract to make sure it was legal, the lawyer who was there when you and Father signed it as witnesses. Well, that was the same lawyer who was waiting for me at the house, and he had more documents, signed by Frank Sefton, documents of ownership. Sefton had somehow sold the lands, the house, even the racehorses that Father had given me for a dowry. And after the lawyer had told me all that, he showed me the door."

"My God. Nowhere to live? Oh Hat, what did you do?"

"What choice did I have? I was forced to go back to the stage ... live on my wits, while the people of Auckland whispered and men—men tried to take advantage... And then your letter came."

"You're destitute?" Royal's voice shook.

"I don't own a single penny. The passage and ... and hiring this brig took the last of my money. The alpacas are our only hope. Without the alpacas, we have nothing."

And Royal lurched to his feet, and vomited over the rail.

Royal still had his head over the side when Valentine

arrived. He had come out of the door that led to the after-quarters, and he had his sea chest on his shoulder, and he was whistling.

The whistle was cheerful, determinedly so, but he had a chastened look. "Heigh-ho," said Valentine as he came alongside. "*Adiós* cabin, and hail foc'sle. Crotchet and I won't enjoy the pleasure of your company at meals any more, Miss Gray."

Harriet said incredulously, "You've been demoted? To the rank of *seaman*?"

"The events of yesterday proved a little too much for our skipper to swallow."

"He's punishing you and Crotchet because you rescued my brother?"

"Well, ma'am," said Valentine, and coughed. "The rescue, as it happened, Miss Gray, was carried out by Captain Dexter himself."

And the rescuer himself arrived on deck, just as Royal backed away from the rail, wiping his face. Valentine disappeared rapidly through the foc'sle hatch, leaving Harriet to counter Jake's black stare.

He snapped, "Where are the alpacas? If, that is, they really exist."

Harriet looked at Royal, who flinched.

However, her brother said gamely, "The alpacas exist, I assure you, sir— and I thank you for yesterday's rescue. I'm sorry if it will make matters difficult the next time you drop anchor in Valparaiso—"

"You're sorry, I'm sorry," Jake barked. "Where are the bloody alpacas?"

'They're up the Tombez River, on the border with Ecuador. A Frenchman has a plantation there, and—"

"They're *where*?"

The word was a roar. Royal said defensively, "I had to put them somewhere safe."

"But Tombez is goddamned thirty days' sail away!"

"I know, and I'm very sorry." Royal sounded tormented, and Harriet moved closer to him, feeling protective of him, and very angry with Jake for being so harsh. "I've had the very devil of a time, Captain. The agents I hired have not been reliable. They supplied me with beasts and then reported them stolen, so I've been pursued by troops as well as marauding Indians. I've been on the run for months, Captain, harried northwards and all the time knowing I had to get to Valparaiso by the end of June. I did what I could, sir!"

Jake's expression grew grimmer with every word. Royal sounded like a guilty schoolboy, Harriet thought, full of hurried excuses, and at that moment she hated Jake for doing this to her brother.

She stared at him defiantly, but instead of noticing he snapped, "So it will be thirty days before I see the sight of even one alpaca. And last night you said the word *llama*, Mr. Gray. How do I know that these alpacas won't turn into common llamas when I finally get to clap eyes on them?"

"There are three hundred alpacas, I swear it. I had to have some llamas, for alpacas are too disdainful to carry burdens. They're wretched beasts, I hate them! My God, you've no idea of the fidget and fuss that alpacas cause — and they're shocking poor dams, in the bargain."

Jake, for once, looked taken aback. He said in a stunned tone, "*Dams?*"

"Damn shocking mothers," Royal said broodingly. "The pangs of birth are enough to make alpaca ewes flee for the distant horizon, and if the lamb drops halfway through the dash the dam don't even notice. It's up to the poor fool of a herdsman to make up for the beast's lack of sensitivity, and more often than not the running dam was picked up by some passing Indian, who would have the face to sell her back to me!"

Jake said with cutting sarcasm, "You mean that you didn't steal the alpacas?"

"Of course I did not! I bought them, as I said, from damnable unreliable agents, who might have stolen them in the first place—but what else could I do? The Indians worship the beasts, and only the backsliders in the tribes will sell them, men as underhand as the agents who talk them into it. And even then I couldn't feel secure, because they constantly tried to steal them back!"

Then, with an obvious effort to contain his righteous anger, he said more quietly, "I regret that I had to take them so far before I dared leave them, and I am grateful, sir, that you have consented to carry them to Australia."

"Consented?" Jake echoed. He shifted, and Harriet found the narrow green eyes focused on her face. Then he said deliberately, "It wasn't quite like that."

Uncomfortably, she listened to him inform Royal just how she had tricked her way into the *Gosling* Company, and then inveigled the men into voting for the proposition by naming the huge reward. Throughout, Royal kept on darting little looks at her.

At the end, he muttered, "Damn devious, I must admit."

"At least your presence on the *Gosling* will give a little decorum to the situation. I assume you want to join the Company? The price of a share is fifty dollars."

Royal winced and shifted, his eyes evading Harriet's. Then he muttered, "I'm afraid I can't afford that."

"What?"

"Collecting the alpacas and getting to Valparaiso took every sou I had."

Jake was frowning, Harriet saw, his narrow eyes studying her face again. He said slowly, "Perhaps your sister has the money?"

She silently shook her head. Buying her own share had been a desperate gamble, because it had taken the last of her scant funds.

She thought Jake's expression became troubled, but when he spoke to Royal his voice was matter-of-fact. "Then

136

you will have to work off your share," he said.

"*Work?*"

"Aye. Do the work of a seaman—go aloft, mend rigging, wash decks, obey orders. Thirty days will work out one share exactly. You'll find it a cure for seasickness, too."

Then he was gone, shouting out to the seamen in the rigging as he headed forward. Royal muttered, "Oh God," and stumbled to the rail again. Harriet listened to the awful retches, and then the spit and curse as he straightened.

"What a martinet," he said with passion. "What a bastard."

Quite involuntarily, she said, "No, no, he's isn't"—but Royal wasn't even listening.

"So I'm doomed to sleep in the foc'sle," he muttered self-pityingly. "They swear I stink, and stole half my clothes and threw them overboard ... oh God, I feel awful. D'you think I'd feel better if I ate some breakfast? Will he keel-haul me if I dare go to the galley and ask the cook for something edible, and maybe something hot to drink? It used to settle my guts first-rate once I managed to keep down a meal on the voyage to South America ... or do you think he'll starve me until I've worked off that share?"

Harriet moved away from him. "You will find," she said stiffly, "that the grub here is excellent—and that Captain Dexter admires a hearty appetite."

138

SEVENTEEN

ROYAL Gray was seasick for a full two weeks — and how the men tormented the poor sad scarecrow. Jake did not find it amazing that the young man should be so thin and ragged, as from all accounts Royal had run afoul of every sharp trickster in the Andes — but the seasickness did surprise him.

"He," he pointed out to Harriet, "has plenty of fresh air."

It was part of the running argument about her campaign to spend the daylight hours on deck, instead of below. The sun shone hot and bright as the brig forged north, and the ribbons Jake had given her were becoming as faded as the straw hat she wore. Her face, in the speckled shade of the hat, was mutinous in the extreme.

She said loftily, "My brother has always been a martyr to *mal-de-mer*."

"Even on the passages to the Cape Colony and New Zealand?"

"Even then."

"And what did he do when he didn't have his head over the rail — take part in plays and read poetry?"

Her glare, Jake thought, was simmering enough to bubble the tar in the deck seams. Harriet snapped, "He does his share of work."

"He does," Jake admitted. After a fashion, he thought.

The day after the brig had left Valparaiso so abruptly, the men had asked for a Company meeting. The wished to protest the lack of alpacas. Where were they? Full up the Pacific coast of South America? It was a scandal! Royal Gray had listened with an air of profound disbelief, but from then on he had certainly worked, knowing very well that the men were watching him very closely indeed. The actor looked such an awkward marionette as he sidled about the rigging that Jake sometimes wondered if he exaggerated his maladroitness on purpose, but he always obeyed orders, and complained only in a mutter. And it certainly provided the crew with amusement. Which was a blessing, on a passage that was as hot and dry and monotonous as this one.

"And I, too," said Harriet virtuously, "am prepared to work."

Jake didn't bother to answer. Harriet had offered to help Bodfish, which had scandalized the steward extremely, and she had offered to help Jake with his account books, which had been easily declined. For all he knew, she had tried the same with Charlie Martin and the logbook, with the same result. But then came the day that he arrived on deck to find her sitting on an upturned bucket, helping the men on watch pick over potatoes.

"But I told you," she said. "I really do want to help."

Jake surveyed the flushed face with no patience whatsoever. Despite the boatloads of fruit and yams he had sent on board at Valparaiso, fresh food was growing short and the potatoes were precious. Taking off the sprouts was a daily task, but...

But he most emphatically did not want Harriet doing it.

Just as he had feared when she had first come on board, the crew was becoming restive. The men had always been over-interested in her, in Jake's candid opinion, and now that the long, dry, monotonous passage had worsened their

140

tempers, jealousies had arisen. When Irish Cookie had enticed Harriet to sit by the galley with a batch of molasses cookies, Bodfish had mumbled and sulked, as only the cabin food was supposed to be good enough for her. Then, when Harriet had chatted to Abner while he was overhauling some blocks on the poop, Tib and Dan had complained, saying that Abner, who was now second mate, had plenty of opportunities to talk to her at the cabin table, so had no right to monopolize Miss Gray's attention on deck. There had been similarly jealous complaints when Harriet was seen chatting to whoever was doing his stint at the helm. Jake had even heard gossip that Pablo had challenged his long-suffering comrade, Joseph Fayal, to a duel, to be staged the next time they were on shore.

Now, he said, "There is no need for you to do anything, Harriet. You own a share — you're the supercargo."

"But the men who own shares work on the brig, and anyway, I need some money."

"*Money?* You expect to be paid?"

"Royal needs clothes. The men threw away what he was wearing when he came on board."

"Oh, for the sake of Jehovah," Jake said with a sigh, and sent her below to choose clothes from the slop chest, the store of clothes for sale to the men.

But soon she was back on deck again. Why did that annoy him so? It was the heat, perhaps, and the lack of fresh water. Everyone was getting cross, and it was unthinkable that he was jealous himself, just because she spent time with the men on deck...

Completely unaware of the progress of his thoughts, she said, "Anyway, how do I know we're heading for Tombez? Because I haven't seen the coast in ages."

Jake lifted his eyes to the heavens, and then said, "We're sailing well offshore to take the trades, or else the wind would be against us."

"But how do you know that?"

"Every seaman knows it. Ever since Juan Fernández steered this course, mariners have known that it is the best way to sail north."

"Juan Fernández?" She was back at her trick of listening with her whole body—was there ever an audience as flattering as Harriet Gray?

"Juan Fernández was a navigator," he said. "He discovered the route that takes advantage of the offshore winds, and he made the voyage to Callao in thirty days. And because it was considered impossible, they tried him for sorcery."

"I don't believe you!"

"Well, believe it," he said, and sent her below.

"Jahaziel," she said thoughtfully the next time he caught her out on deck. "What do you think of those yarns of gold?"

"Gold in California?"

"Yes."

"I saw no gold rush the last time I was in Monterey," he said.

But he had most of his attention on the sky. Gray pillows of cloud were piling up on the horizon, promising cool rain. The men were watching them as hopefully as he was.

"Gold rush?"

"It's as good a way of putting it as any," he said.

Gold rush. Man's eternal greed for gold, and the race to get to the yellow stuff first. Jake thought of the Conquistadors, and old Schouten's journal.

She said, "But you don't believe there is one?"

"If those gold yarns were true, do you really think those sailors and soldiers and marines would be content to stay in Valparaiso, even with the excitement of a desperado on the loose? What soldier would be satisfied with twenty cents and his rations every day, if that gold really did exist?"

"Perhaps they haven't heard the stories yet."

The heavens opened while the watch was shortening sail. The clouds were thick white at the edges of their dark gray masses, and the rain hissed down and bounced merrily on the decks. The men in the rigging cheered, and held out their hats and then tipped them over their heads, and the watch below came yodeling up on deck and capered in the rain. Royal Gray was with them, his thatch of stiff beard pointing exultantly up at the sky—and there was Harriet, too, on the afterdeck.

Jake stared in disbelief as she spun in circles, holding up her arms to the sky. He hadn't realized that she, too, wished for rain, not until he saw her now, her hair streaming down her shoulders and back, the gold darkening with wet, the rain running down her upheld arms and soaking into her gown. For God's sake, she looked twelve years old!

No, she did not. Her dress clung as it became sodden, clinging to her long, narrow waist, her firm round buttocks and pert breasts, making it obvious that she didn't wear corset stays. He moved quickly, heading up the ladder from the amidships deck to hiss at her, "For God's sake, get below!"

"But I'm wet already, Jake."

She most certainly was. The voyage and the good food had done well by her, a primitive part of his mind decided. Her skin was radiant, she throbbed with life, her breasts had enlarged. Behind him, on the foredeck, Cookie was waiting with bars of yellow soap. Jake urged her to the ladder, jumped down after her, reached out, grabbed the afterhouse door open, and gave her a push to send her on her way down the steps into the passage to her stateroom. And with a backward scowl, she went … only just in time.

Cookie tossed the soap, and the men caught the bars. Rain splashed down as they wielded the soap, scrubbing the clothes while they were still on their bodies, and then casting them off and scrubbing their skins. After that, they stopped up the scuppers so the rain could not run away, and they tossed each other into the shallow bath that the trapped rain made, rinsing themselves and the soapy clothes. And then they ganged up on Royal Gray.

He took one look, and ran. They chased his frantic lean buttocks round and round the masts and decks, and then they caught him and felled him. They scrubbed him hard and he cursed most wonderfully. "Crack your bottom cheeks!" he shouted, and, "Drench your balls, and drown your cocks!"

This caused gales of laughter, for Royal's cock was as long and thin as he was. They rinsed him and then scrubbed him again, until they all decided that they had got rid of his stink. Jake Dexter, clean and naked as the day he was born, declared it was a moment to splice the mainbrace, and the boys unstopped the scuppers, and let the soapy water out, and then sat around savoring the good dark rum.

Harriet was rather distant at supper, Jake noticed. He wondered if she was scandalized. Perhaps, he thought, she was upset that the men had treated her brother so roughly. But Royal would do a great deal better on the brig now, because it had been a kind of initiation rite.

Then he was distracted by Chips, who knocked at the mess cabin door to announce that the men had asked for a meeting of the Company. "What now?" said Jake.

"Abijah asked for it," said Chips.

"Oh dear," said Harriet, who had overheard.

They held the meeting on the open deck, because the rain had gone away, leaving the planks clean and steaming. The sun was heading for the horizon in a blaze of red and orange, and the formalities of the opening and the reading of the minutes seemed as endless as ever. But at last they came to the sailmaker's problem — which, as Harriet had guessed, turned out to be herself.

"Miss Gray spends too much time about decks, sir," said

Abijah Roe, and sniffed.

"Well," said Jake, and grinned triumphantly at Harriet, who lifted her head and sniffed, too.

Then she turned her haughty stare on Abijah. "And your reasons, Mr. Roe?"

"It don't allow the crew no privacy, Miss Gray. It ain't decent."

"*Decent?*" Harriet's voice rose in outrage. She was on the verge of another dramatic scene, Jake decided, and watched her in enjoyable anticipation.

"We can't even wash in peace and quiet, Miss."

"Peace and *quiet?*" Then Harriet said, "I apologize," in a tone that was not apologetic at all. "No doubt, Mr. Roe," she went on, "you are thinking of the massed communal bathing I overheard this afternoon, and undoubtedly you feel a proper embarrassment that a lady was a witness — an *invisible* witness — to your fun. I appreciate your sentiments, sir, but please do not feel ashamed on my account. In future, as long as I am warned, I will take take great care to keep my decent distance — though as a *gentleman* as well as a sailmaker, Mr. Roe, it would be courteous of you to make a canvas tub for me, so that if the heavens should pour down like that again, it could be filled for me, so I could take a bath of my own..."

Abijah's mouth fell open as he slowly absorbed the fact that somehow her apology had reflected on him. He went red, and Jake heard Royal Gray let out a muffled snort.

Then the sailmaker rallied. With another sniff, he turned to Jake and said, "I would make a canvas tub for Miss Gray if you *ordered* it, sir. But it ain't just the bathing, Captain Dexter, but the calls of nature, too. Miss Gray can't help but see which men are relieving theirselves in the bows."

Jake winced, but Harriet didn't look at all shaken. She tilted her chin and said distantly, "If that is your problem, Mr. Roe, then please don't feel any concern on my account, because I have too much sensibility to notice such things, I assure you. Though you consider yourself a *gentleman,* you seem to forget, sir, that I am a *lady.*"

And that was that. Harriet had won the battle, lock, stock and barrel. The meeting broke up with a lot of muttering and disapproving looks at Abijah Roe. But Jake felt he had won a point in his own personal argument, too.

"See?" he said triumphantly as Harriet passed him on the way to the afterhouse. She merely cast him a disdainful look, but next day she was on deck again, though at the taffrail in the stern, with her back firmly turned to the men.

Jake came up to the rail beside her, and said, "What are you doing?"

"Fishing," she said, and she certainly did have a line in her hand.

And she was there again the day after that, and he couldn't complain, because she wasn't talking to any of the men, and her pursuit was so innocent. And it was no use pointing out that it was useless to try to catch fish with a line from a moving vessel, as she merely chose to disbelieve him. "It's so long since I ate fresh fish," she said plaintively. That evening, when a flock of flying fish skimmed twenty feet above the waves as they were pursued by a huge leaping albacore, she watched them wistfully, and next morning was back at the rail with her fishing line.

The men saw it as a joke. Next night a flying fish missed its mark and landed on the planks, and in the morning Irish Cookie sent the fish, nicely fried, to the after cabins for Miss Gray's breakfast. Bodfish presented it to her with a flourish, after he had tastily decorated it with paper frills and a few leaves from the sweet potato vine he grew in a pot in the pantry. Harriet declared it delicious, and Jake laughed and said, "I'll show you how to catch flying fish properly."

In the evening the brig *Gosling* was hauled aback so she barely moved through the starlit waves, and one of the halfboats was hooked onto the falls, ready for lowering. Harriet was ushered into it, and Jake stepped in with her, working the falls as the boat was dropped down to the water. He was barefooted, and wore duck trousers and a loose French shirt. Everything was very quiet, except for lapping against the planks, the click of the boat as it touched the hull, and the murmur of the men who were gathered at the rail to watch.

Jake left the boat hooked to the falls. Then he padded about the boat, as Harriet watched him. A short mast was stepped and fidded, and then he hoisted a four-cornered sail, and adjusted it so it didn't take the wind. He lit a lantern, and told Harriet to hold it on the other side of the canvas.

"And keep down low," he said.

"But why?"

"You'll see." The light made the sail luminescent, and he watched her silhouette, a ghostly shape cast on the lit canvas.

Moments plodded by, and she said, "Is this one of your tricks, Jake Dexter?"

He grinned, and said nothing. Then all at once a silver-fletched arrow sped through the air, crashed into the sail, and dropped like felled bird into the bottom of the boat.

"Jake, what the devil was that?"

It was a flying fish—and it was rapidly followed by another, and another, and two dozen more. Jake shoveled them into bags as they dropped, too busy to talk. Within ten minutes he had enough for a fresh mess for all—and a two-hundred-pound albacore came hurtling through the night.

Jake's only warning was the swish as it left the water. He threw himself forward to knock down the sail but the huge fish hit it like a cannonball first. Jake plunged right through, grabbing Harriet as he went. His body thumped against hers and he felt the whoosh of her breath. Then his scrabbling toes felt the boat tip and capsize. Somehow, he reached up with one arm, the other still holding her, and grabbed the boat falls.

He gripped and hung on grimly, and felt the jerk as the boat became unhooked and turned upside-down. Harriet's body was taut with shock. He had one knee thrust between hers to stop her from slipping, and his arm socket grated with the double weight. His pulse thumped deafeningly in his ears and he could feel the flutter of her breath. She moved against him, wriggling wildly, scrabbling for a hold on the rope, and they began to spin slowly, held only by his single hand.

He could feel her straining upwards. Then she set a foot on his knee, and straightened her leg. For an awful moment he thought he was going to lose his grip, but with a lunge she had a hand on the rope as well. Then the worst of the strain was gone.

She wriggled further upwards, moving against him, and suddenly his mouth was in the curve of her throat, open, gasping for breath. Shocking excitement surged inside him; he was gripped with heat; all he wanted to do was close his teeth, gently, close his jaws softly on the smooth taut skin and hold her still while … while…

She lunged again, and got a grip on the rope with both hands, easing the strain still further, and he could feel the rope move as the men on deck began to haul. They spun; she was leaning outwards, her lower body fitting close against his; surely she must be aware…

She leaned back further, ever more precipitously, as she turned her head to look down at the sea.

"*Goddamnit!*" she exclaimed. "We've lost our fish!"

Her mind was entirely on the lost catch. Jake began to laugh helplessly. Within the space of a moment he had been overwhelmed with a hot, primitive lust for her — swinging one-handed on a rope, for God's sake! — and now as the men hauled them up to deck he was shaking with mirth.

"You ought to watch out for them albacore, sir," said Chips as Jake settled Harriet on her feet and straightened.

"Indeed I should," Jake agreed.

"You could've been killed, sir, and even worse still, Miss Gray might've been drowned."

"You're right," said Jake.

When he had finished laughing, he and the men turned their attention to the capsized boat. It was righted and baled out, and another good haul of flying fish trapped, this time with due caution in the matter of albacore. Then the *Gosling* Company debated the idea of having a nice swim, but the sharks had come sniffing around, so Jake ordered them to make sail, instead.

Two days later the coast of Peru was raised. Next day, in the late afternoon, they reached the mouth of the Tombez River.

EIGHTEEN

F IVE men went in the whaleboat with Jake Dexter. Royal was there, of course, to lead them to the Frenchman's plantation, and there was Pablo to interpret, if necessary, along with Joseph Fayal, in case someone needed to speak Portuguese. Valentine and Crotchet went too, the boy from lower Carolina being included for his French.

It was just dawn. The rest of the ship's company had gathered at the rail to watch them go. Jake frowned as he looked at the muddy yellow surf and past the surf that broke over the bar to the unmoving green jungle. The last time he had come here for wood, water, and fruit, there had been seven ships outside the sandbar. Now, the *Gosling* was the only vessel.

There was no wind at all, so the only sounds were the crash of the surf and the whisper of myriad leaves and insects. As the men arranged themselves on the thwarts and took up their oars, Jake looked up to the rail, where Harriet was gazing down at him, looking worried.

It seemed strange to have an anxious girl say goodbye. The last time it happened… He pushed the thought away, and reached up for the rifle that Charlie Martin handed down. It was a pretty piece, French in manufacture. It had mother-of-pearl ornamentation on the stock and a brass plate on the butt, engraved with a scene of ships at battle. Jake set it down by his knee and braced the steering oar in his armpit.

The surf was high on the sandbar, snapping up mud and spray. Royal was the nearest to Jake, and Jake put his hand on the end of his oar, to give him the timing of the stroke. The boat jumped and jinked and took in water, and then with a lurch they were over, into the mirror-calm river right on the other side of the breakers.

The river was narrow, so narrow that Jake could have touched either bank with the tip of his twenty-foot sweep. It also curved, so that within yards they were surrounded by overhanging trees, and it became like sculling through a green tunnel. The local birdlife suddenly became raucous — brilliant parrots and macaws racketing about the trees, accompanied by unseen monkeys. Palm fronds leaned far over, threatening to swipe off Jake's hat.

The water was the color of well-stewed tea, dusty with pollen on the surface, so that the reflections of flowers and foliage were in shiny pools, like oil. The tide was so low and the river so shallow that they were in danger of running aground, so that Jake had to keep a sharp lookout. the roots of the riverbank trees were exposed, and the clumps of dead vegetation that floated with them caught in the roots, revolving. The smell of mud and decay and rampant vegetation was thick, almost palpable. Insects whined and alligators floated like fallen trees, watching the boat pass with cold bubble eyes.

The men rowed slowly, for the wet heat was clinging and oppressive. Then, at last, on the dozenth muddy bend, the piles of the first houses came into sight. More spiles were set in the middle of the river, slimy and green with thick algae. As Jake knew from much past experience, these were for the boats that came up the river to collect fresh water. The boats towed empty barrels like beads on a string, and after tying to the spiles they were tipped so that only the bung-holes were exposed, and the water flowed into the open tops. Full, the barrels were righted and closed up, and towed back downriver to the ships. The last time Jake had been here the boats had had to wait in line to get at the spiles. But now the river was deserted.

He looked about slowly, carefully, trailing the blade of his oar, listening to the silence with the hackles rising on the back of his neck. The last time he'd been here the landing pier had been noisy with urchins and touts, but now there were just a few thin, cringing dogs. The boys were looking about apprehensively, too, and when a bird called right above they all flinched with fright.

Carefully, very quietly, the oar blades touched the water. The boat drifted on against the slow current. "Wa-ay enough," Jake said, and the boat arrived at the stage with the slightest click. He was the first to clamber out, and once the boat was secured he stood still, looking around, listening ... to nothing. All the huts were empty.

The inland town of Tombez was three miles from the landing. Usually there were horses for hire. Now the men trudged uneasily up the sodden mud and grass of the bank to the much drier track, which led through tall rustling fields of sugar cane. The stiff drab-green leaves were shoulder-high, and the plantation seemed as deserted as the landing. When two women came out of the cane ahead, the men jumped with surprise.

The women seemed equally nervous. They wore loose clothing in the South American style, and had the familiar hungry South American look. They were dirty and soil-smeared and one carried a mattock over her shoulder. When Pablo teased them in Spanish they relaxed and even giggled, and the young one seemed willing to go back into the cane field with Valentine, but they didn't seem able to say where the men who lived in the huts by the landing might be. All Pablo could find out was that the men had all packed up and gone, taking the horses with them. Their women and children had moved inland, either to the town of Tombez or to family farms.

But why had the men disappeared ... and to where? Jake tipped his hat back, staring down at the bland faces in puzzled frustration, and then, slowly, his nape crept with an indefinable sense of being watched.

He turned his head quickly, and saw Joseph turn his head too. The Portuguese had sensed the intruder even before he had; Jake could see the whites of his wary eyes. Then he saw the man who watched them from further ahead, standing in the middle of the track about fifty paces away.

An Indian. An Indian, unmistakably, but a man unlike any Indian Jake had ever seen before. He was short and squat and nut-brown, red-cheeked, almond-eyed, and dressed in many square-shaped colorful garments, with a braided cap on his bullet-shaped head. He stood very still. Jake wondered how long he had been there.

He said to Royal, "Who is he?"

Royal shrugged. The movement was nonchalant, but Jake could see gooseflesh on his forearms.

"Where does he come from?"

"How would I know? From high altitudes, probably from the Altiplano."

So that accounted for the bright red cheeks and barrel chest. Jake slowly led his party forward. The Indian stood to one side as they arrived, saying nothing and watching unblinkingly as they passed.

None of the men said a word, and Jake thought they were all very nervous. The women paid the Indian no attention, and did not seem to be afraid at all. Then they emerged from the sugar cane fields, leaving the Indian behind.

After walking so far through the tall gray-green leaves and stalks, the dry reds and yellows of short, sere grass hurt the eyes. To their left, a pale thorn hedge led to a farmstead of sorts. Jake could see a few trees, and the roof of a barn. The track they had been following ran straight ahead, arrowing through parched plains toward the town of Tombez, which was still invisible in the distance. High in the glaring pallor of the sky, an eagle clung to an invisible current of air, its wings widespread.

After the rustle of the cane, it was very silent. The hot air was thick with dust. Jake grimaced, and said to Royal, "Where is the Frenchman's plantation?"

Royal came out of some grim reverie, and said, "Four miles."

"Beyond Tombez?" Jake stared up the long pale streak of the track, his eyes narrowed against the glare.

"No — that way." And Royal pointed to their left.

That way was past the thorn hedge and the farmstead. This track was wider than the other, and deeply marked with a double rut as if wagons often passed that way, and Jake had assumed that it belonged to the farm. Evidently, however, after leaving the trees and the barn it went on and on for at least four hot and dusty miles.

Then Jake became aware that one of the women was pulling at his arm. She led the way up a side path past the hedge and along a post and rail fence to the trees, which turned out to be a mango and two tamarinds. The trees grew in a paddock where a couple of oxen grazed. Just beyond was the shed, and the two women urged Jake that way.

In the shed, it was very dark after the bright sun outside, but when Jake's sight adjusted he could see that there was a cart there, and that other equipment was stowed at the back. Harness dangled from dusty rafters. The two women intimated that the cart and the oxen were available for hire, and that they could negotiate a price that was ridiculously cheap. Their smiles had a nostalgic air, as if they had almost forgotten the pleasure of striking a bargain with visiting skippers.

Jake surveyed the cart doubtfully. The oxen would undoubtedly be easily caught, but hitching them to the cart was a different matter entirely. The yoke that the two women rummaged out was enormous, made of wood, and very heavy. The wheels of the cart had been made from rounds sawn out of some great log, and the axle tree, also made of wood, was at least ten inches thick. The cart itself was made of more heavy timbers, and was such a cumbersome object that it was a wonder to Jake that there were oxen strong enough to draw it unloaded, let alone when it was piled up with freight.

He shook his head, but gave the the women a coin to thank them for their trouble. Then he walked back past the fence and the hedge to where his men were waiting for him.

When he arrived, Royal roused himself, and led the way up the double-rutted track. Past the field with the oxen and the trees they trudged, and then Royal came to a sudden stop.

The Indian was standing in the middle of the trail. Just as in the cane field, he was fifty paces ahead, standing and waiting for them. It was uncanny, almost frightening, and Jake could hear Valentine whistling under his breath, as if in self-reassurance.

Once again, as they arrived alongside, the Indian merely stepped out of the way. Then, standing still, he watched them impassively as they passed. Jake could hear the uneasy comments of his men, and when he looked back, the Indian was following them again. It was peculiarly chilling to be dogged thus by one silent man who kept an even twenty yards to the rear. The back of his neck felt stiff.

The sun beat down from the pale sky. Time ticked by, a hot monotony of putting one boot in front of the other. When Royal stopped, Jake almost bumped into him. He looked up and around, and the landscape seemed the same as ever. Then he saw the path that straggled off to the left.

The path had an adobe gate in the Spanish style,

crumbling but whitewashed, and with a few terracotta tiles on top, but the path itself was just cracked clay, scattered with small pebbles. It led past a weather-silvered fence to a clump of huge dusty trees and a glimpse of a large, low whitewashed building. Jake could see cattle grazing in the distance, and the wavering, heat-muddled shapes of the low roofs of pigsties, but the field between the track and the hacienda was empty, a sere, brown, empty pasture.

Jake said sharply to Royal, "This is the Frenchman's place?"

"That is his house, yes." Royal spoke confidently enough, but his face was apprehensive and worried. His eyes looked as reddened by dust as Jake's felt.

"Then where are the bloody alpacas?"

"How would I know? They must be in another field." Royal set off through the archway and along the path, and Jake and then the others walked after him. When they arrived in the shade of the trees it was like a blessing.

Then Jake heard a loud grunt, a whistling kind of grunt. He jumped with surprise, and turned to peer narrowly into the tamarind thicket. As his sight adjusted, he saw an animal ... five animals, peering haughtily back at him.

He had never seen animals like them. Their fine dark eyes had miraculously long lashes. They had long, elegant necks and imperious expressions, and reminded him somewhat of Harriet.

He said to Royal with amusement, "So that's what alpacas look like."

Royal said flatly, "No." His own expression was eloquent with disgust and dislike. He said, "They're llamas."

"Then where the devil — ?"

Jake stopped short, for he had just seen the Indian again, the same Indian who had followed them from the river. He was walking across the empty field, his squat shape dignified, and he was walking to join a group of Indians who looked just like him. Where the hell had they come from? Or had they been there all the time, blended into the landscape like the llamas?

Jake swung round and demanded of Royal, "Do you know those men?"

"I don't know!' Royal sounded caged, like a lion. "My agents bought alpacas from Indians who looked like these Indians, but they all look the same to me. Unless I'm right up close, I can't tell them apart."

"So where is the Frenchman?"

"He must be in the house."

The house stood to one side, an ancient structure built of solid adobe, many of the roof tiles gone. Royal walked right up to the door and hammered loudly. The door creaked slowly open, hinges grinding. There was no one behind it. The room was empty. The door had opened by itself, with the force of Royal's knocking. When Jake went inside and searched, he found the whole house echoing and vacant. There was a distinct air of dust and desertion.

He came out and said again to Royal, "Where is the Frenchman?"

"I don't know!" Royal shouted.

And a man came from round the back of the hacienda, saying in a Yankee accent, "Be you after M'sieu La Plante, sirs? For if you are, then he's gone."

Dead silence. Jake's hand was gripping the stock of the rifle that was propped on his shoulder, but the newcomer merely grinned obsequiously.

He was a man below the middle height, dressed in a short, furry jacket and canvas trousers, with a striped shirt underneath, and a kind of leather apron over his middle. His countenance was far from prepossessing, his features being snub, and his small gray eyes restless and inquisitive. One tooth was missing in the front of his ingratiating smile, and by his side hung a seaman's cutlass. By the smell of him, he had just come from a pigsty—and he looked rather like a pig, too. He wore a fur cap, from beneath which his red hair stuck out in bristles that stuck all over his face and head.

Royal exclaimed, "Who the hell are you?" — and then, in the same breath, "Never mind that, where the hell are my alpacas?"

"You mean those woolly beasts, sir? Ah, they went."

"They *what?*"

"They were pastured in that there field when M'sieu La Plante went off and left me in charge, sir, and then a lot of them Indians came and sorted them into a flock, and off they trotted."

And this odd-looking character gestured at the Indians in the middle of the paddock, whose sudden materialization didn't seem to worry him a whit.

"*You let them steal my alpacas?*" Royal was scarlet with rage and consternation. "You watched them take my alpacas away and did nothing to stop them?"

"Well, no, I confess not, I didn't do nothing. I didn't do nothing at all."

"But I paid La Plante to look after them!"

"But you must admit, sir, that you never paid me."

"How the hell could I? I've never seen you before in my life!"

Royal was shaking with rage; Jake could see the veins sticking out on his neck. "Those alpacas were my rightful property!" he shouted. "I paid good coin for them — and I paid La Plante the last of my cash to take good care of them! So where the hell is the bastard?"

The newcomer didn't answer. Instead, looking alarmed, he gripped his cutlass — and with good reason, because Royal was taking a furious step towards him. Jake was just preparing himself to prevent imminent murder when Royal, utterly unexpectedly, whirled about and vaulted the fence.

The llamas snorted and scattered, and Royal set off in a headlong sprint for the Indians. "Those alpacas were my property!" he shouted. "Those alpacas belonged to me, by damn!"

159

The words, like his expression, were thunderous. Fearing a battle, Jake vaulted the fence after him, but the Indians merely stood and waited. And when he arrived in front of the group, Royal merely skidded to a stop.

"I paid good Chilean dollars!" he shouted into their impassive faces. "I paid all the money I owned in the world, gave a twelve-month of my life, and where are my bloody alpacas? My God, when I think what I suffered, endured! Am I to profit nothing, naught for all my investment? My God, I could drink hot blood!—for I have done such bitter business as the day would quake to look on, yet without my alpacas I have gained nothing—nothing!"

Jake came to a stop, too, and propped his rifle butt on the ground, holding the barrel as he listened with interest. It was marvelous thunder, he decided, fully worthy of a Gray, rich from quotations from past dramas. Then Royal abruptly changed to another language, one that Jake had never heard before in his life. He supposed it was the Indians' dialect, but it inspired as little response as the English.

The Indians merely listened, their brown unblinking eyes attentive, their brown faces impassive. They didn't even speak when Royal ran out of steam and out of words. Instead, there was silence, a long, polite pause.

Finally, having evidently decided that Royal was not going to say any more, one of them spoke. It was in the same strange language, and was a lengthy speech that sounded very solemn and formal and elaborately courteous. Royal kept silent, but went so purple in the face that Jake wondered if he was going to throw a fit.

Then at last the Indian spokesman was finished. He didn't seem to expect a reply, because he bowed, nodded regally at Jake, turned, and headed back across the field, followed by his fellows. It was startling to see how quickly they vanished. One minute they were there, and the next they were gone.

Jake returned his stare to Royal, and said, "What the hell

was that all about?"

For a moment Royal muttered foully to himself instead of answering, but then he said, "The bastard scolded me for what he called my *theft* of their precious bloody alpacas—he made me feel like a guilty schoolboy! And then had the sauce to sympathize! To make up for my loss, he gave me a present."

Jake said, "What?"

"He gave me the goddamned llamas. Five useless bloodyminded pack beasts! I'm ruined, Jake, ruined! My God, when I think—"

Jake stopped listening. He turned on his heel and set off to the clump of trees and his waiting men.

The stranger was still with them. The ingratiating smile slipped a bit as Jake strode right up to him, and he lifted a defensive hand, but Jake simply demanded, "Where has the Frenchman gone?"

"Why sir, he'd gone with all the other men from these parts, off in a rush with them all. He gave me this farm for a song, such was his hurry. Why, sir, they all bought berths on the ship, and they've lit up and gone to California."

"*Where?*"

"California, sir, after the shining gold."

Gold. The word dropped into the stunned silence.

Then Jake said, "Who are you?"

"Why, you can call me Honest Mill Mason, sir, late of the American forces in the Mexican War, stationed on the flagship *Ohio*, sir, only what I somehow missed the ship in Callao."

A deserter, Jake thought, staring at him, a man on the run. Then Mason said, "D'you think these tales of gold might be true, sir? I didn't believe them at all, but now I think I might be changing my mind, and why, sir, you may well ask, sir, but none of them have come back."

Jake paused, and then said shortly, "Tell me these tales."

"Ah..." said Honest Mill Mason, and drew a long

161

breath.

And they all listened to the tales he said he had heard, and they were marvelous tales, too.

One was a yarn of a Mormon settler in the Sacramento valley who had been there for years, and whose wife was an idle fire-spannel of a woman, who put the sweepings of the cabin floor into a cask outside the door, instead of throwing them out properly. "Well," said the Yankee deserter, "when he heard about the gold, her husband took those sweepings and panned them out, and made himself two hundred dollars. Or that's what they told me. And there's another tale about a man who picked up a rock to throw at his mule. As he hefted it, he thought to hisself that it were unnaturally heavy, and when he looked at that rock it was a two-pound nugget, perfectly pure."

And so his stories ran on. According to what Honest Mill Mason had been told, and related now, men dug in the mountains that overlooked the Sacramento Valley were able to wash out thirty or forty ounces of gold a week, which Jake knew was the equivalent of a year's pay for a well-regarded tradesman back in New England … but he didn't want to believe it could possibly be true. He didn't want to believe that Captain Mervine of the frigate *Savannah* had been so wrong—he didn't want to believe that while he'd been setting a course from Lahaina in January a man called Marshall had found gold in a mill-race on the American River … that while the *Gosling* Company had been digging fruitlessly on Judas Island, other men had been digging most profitably up the Sacramento Valley. He didn't want to believe that the shrewd Mormon trader, Sam Brannan, might, after all, have been telling nothing but the truth when he'd run about with his shouts of gold, gold, gold on the American River.

But, as Honest Mill Mason had pointed out, the Tombez River men had gone and none of them had come back. And Jake knew that it made no difference if he believed the tales

162

or not, because he could hear the excited mutters of his men, and knew it would go to the Company vote, and what the vote would be. Gold, gold … it was the greatest adventure, and adventure was the reason the men had joined the *Gosling* Company, along with the lure of a fortune.

And, Jake thought dryly, the tales of gold would save Royal Gray's skin. The talk and the excitement and the voting would distract the men from the righteous anger that they would have otherwise taken out on him. Dear God, he thought, the alpacas might have seemed a crazy scheme, but at least that plan had a guaranteed outcome. Half a million dollars! — and all they had in their place were five reputedly useless pack-beasts. The llamas.

Pack-beasts. He turned to Mason and said sharply, "Why did the men take the horses?"

"The tales also said, sir, that there be a grave shortage of mules and oxen and horses in California, on account of carrying all the gear to the mines, and the carrying of all the gold out. Why, they said, sir, that a captain who took horses to 'Frisco sold them for two hundred each!"

Jake stared. In some contrary way, this convinced him more than anything else he had heard that the tales of gold were true. Two hundred dollars? Each?

He turned and studied the llamas very thoughtfully indeed.

NINETEEN

IT was late afternoon when they reached the *Gosling*, and the tide was on the turn. The swell carried them over the sandbar with scarcely a hitch, but Jake didn't notice, because his entire attention was fixed on the dramatic change that had come over the scene since the early morning when they'd left.

The brig was surrounded by a host of ramshackle coastal craft. The men who had remained on board were lined up at the rail, keeping off the horde with aimed muskets, while the gaggle of boats hovered underneath. Not one of the South American craft impeded their return to the *Gosling*, holding back instead, but the moment the whaleboat touched the side, they gathered close again.

Jake scrambled very quickly up the side to the deck. He made straight for Charlie, and said, "What happened?"

"They came about noon, sir." Charlie was hauling at his beard and looking extremely hot and sweaty. "Bill was up the forepeak when he started hollering that pirates were on the way, and afore we knew it, there they were. They seem extreme excited, and so I held them off until you come, sir."

"Excited? What about?"

"The Lord alone knows, for the only word they shout is *California*."

California? Jake looked at the craft, all full of hopeful-eyed men, who stared back beseechingly.

"They seem peaceable enough, sir, but I was not prepared to take any risks."

"And you were absolutely right." Jake deliberated, and then sent for Pablo. "Tell them," he said, "that they can send over a spokesman, but no more than one from each craft."

The commotion that followed Pablo's shouted message went on a long time. Jake waited as patiently as he could, despite the ache in his back and feet and the dust and sweat that coated every inch of him. Meanwhile, he listened to the babble about decks, as the men who had come in the boat with him told their news to those who had been left behind — the word *California* predominated, and the air fairly vibrated with excitement.

Royal was in much more serious conversation with Harriet, he saw. As he watched, she went red, and ran below. He thought she might be crying with shame and frustration that she had brought them all on such a wild goose chase. And then he thought it was a good thing she was out of sight, because the South American delegates were clambering on board, and shoving each other to get to the front of the mob.

At first look, they all appeared the same — all black-haired and wearing some form of the local costume. Then, with years of summing up men as they applied for a berth on his ship, Jake saw the differences. Some were very young and callow, though they strutted proudly, while others had a weary seasoned air. Some were obviously used to spending, for they had the sleek but furtive look of those who owe much to merchants, while others had the hollowed cheeks of habitual hunger.

Then at last, the final delegation arrived — and numbered six, instead of the stipulated one.

"You," said Jake sharply, and pointed. "Step forward."

Instead, the whole crowd shifted, moving away from the

new arrivals so that the six men stood isolated. They smiled insolently at Jake, and Jake stared grimly back.

So, he thought, here were the cocks of the farmyard, the bosses of the perch. These six men had the arrogant look of bullies and bandits. Their leader stood a little forward, brace-legged in tight black trousers with gilt buttons down the seams. All six wore these calcineros, the bottoms of the trousers left unbuttoned to the knee, so that bright silk linings and chipped and scarred riding boots with six-inch spurs could be seen. They had striped serapes pinned to their shoulders, and knives and pistols thrust into the stained silk sashes about their waists. They smirked, but did not quite meet Jake's stare.

Jake said, "Your names?"

The leader knew enough English to answer. He spoke for all of them. They were brothers, and they were all called Murieta. The leader called himself Don Joaquín.

Jake believed the relationship, because the stubbled faces were all alike, but he disregarded the Don. These men weren't quality—they were from the lower classes, definitely. *Bandits*, he thought again.

Like all the men in the hastily gathered craft, the Murietas came from the Gulf of Guayaquil. So the news of California had passed from Peru to Ecuador, Jake reflected. That was not surprising, for it must have perplexed the neighboring state to guess where the Tombez men had gone. What did amaze him was that the arrival of the *Gosling* had been reported so quickly.

"Our business, Captain," said Joaquín Murieta in his heavily accented English, "is of the most profitable. For you." He had a way of splitting up his sentences in a curiously threatening manner. "All we demand is passage. To 'Frisco. At good price, very good profit. For you. That is what everyone here wants. But our price is better."

Jake paused. All the Ecuador men on deck stood still, staring at him, silent and waiting.

"Well, señor?" said Joaquín Murieta.

Jake calmly and deliberately looked away from the crowd on his decks, at the jungle and the sea. The punctual late afternoon wind had arrived. It brought a wave that lifted and broke on the bar, the first crash of a continuous rush and thud of surf. The sound of the water seemed loud, because of the waiting silence.

Finally, he looked at them all, and said, "I will tell you what I have decided in the morning."

Joaquín Murieta sneered, "You need so long? To make up your mind?"

"I do," said Jake. "And in the meantime you can all get the hell off my brig."

The meeting of the *Gosling* Company was scheduled for the hour after supper. Harriet went up to deck ten minutes early, and stood at the rail, staring out to the open sea.

Somewhere over the far horizon New Zealand lurked— New Zealand, where she had endured gossip and scandal and saved what pennies she could. The alpacas … she didn't even know what alpacas looked like, precisely, but for more than a year they had been her only hope. All that time, she had waited for Royal's letter, and while she had waited, she had dreamed.

Now, she wondered what exactly she had dreamed. The pictures in her mind had changed all the time … Europe with Royal, or back to England, or maybe even the Cape Colony, where the Grays had been so popular… Wherever they went, they would be rich with their share of the reward paid by the British Government and the Bradford merchants, rich enough to set up a theater and become famous. England would have been a good place to go, because it was so unlikely that Frank Sefton would pursue her to the country he hated—if he ever took it into his head to make her life unbearable again.

But her dreams didn't signify any more. The alpacas had

gone. Perhaps they had never existed. She had involved Jake Dexter and his Company in a dream. She heard the men assemble, and braced herself for the *Goslings'* recriminations.

Instead, astounded, she saw broad, approving grins. Then, as the business of the meeting dragged on, she realized that the men were delighted that she and Royal had brought them to a place that was so convenient for a venture to the diggings of California — delighted! She was so amazed by this that the motions and voting passed her by, and then, belatedly, she understood that the Company had voted to sail to San Francisco.

Then Jake said, "There is also the business of those gentlemen over there." He nodded at the assembled craft, now all lit up with little fires as the occupants cooked their supper.

Puzzled, Harriet said into the general silence, "What do you mean?"

"They all want to come on the *Gosling* to California, and they are happy to pay for the passage."

"But … surely…"

"What I tell them," he said, "is up to the *Gosling* Company." And he looked at the crew.

Harriet stared at his turned head, horrified. The voyage to 'Frisco would take three weeks, or so Bodfish had told her. Maybe longer. Which meant three weeks or more of a gaggle of insolent male strangers on the decks of the brig — which had become her home. The realization was like a punch in the stomach.

She cried, "We must not carry them!"

All the men looked at her. Abijah Roe said, "You ain't got no vote, remember, Miss Gray."

"But I do have a voice, Mr. Roe — and I do have a mind, to think."

That mind was flying with desperation, hunting out some logic that would forestall the decision to carry the South Americans to San Francisco. Then she had it. She said calmly, "Why carry passengers—when they won't bring us any profit?"

"What do you mean, Miss Gray?" said Charlie Martin, very puzzled.

"Those men out there will give us coins to carry them, probably more than they can afford. You could charge them one hundred dollars a head! But what would that profit you, when you get to California, where people deal in gold, not coins? No one is going to be very impressed with a sackful of Chilean silver dollars!"

A babble set up—and just as abruptly stopped, as the men understood her logic. They all looked at Captain Dexter, who shook his head and said, "My God, she's right."

Harriet savored victory. "After all," she said, "those captains who carried men from here haven't come back for more of their business."

Everyone nodded and laughed. The mood was with her. Then Jake said thoughtfully, "There is something we've forgotten."

Silence. They all looked at him and waited.

"The ship that came with the news of the gold. It was calling here for provisions to take back to California."

Silence, and then a babble. Provisions! Fruit, vegetables, salted pork, rice and flour. What price would they fetch in San Francisco? The imagination was their only boundary.

And so, after a lot of discussion, the decision was made—to take on the Ecuadorean men, but not charge them money. Instead, they would buy their passage in bananas, salted pork, vegetables, and lengths of sugar cane. Berths could be put in the hold, and Cookie and Bodfish and Chips and Abijah all volunteered to sling hammocks in the forecastle, freeing up the steerage for passengers who were willing to pay more than the common rate to travel in reasonable style. Harriet looked down at her hands, feeling depressed and tired. It didn't matter that she had no vote. It would have been one vote against many.

TWENTY

NEXT morning, Jake, through Pablo, sent a message that he had made his decision, and that one man from each craft could come to hear it. Just one, as a representative of the rest. And that stipulation, he said firmly, included the Murietas. Harriet listened, hidden in a corner by the taffrail.

The boats had bobbed away from the brig with the changing tides of the night. Now, as the word passed along, men hurried to get them closer. Again, they vied and pushed to be on board first, and get closest to Captain Dexter. And, as before, the Murieta delegation arrived last. This time, there was just Joaquín Murieta, which seemed hopeful. When he looked about, though, Harriet inadvertently met his challenging stare. He preened, tucking in his tightly clad buttocks and jerking his loins in her direction. She quickly turned away. When she looked back, Jake Dexter had arrived on deck.

He stood facing the crowd, in the stance she knew so well by now—hat tipped back, legs braced apart, thumbs hooked into the loops of his belt. He was taller than any of the other men there, rangy in buckskin trousers and thin leather weskit over a full-sleeved French shirt. The sleeves of the loose shirt were pushed up to his elbows, and dark hairs gleamed on the brown skin of his forearms. He looked experienced, very competent and businesslike, she thought.

She listened to him explaining the system of payment for passage to San Francisco, while Pablo translated. The cost of passage had been fixed at one hundred dollars per head — one hundred dollars' worth of provisions.

The silence was blank and uncomprehending. She listened to Jake and Pablo explaining how, as the provisions came in, Mr. Bodfish, the ship's purser, would inspect each load and put a value on them, and give the owner a promissory note in exchange. All kinds of goods would be acceptable — potatoes both Irish and sweet, rice, flour, salted beef and salted pork, vegetables and fruit, including as many oranges as possible, and bananas if they were green. Live animals would be accepted, depending on space, and as the brig would be carrying five llamas to California, fodder would also be acceptable. Wine, molasses, the local brandy, and sugar would all fetch good prices — but all payment would be made in promissory notes.

Those men who had collected one hundred dollars' worth of notes would have a berth in the hold. He would have to have his own bedding, and cook his own food, which he would carry as well. An extra thirty dollars would earn a place in the steerage — the deck between the hold and the upper deck — with meals provided, which would be served at the cabin table after the captain and his officers had eaten.

Once the brig was full the *Gosling* would sail, he concluded. But those men who had not accumulated enough notes to buy a space on board would not be cheated. They would be given money in exchange for their notes.

Jake stopped, and so did Pablo. Then there was a silence … a silence that became menacing, as the Ecuador men looked at each other and shifted and muttered proudly. This proposition to trade in foodstuffs, it seemed, was an insult to their manhood. The hairs on Harriet's forearms shivered with a sense of danger.

172

Joaquín's sneering voice said, "Salt beefs, you want? Salt porks?

"Yes."

"Potatoes?"

Jake nodded. Harriet watched the hands on his belt curl into fists.

"Beans? Fruits? Flours?"

"Yes." He nodded curtly at each word.

"*Caray*, sir, we do not deal in such things."

Caray. Harriet had never heard the word, but it was obviously an insult. The Ecuadorean men all looked at each other. She saw the *Goslings* sense the threat growing in the air, too, and shift so they made a coherent group, surrounding their captain. A fight was in the offing she thought, and wished again she had not come up on deck.

Jake Dexter did not move, His right fist had dropped from his belt, and touched the wall that was the break of the poop. The broad back was alert; she could see the tension in the kite-shaped muscles.

Joaquín Murieta sneered into the silence, and said again, "*Caray*, I do not." And he thrust his hand inside his shirt.

There was a hissed intake of breath, as every man watched the movement. Instead of a weapon, however, Murieta produced money. He pushed his closed fist towards Dexter, and Harriet could see the glint of coins between his shut fingers.

"Take," he said. "Money. Plenty money. Enough. My brothers, me, all six, in steerage. Eat at cabin table."

Jake said curtly, "You do not seem to understand the arrangement. I take no money. Only notes that have been exchanged for provisions."

Murieta's tongue clicked on his palate, in the Spanish gesture of contempt. He open his fist little by little, so that coins dropped to the deck. Some fell with a single rattle, while others rolled to a wobbling stop. One ran all the way to the scuppers. Most of the Ecuador men were grinning.

At last, the sounds stopped. Jake had not moved. When he spoke, everyone had to strain to hear.

He said, "And still you do not understand. I do not accept money. I accept only notes. Coins are useless to me. Take that money away."

Joaquín Murieta shook his head, spat, and moved to the gangway rail. "Pick it up, Captain," he said. "We will be here, yes. When you sail."

Jake moved. He gripped the rifle that leaned on the wall, swung it up and around, and said very crisply, "Hold it."

Joaquín Murieta kept on going. Breaths hissed all about the deck—and Jake pulled back the hammer.

The metallic click seemed very small to Harriet, but Joaquín Murieta stopped at once. Then he turned, his eyes burning.

Jake said softly, "Pick up the money."

"Señor…"

"You heard me. Pick up the coins and get the hell off my brig."

Silence. Every man on board was rigid. Then, slowly, Joaquín Murieta knelt. He picked up the coins. He even found the one in the scuppers.

Then he went. It was as if a spell was broken. Harriet heard breaths let out. The Ecuador men all shifted and a babble of talk began. Somehow, she thought, they all looked smaller, as if the defeat of Joaquín Murieta had diminished them all.

"Pablo and Mr. Bodfish will explain it all again, if necessary," Jake said briskly, and then, without another word, he walked to the afterhouse door, and went inside.

Bodfish certainly had to explain it all again, as the Ecuador men insisted on considering the system income-prehensible. If he had had any hair to pull out, he certainly would have done it, while Pablo was reduced to despairing gesticulations.

174

Harriet forgot propriety and tried to help them, but she fared just as badly. She tried to explain in her clear ringing tones, but they merely grinned and made sheep's' eyes at her. And then Jake Dexter, having heard her through the skylight, made an abrupt appearance on deck.

"If you want to help," he said. "There is work waiting in the pantry."

Horrified, she said, "But what could I do there?"

"What Bodfish is normally doing."

"*Cooking?*" She was appalled.

"That's what I had in mind," he told her. "You've said so many times that you want to be useful, and now is your chance to prove you meant what you said."

"Well, I hope you don't regret it," she muttered, and flounced below.

Once in the pantry, however, her problem became acute. The steward was in charge of cooking the fancy food for the cabin table, as well as bread and cake for all hands, and Harriet knew with a sinking heart that she was no kind of fancy cook.

She could buy a pie and a mug of milk or ale, and rig a curtain in a dank and dirty backstage corner so she could be reasonably private while robing or disrobing for a part; she could learn that part in less than three hours and go straight on the stage and play it; she could, indeed, play four different parts in the space of one week, and groom a horse, and act from the back of that horse if need be—but persuading dough to rise and then baking it into a fancy soft loaf was beyond her. Nevertheless, she put her attention to a bowl, a spoon, and some flour.

The result was not encouraging. The bread did not rise and tasted strangely metallic, and subsequent efforts were no better. Predictably, the Company held a meeting to complain about it.

"A man cannot work with such ballast in his belly," said Abijah Roe, and everyone agreed.

175

The *Gosling*s had all been thoroughly spoiled, Harriet decided, but there was nothing she could say in her own defence. The men were certainly working very hard. The coastal craft had sailed away as the Ecuador men finally understood the system, but the brig still rang like a barrel of nails with unstowing the hold, ready for the provisions to arrive. As Harriet struggled in the pantry, she could hear the commotion as the half-cargo of lumber was heaved on deck, and the sawing as planks were made ready for the manufacture of berths.

Over the next two days Bodfish took back most of his job, and she did her best to learn from him. But no sooner had she begun to pick up the niceties of proving dough than the Ecuador craft began coming back. They arrived in gaggles, loaded to the gunwales with vegetable stuff, which Bodfish assessed, and then exchanged for notes, which they counted several times, before sailing off for more. Sacks arrived with corn, both grain and ground, and little barrels that oozed molasses and brandy. Sacks of coconuts came too, and sugar cane, gourds, squashes and bananas, along with boxes of oranges, and Bodfish was fully occupied inspecting each lot as it came and allotting a value to each load.

Harriet loved to watch the process, and wished she had the time to do nothing else. The South Americans hovered in eloquent suspense as they waited for Bodfish's judgment, watching every motion and unconsciously imitating every expression that crossed his magisterial face. They smiled eagerly when he smiled, and frowned piteously when he frowned. Then, when he pronounced his decision, the heavens were called upon to witness the unfairness, and every saint called upon to see their wretched lot.

As the weeks went by the salted meat arrived too, coming from the hinterland of Tombez. Bodfish went on shore and took up his office work in the hayshed near the sugar cane fields, so Harriet was deprived of even his advice.

"I would have thought," said Jake, "that with practice even you would have improved."

Harriet ignored him, concentrating instead on Bodfish's neatly written recipe. Surely, she thought with despair, she could make some passable biscuit. The loaves she had produced that morning had been almost inedible, and she had to do something to redeem herself. It was hot below and noisy, too, with the clatter on deck, and her hair straggled down and stuck to her cheeks, and the strings of the apron Bodfish had given her had come untied.

"Did you never learn to cook?" asked Jake.

She said briefly, "No," and wished he would go away.

"But your mother…"

"Never learned to cook, either. She never had the need. She was one of London's great beauties, much in demand at the court. You forget that I am an actress, Jake, you forget that I come from an acting family. Why, for that matter, we never had a kitchen, or a pantry, because we never had a real home."

"Where is your mother now?"

"She died when I was ten."

"I'm sorry to hear that."

Jake was behind her so that she couldn't see his face, but his tone was soft, more than polite. Then she felt tugs and realized he was gathering up the waist strings of the apron, and tying them up. It felt odd—matter-of-fact, and yet intimate enough to make her shiver inside.

Then she heard him say, "And your mother was an actress? Should I have heard of the famous Mrs. Gray?"

"Of course," she said, neglecting to add that her mother had not, in fact, been married to her father, though they had traveled and acted as a couple. "We were a stage family, with stage traditions. And my mother was indeed famous. She was very talented. People travelled miles to see her on the stage—not just because of her beauty, but because of her

177

reputation as a fine actress, too. But she never cooked. Acting families don't need to cook, Captain Dexter. They spend their lives in boarding houses."

Harriet could feel the bow being patted neatly into the back of her waist by those firm, long-fingered hands. She felt a strange warmth where his fingers rested, almost electric, and she suddenly wondered what would happen if she turned round while he was so close to her. If she turned into his arms, she thought, and remembered the ardent, inadvertent embrace on the darkened deck of the *Nympha*. There was another shiver deep inside her, a dangerous shiver of primitive awareness, something that urged her to do it.

Instead, she kept very still, and found herself talking a lot, to conceal her errant thoughts.

"We had our favorite boarding houses," she told him, as she kept her head bent and her eyes on her hands in the bowl of flour. "Or my father did, for we had our regular tour of the provinces, and always returned to the ones he liked. There was a Mrs. Grubbins in Bristol who was famous for her pies — and my father was particularly fond of a Mr. Kelly who had a deft hand with our horses. He had an even defter hand with a bottle of port," she confessed. "And then in the London season we stopped with my great-aunt Diana, in her house in Redcliffe Square. She was an even greater beauty than my mother, in her time, and even as I remember her in her advanced years, she was magnificent. And she had a very severe housekeeper, a paragon called Mrs. Pink, who ruled my aunt with an iron hand, and had a weakness for a bottle of port. She was only lenient with my father."

"Because of that fondness for port?" There was a warm chuckle in his voice.

"No doubt, though I have to admit that he was a very handsome man, even if he was my father," she said, and heard him laugh again.

"And in New Zealand?"

Harriet stiffened. Why did he ask that? She gripped the

178

spoon she was holding so hard that it hurt her fingers. She thought Royal must have told Jake about Sefton, and how he had left her. She remembered the pity and salacious speculation in other male faces, and thought she couldn't bear it if she glimpsed the same expression in Jahaziel Dexter's eyes.

She kept her focus on the spoon, and said very carefully, "When we arrived in New Zealand we stopped in a hotel."

"No servants?"

"Of course we had no servants—none of our own, that is. But the hotel had maids and cooks. What do you mean?"

"I was wondering how you coped after your father died."

Jake's voice was merely kind, but her eyes stung. He was the first person ever to ask how she had managed. Even Royal hadn't thought to wonder.

She said, "I acted. After all, that is all I can do. Manager Buckingham was pleased enough to employ me."

"At the Fitzroy?"

"The very one. Green room it did not have, nor any kind of apartment for robing—it was a dirty, flea-abounding, ill-lighted stink-hole, but it gave me employment."

"And how much money do you get for that kind of life?"

She shrugged. "Money. You don't really think of it as *money*. Lodging at a boarding house is included, and meals of a kind, and stabling, if you have a horse."

"Did you have a horse?"

"Not then."

Silence—a silence that dragged on. Despite herself she turned and met his eyes, fearing what she would see there. Jake's expression was wry, his head a little on one side as he studied her. She could smell his distinctive scent of clean soap and warm leather, and was more conscious than ever of the close quarters of the little pantry.

Again, there was that primitive urge to move into his

179

arms and lift her face to his…

He said, "How much?"

"Ten shillings a performance." Two dollars, fifty cents.

"Not much."

"Well, I could only afford one share in your company, remember."

She had tried to keep her tone light, but to her disgust, her voice wobbled a little. She thought of the gossip that had run about in Auckland, of the men who preached against actors, of the editors who called that theater, *The greatest threat to public morality in the whole of the colony.* She thought of the men who had sent her flowers and poems and sly propositions, many of them the same men who had preached against her, and who certainly ignored her in the open street, and she braced herself to counter Jake's pity.

Instead, he meditated, "So you had no time to practice cooking biscuit … and nicely cooked biscuit is a great weakness of mine, I must confess."

She said sharply, "And you don't trust me to cook it the way you like it?"

"I'm afraid I do not. I've never tried my hand at biscuit, but I see that Bodfish has written that recipe in a perfectly legible hand, so if you will excuse me…"

"With pleasure," she snapped, and left without wasting another word.

TWENTY-ONE

TO Harriet's chagrin, the biscuit proved excellent, and Jake Dexter was as smug about it as a cream-fed cat. Charlie Martin's compliments flowed, and he became more and more complacent.

But then, "I saw such a sight this day," Charlie added. "Such a gruesome sight you would never believe, and that in a cask of salt pork."

Jake said, "What?"

"On shore, in Bodfish's shed, what he calls his store. The carts come in laden with barrels of salt pork and beef, and because there's so much coming in all at once it's impractical for him to have all the kegs opened, so he chooses one at random, and judges the whole by that. And today the sample tub turned out to be full of heads. There were even rings in the snouts, all gone greenish. The owner roared his astonishment, but Bodfish held firm, and ordered them all taken away."

"As severe as Mrs. Pink," murmured Jake, and raised a crooked eyebrow at her, which Harriet haughtily ignored. The aspersions on her cooking rankled, and as far as she was concerned Captain Dexter the consummate biscuit maker could do all the fancy cooking, and welcome.

Jake was far too busy to do anything in the pantry,

however, as he was supervising the stowing as the goods came in. According to his directions, the bags and sacks and barrels were stacked in the hold, along with casks of water, and when the lading had reached a stated level, Chips and Jonathan laid boards on top to make a kind of floor, with a hatch so that the goods could be reached and broken out, as necessary. Once the floor was finished, they built berths along the bulkheads, with a long, rough table along the middle, lined with benches on both sides. It was going to be cramped, crowded accommodation, especially as the passengers who bunked here were providing for themselves, but it was obvious that the South American Argonauts would put up with just about anything, just to get to California.

So Harriet was left alone with culinary duties again, to cope as best she could with making something edible out of the goods that came in — and it had to be something edible for the entire crew. Irish Cookie was summoned to help Bodfish on shore, and so she was put in charge of the galley, as well as the pantry. Every morning sacks of fruit and vegetables were dumped by the galley door, under the forecastle deck, leaving her to sort out what to do with them. Gallingly, there was the constant nagging knowledge that if she made a blunder, the Company would hold a meeting to complain — and some of those fruits and vegetables were exotic enough to be completely unidentifiable.

Bananas and coconuts and oranges were easy, as she knew coconuts and oranges and bananas, even if some of the bananas were the size of baby fingers, while others were enormous, with huge, woolly spiders lurking in the bunches, which leapt out and made her scream. Mummy apples arrived, looking like pumpkins which could be stewed, but collapsing into syrup as soon as the water came to a boil. There were other strange fruits called *apple*, too — sweetsop, soursop, cherimoya and pawpaw, which proved just as challenging, until she learned the hard way that they were supposed to be eaten raw.

Alfalfa came as a fodder for the llamas, and she mistakenly tried to cook it as a vegetable, which almost triggered a mutiny. She made stews out of vegetables which came out as strangely colored soups, and soups which thickened mysteriously into stews. Some sweet little berries looked just right for pies, but when Charlie Martin tasted one his lips blistered and his language was most unhandsome.

Mortified and exhausted, Harriet left the table and slammed into the pantry. Beyond the partition she could hear Jake Dexter laughing. She put her apron over her head and dissolved into furious sobs. When he discovered her in this humiliating state, Charlie Martin was most contrite and begged her pardon often. And Jake Dexter, when he had got over laughing, suggested she might like to go in Valentine Fish's boat for a jaunt on shore, not having been up the river yet.

Harriet went willingly enough, though—as she reflected as the boat set off—it was an odd circumstance that this was her first trip ashore in more than four months, and yet, while she had yearned to get off the whaleship *Humpback*, she had never felt trapped on the brig. She held onto the side of the boat and looked about with interest, as Valentine Fish at the steering oar broke into song:

> *My creditors gave me just a week, to pay them what I*
>   *ought*
> *So I thanked them very kindly, and sailed to Tombez*
>   *port.*
> *Now I sail to Sacramento, where once the river rolled*
> *To fill my trouser pockets, with the bright and shining*
>   *gold!*

Sacramento, she thought uneasily. The Sacramento valley, surely, was some distance from San Francisco. What would Jake Dexter do with the brig if the Company voted to leave the *Gosling* to go up the river to the mines? It was inconceivable that he would abandon his ship, an even more appalling notion than carrying a load of South American men to San Francisco. Surely he wouldn't do that, as the *Gosling* was his home, as well? She turned her head and watched her home as the boat lifted and dropped over the sand bar. Then the men pulled about a narrow curve, and the brig was out of sight.

Cool green enfolded them. Insects as large as reef fish buzzed and hovered just overhead, and long fronds leaned down and touched the river surface and caressed the river current. Tib and Dan pulled strongly at the oars, and she could hear them grunting with each heave. Alligators floated balefully, and —

"Beneath a hot and burning sun, I'll work for many a day," sang Valentine —

Certain sure I'll strike it rich and soon be sailing away
I'll find a monstrous heap of gold and dig it with my
* hands*
And get some boards and box it up and sail for Yankee
* lands!*

Then the boat touched the landing. Harriet stepped carefully from the boat to the pier, and climbed up the bank to the track with her skirts held high. The smells of warm dirt and slime and pigs and rotting leaves and squashed bananas rose with every step. Then she was on the path trailed through a sugar cane field, and she was surrounded on both sides by stiff gray-green leaves that grew higher than her head, which clashed and rustled as the breeze eddied and lifted the dust. Valentine and the other two were still on the landing, so she walked alone.

It was hot enough walking through the dry and dusty cane, but when she arrived at the end of the sugar plantation the sun beat down and enervating heat enfolded her. A path led off to the left, heading for some trees and a barn, and so she followed it. If she could find Bodfish, she would be able to ask some advice about cooking strange vegetables, she thought.

Then she saw Royal sitting in a field, in the shade of a thick thorn hedge. Five strange beasts were grazing nervously nearby. She walked on until she reached a railed fence, climbed over it, and walked back to join him.

'What are those?" she said.

"Llamas."

She walked up to one, and the beast skittered off a couple of feet. Then it was still, and they stood and looked at each other. Llamas, she thought, the sheep of the Andes. Captain Schouten had drawn some on his map, in the company of bears and dragons. After a moment she circled the llama, her head on one side, and the llama kept still, turning its head on its long flexible neck to meet her eye-to-eye throughout the inspection. Captain Schouten, she remembered, had wondered in script if the llama fleece had been used by the Indians to sieve the fabled gold, and the wool on this beast looked thick and dense enough to serve that kind of purpose.

Gold, she thought, *gold.*

She sighed, turned away, and sat down on the stiff, short grass by Royal. "You know," she mused aloud. "Those llamas remind me of great-aunt Diana. She had just such a neck, and the same sloping shoulders and dark eyes with long lashes, and the same haughty expression."

Royal favored this with no more than a bad-tempered grunt, so she said, "Do alpacas look like llamas?"

"It wouldn't have made any difference if the alpacas had been here," he said instead of answering. "The *Gosling* Company is dead set on chasing to California, to mine a fortune in gold."

"I know," she said sadly. She wondered what Captain Schouten would have made of California, but knew beyond doubt that he would have believed the tales without the

185

slightest hesitation.

She looked about, and saw Bodfish standing in front of a big, ramshackle shed. That, she deduced, was his store, but the area in front of it was empty, so she wondered if all the provisions had been loaded already. Three South American women had arrived at the fence and were standing still, staring at her just as inquisitively as she had studied the llamas.

Harriet gave them an uncertain smile, but got no response, the women moving on, instead. So she turned to Royal, saying, "Who tells these tales of gold in California, anyway?"

"A man by the name of Honest Mill Mason."

"*Who?*"

"He's a deserter from the American man-of-war *Ohio*, so who can guess what his real name might be?"

"Do you think he's really honest?"

Royal shrugged. "The tales he relates are incredible enough, and they are secondhand, too, come from the crew of the ship that came in for provisions and took all the local men away. But everyone believes him — because those locals have never come back. If the ship didn't wreck with all hands, they must be digging away in the hills of California."

"Where is this Honest Mill Mason now?"

"Back at the Frenchman's plantation, spinning his yarns. But he's also killing pigs and rendering them into barrels of salt pork. Soon, he reckons, he'll have enough to pay for his way to California on the brig."

"Why didn't he go on the ship that came for provisions, with all the other local men?"

"Because he thought it was all a nonsense, but since then he's become a believer."

"And do you plan to chase these gold tales, too?"

"I'm one of the Company, so I will do what they do — and don't look at me like that, Hat. It's all your fault, admit it."

She said furiously, "And what happens to me while you go off to the diggings, Royal?"

"Jake Dexter will look after you," he said—and then, so suddenly and casually that it took her breath away, "I assume he is your lover, Hat?"

She flushed hotly. "Of course he is not! And I think poorly of you for saying that, brother."

"Why so? It would surprise no one if you became his mistress. Some of the men reckon you're his already, and the others are laying bets on it."

Oh God, she thought, and shut her eyes.

"So shocked, dear sis?" he jibed. "You're an actress—an actress!—so it's expected behavior. You're pretty, and he's good-looking, in a rugged sort of way, so you can't blame the boys for jumping to the obvious conclusion. And it runs in the family, admit it."

Harriet grimaced, because he was right. Their father was handsome and their mother was a famous beauty, and they had never bothered with a wedding. And, despite their fame as a couple on the stage, there had been many whispers of dalliances. And great-aunt Diana... When the old lady, still elegant, still beautiful, had passed away, they had found out just which prince of the realm had supported the household in Redcliffe Square. The royal descendants had politely and firmly stated the facts, and taken the mansion away. It had been the major reason for trying a new start in the colonies.

"It's just part of life as an actor or actress, dear Hat, and you know that even better than I do. Why, I'd wager all the gold in California that you had more than twenty offers of maintenance after it became apparent that Sefton had gone off-stage. Am I right? I bet I am!"

Harriet pressed her lips together, remembering all the men who didn't deign to recognize her in the street, but who had thronged adoringly at the stage door. Bouquets with little notes of assignation had been tossed over the whale-oil footlights. If she had been a sporting woman, she could have

187

lived in what passed in the colonies for luxury, as the kept mistress of one of the notables.

She said, "So that's why you've never asked me how I managed after Frank left."

"Well, dear Hat, I do have an ounce of tact, you know."

"I can't say I've ever noticed that," she said sharply. "And, as for Captain Dexter, you can put that idea right out of your head. He's not that sort of man."

He laughed. "You really think so? He looks adventurous and dashing enough to me. And I've seen the way he watches you, sis."

Was it possible? Would Jake Dexter have kissed her if she had given into wayward instinct, and turned into his arms as he tied her apron strings on that day in the pantry? Would he have carried her off to his stateroom, and tumbled her into his bed? Of course not—he had purely been motivated by a craving for well cooked biscuit. What nonsense, she thought, and pushed sensual images out of her mind.

She snapped, "You heard him for yourself when he said that your arrival on board was well-timed, because it made the situation more respectable. And you've seen him order me below, and you know how much he hates to see me about the decks. He treats me like a child!"

"It's a game, Hat—he's teasing you! And enjoying it, too. And how old did you say you were, when he asked?"

Harriet looked away and muttered, "Almost nineteen."

"What? If my memory serves, and I am sure it does, you're only two months past eighteen."

"I'm nearer nineteen than twenty, Royal."

"Such sophistry," he derided. "Hat, my dear, you really are a child." Then he clambered to his feet, saying, "Enter the star of the show."

It was Jake himself, arriving at the end of the track with a group of *Gosling*s. Harriet scrambled up, feeling most uncomfortably flustered. To avoid looking in that direction, she turned to Royal and said, "What's up?"

"We're collecting the llamas, sister mine, and taking them out to the brig."

"Already?" She was dismayed, because she hadn't realized that the day of sailing was so near.

Royal, however, looked animated. His pointed straw beard jutted at he contemplated his little herd, preparing himself for battle. The llamas seemed to scent this, because they skittered and pranced.

"We must introduce 'em to their transport, sis," he declared. "They must become submissive to their lodgings. Like women, dear Hat, they must learn duty and patience. Their digestive systems must become resigned to the peculiar motion of a ship."

"What nonsense you talk," she said.

"Not nonsense at all. Tell me, Captain," he said as Jake arrived, "have you ever seen a seasick llama?"

"I have not," said Jake.

"Neither have I, sir, neither have I — and I would like to avoid the experience, by starving them for twenty-four hours before we sail, to render their systems barren."

"Something a certain man would be wise to emulate," Harriet said tartly, but Royal ignored the taunt, loping over to his llamas instead. The llamas backed off and then trotted away, keeping just out of reach, their long necks swiveling to keep everyone in view.

Bodfish arrived down the path from the barn, and said, "Can I help?"

"With pleasure," said Royal.

He began to sweep a bow, but a llama chose that moment to make a bid for freedom, breaking into a gallop as it headed for the hedge. To Harriet's incredulous amusement it cleared it in one agile and completely unexpected bound, proving to them all that the llamas had remained in the field purely in a spirit of cooperation.

The other llamas bolted after their leader, followed by a

mob of shouting men, with Royal at their head. Dust rose, veiling the struggle, and when it cleared the llamas were more or less in a group, trotting down the middle of the cane-field track.

Everyone walked slowly after them. The woolly beasts walked mincingly, on fat trotters, their lashes fluttering as they looked this way and that. Their long necks bobbed like the necks of swans. One tried to bound into the cane as the river came into sight, but Davy Jones Locker stepped in front of its wayward path, with a long arm thrust out. The llama turned a complete circle in mid-air, and dashed full-pelt for the river, heading for the landing stage and followed by its fellows.

"Yo ho!" Royal cried, whirling his hat in triumph. "Got them, by thunder, and never was easier!"

And a large alligator swirled in the river.

The llamas all jumped straight up into the air, and when they came down the group split up. Two shot back up the trail, leaping Davy's outthrust arm easily, two dashed away upstream, and the fifth ran around in circles and then lay down with its neck stretched out, emitting heart-rending groans. When Royal went up to it, he was greeted with a stream of smelly green spit that smacked right into the middle of his chest.

With a terrible curse he flung down his straw hat and stamped on it. "Oh mighty Gray," he roared at the indifferent sky. "Have we sunk so low, are all our plans and schemings, our glories, triumphs, dreams, all shrunk to this little measure, that we should be humbled so by a pack of bloody llamas? Unfair!" he cried.

"Such eloquence," sighed Bodfish, who was a fan of the stage. Jake Dexter, predictably, was laughing helplessly.

Then the alligator sounded with a loud slosh, and the prostrate llama surged to all four feet and took off, apparently straight up in the air but landing down the track before disappearing fast. All the men halloa-ed, and raced off after it, with Bill the steerage boy in the lead.

Catching them was a lengthy business, but the *Goslings* enjoyed it, judging by the commotion. In the end Harriet clambered into the tied whaleboat to watch, as every now and then a llama galloped into view, hotly pursued by a *Gosling*. For a long time she thought the llamas had won their freedom, but to her surprise they eventually reappeared as a group, to be herded onto the landing stage.

Even then, the job wasn't easy. The animals had to be felled, and trussed and tied, while all the time the men dodged flying green spit. The first was lifted, Harriet hastily quit the boat, and the llama was deposited in her place. The other llamas put up an even bigger fight. One broke loose from the hold of three ropes, and to her secret pleasure Abijah Roe was kicked fair-square into the river, but at last the two boats were loaded, bobbing frantically with llama struggles. There was scarcely any room for the oarsmen. Obviously, some of the party would have to stay and wait for a boat to return.

Harriet, Bodfish, and Davy Jones Locker all volunteered, and Jake Dexter joined them. Silently, they watched the boats' erratic progress until they breasted a curve and were out of sight, and after that it was very quiet. It was late afternoon, and humid in the shade of the riverside trees. Insects hovered with only the faintest noise, and even the birds were silent. The river rippled on, like time. When Jake turned and headed up the track through the sugar cane on the way to Bodfish's store, Harriet followed him.

The sugarcane stalks leaned back and forth in the small dusty wind, and made a rustle that clattered secretly in their massed ranks of leaves. Then, all at once, Bodfish was walking beside her, as the path widened out.

"So we sail tomorrow," he said. "Or the day after that, at the latest. I anticipate trouble with the South Americans, Miss Gray, and I don't mind admitting it."

"Yes," said Harriet.

191

"Such men can be quarrelsome and vengeful. We will be lucky if there is no murder on board. The females, on the other hand," Bodfish reflected, "are generally lively, beautiful and interesting."

"Yes," said Harriet again. She held up her skirts with both hands and watched Jake Dexter's broad back as he walked ahead of them, the black shadow of his wide leather hat bobbing easily with his strides. She thought that the women who had stopped by the fence to inspect her earlier had been too weathered to be beautiful, but it was rather too hot to think.

"The premonition of trouble is constantly on my mind, Miss Gray."

"Yes," she said, yet again. She could hear the quiet plod of Davy's feet as he brought up the rear. The ex-slave was as silent as their captain.

"The evenings will prove the worst," Bodfish dolefully continued. "They will gamble and fight, and be altogether restless. The Spanish," he said with heavy disapproval, "are always thus inclined. They wake up with coming of dark, when more practical men have done their day's work, and instead of resting they sing, Miss Gray, they fight and generally make an unholy ruckus."

"But what can we do?"

"Why, we entertain them, Miss Gray!"

"I beg your pardon?" she exclaimed, astonished, and saw Jake Dexter turn his head.

"We preoccupy those dangerous evenings. We have the best shanty-man I ever did hear, in the person of Mr. Fish, and we could read poetry, and you and Mr. Gray could act small interludes from Shakespeare."

"A good idea," said Jake, but then added, "Except for the slight problem that they don't understand much English."

"But that don't signify, sir, for even those of Spanish blood are conscious of the grateful favor of being privileged enough to view true art."

They emerged from the cane field. Away from the cane the dusty air was so sun-scorched that it was almost unbreathable. In the far distance, beyond the barn and the trees, a laden ox-drawn cart was lumbering towards them, making the only movement in the landscape.

Without a word, Jake led the way along the fence and the hedge to the shed where Bodfish kept his store. The cart had been two hundred yards off when Harriet had first seen it, but by the time they reached the shed, it was much nearer. Harriet could hear the plod of unshod hooves and the rumble of solid wooden wheels.

She kept on walking into the dusty dark of the barn, and behind her, the squeak of the wooden wheels stopped. The cart was right outside the shed, and she could hear the oxen breathing. Bodfish had stayed outside, and when she turned she could see the hot sun reflecting on his shiny bald head. Far above in the sky an eagle hung, its outspread wings quite still.

There were three men on the bench of the cart, Spanish, with their huge sombreros pulled low so their faces were hidden in black shadow. When they got down she saw that their calcineros were dirty and dusty, with spatters of blood or grease all down them. Then one pushed his hat back to stare at her, and she saw it was Joaquín Murieta.

Jake was standing out in the sun, next to Bodfish. He was brace-legged, his own hat tipped back, his fists set on his belt.

Joaquín Murieta said to him, "Salt porks. From the La Plante man's plantation." Then he pointed back at the cart with his thumb poked over his shoulder.

Harriet looked again at the cart. It was heavily loaded with barrels, the fat short barrels that were commonly used for salt meat.

She heard Jake say, "Is Honest Mill Mason still there at the plantation?"

Joaquín Murieta's teeth gleamed, and Harriet thought with a shiver that he was looking at her, not Jake, because he merely said idly, "Capitán?"

"I asked about the man who looks after the Frenchman's estate. An American solder who calls himself Honest Mill Mason."

"Ah…" Joaquín looked vague. Then he poked his thumb again, presumably in the direction of the plantation, in the same gesture he had used to point at the barrels of pork.

Bodfish cleared his throat, and everyone looked at him. He said, "You know my system? That I choose one barrel at random, and open it for inspection?"

The Murietas nodded in unison, smirking confidently. Bodfish didn't move, and said nothing. Everyone waited, as he looked at the cart. It was almost as if he was looking at the cart to avoid meeting Joaquín Murieta's challenging eyes.

Harriet looked at the cart herself. The barrels seemed identical to each other. Their staves were delineated by black lines where the brine still darkened the cracks. The wood of the round tops of the casks was dried to a gray shade by the dust and hot sun. The trees in the paddock by the shed rattled in a sudden little gust, and Harriet heard thumps as mangoes dropped onto the roof.

Joaquín finally moved. Impatiently, he said to Bodfish, "Which one we open? Why do we wait? You choose any one you wish, quick, quick." The tone was bullying.

Harriet saw Jake Dexter shift uneasily, but he said nothing. And still Bodfish hesitated.

Joaquín said, "That one?" — and moved. His hand *moved*. A flash of hard light left his hand and one of the barrels thumped. Harriet's mouth went dry.

The flash was a knife. It stuck, vibrating, in the side of the cask that had thumped. The steel of the quivering blade caught the red light of the lowering sun. Had she seen

Bodfish flinch?

Harriet thought so, because Joaquín grinned. He said, "We open that one?"

"No," said Bodfish, and had to clear his throat to speak again. "That one," he said, and pointed at a barrel that was well away from the singing knife.

Joaquín did not seem disappointed. He and his two brothers teetered the chosen cask off the cart and onto the ground. Neither Jake nor Davy moved to help them. The Murietas opened the top and stood back and one of them reached up and pulled the knife out of the first barrel. It left an arrow-shaped mark where it had stuck.

The opened cask held good pink pork, the best Harriet had seen. She watched Bodfish nod, and would have believed him perfectly matter-of-fact, except that his fingers trembled as he wrote out the notes.

When the Murietas heaved the rest of the load off the cart Jake and Davy still did not move to help. There were twenty casks, and Harriet wondered tensely what each was worth, and how many berths on the *Gosling* they would buy. *I anticipate trouble with the South Americans, I don't mind admitting that I do...*

Yes, she thought.

When the cart finally ground off along the track it was growing dark and rapidly cooler. Birds began to call eerily, crying, *Whip, whip, whip poor Willy, weep, weep, weep, poor Willy ...* and the hairs on her forearms were rising.

"What kind of bird is that?" she cried—or tried to cry, except that her voice came out as a whisper.

Davy moved in the dimness of the barn behind her. "Why, they be goatsucker birds, Miss Gray," he said in his soft, hesitant voice. "In Guyana we say they be the ghosts of poor dead slaves."

"Oh dear lord," she said, shivering, and moved closer to Jake.

TWENTY-TWO

AT dawn next day the South American Argonauts returned to take up their berths, arriving in dribbles. Small craft came in by sea, or down the river, and other groups came down the coast.

There were small boys and grandfathers on the boats, as hands to sail them back home, while the expectant young men had precious handfuls of promissory notes, some folded so constantly that they threatened to fall apart. Those who did not have notes, or enough notes, brought more provisions, so that Harriet was forced to cope with even more foreign fruit and vegetable matter. There were sacks of strange nuts and corn in bright unfamiliar shades, and smoke-dried strips of what she was assured was meat, but looked a lot more like leather.

More familiar looking meat was brought in a living condition, including a gross of furious hens. To Harriet's relief, Chips took these over. He made coops by the simple means of putting two barrel hoops crosswise and weaving them into a globe with rope yarn. Then the trapped, indignant hens were slung from nails hammered on the outside of the stern. Another man brought a live bullock that had to be heaved up with the windlass. Within moments he was lowing sadly in the pig pen, with small black pigs running about his feet, squealing their own protest like rusty hinges. The llamas, who had their own pen on the foredeck, and had adapted to it amazingly well, merely lying down with their necks stretched out, humming to each other, all stood up to have a look, which disturbed the pigs even further.

Then it was another dawn, and the tide was on the turn. The sky was as pale as new milk, and the offshore wind gusted, fair for a swift passage to California. Thank God, thought Harriet, because the time to weigh anchor had come without the reappearance of the Murietas.

"All hands on deck, the first mate cries," sang Valentine Fish —

> *His shouts like thunder's roar, suh!*
> *All hands on deck, brave boys reply*
> *'tis the signal for California!*

Men heaved at the windlass and the men aloft loosed the canvas. The Argonauts packing the rails cheered and waved their hats, and fired pistols in the air. The brig vibrated with excitement, as well as the raising of the anchor. Harriet couldn't help but creep up onto deck, and hide in a corner by the afterhouse.

> *Go loose your tops'ls, boys, he cries*
> *Fly-jibs and jibs let go, suh!*
> *Haul home those sheets, I say, brave boys,*
> *And for 'Frisco gold we go, suh!*

Then all at once the shanty stopped short. The men in the rigging were staring sternwards, shading their eyes. A whaleboat was coming down the river. It crested the bar, took on water, and jinked. The oarsmen baled and then pulled again, steering for the brig. Everyone watched in silence, and the thump as the boat touched the hull of the brig seemed very loud.

Harriet heard Charlie, on the afterdeck, say to Jake in a low voice, "It's the Murietas, Captain." Then she heard the thump of boots as the Murietas climbed on board, and after that they came into sight.

Their expressions were challenging, their grins derisive. They looked filthier than ever in the clear dawn light. These, Harriet thought, were the descendants of the Conquistadors. Their ancestors had lit slow fires under half-throttled Indians, thirteen at a time to commemorate Christ and his twelve disciples, and they had forced Indian women to watch while their men were roasted and their babies spitted alive. Men like these had seized harmless nuns on Judas Island, and buried them alive in a fury, because the nuns had refused to tell them where the Panamanian gold was hidden.

Harriet saw Jake Dexter walk up to the Murietas, and stand in front of them.

Joaquín said, "We come with notes, enough, yes. Enough for passage to 'Frisco."

The papers he thrust at Jake were fouled with dirt and grease. Harriet, frozen, watched Jake count them. Then he said, "Yes, there is enough here for six berths in the hold. More than enough."

In the hold. Thank God, she thought. The prospect of these men eating at the cabin table was too awful to contemplate.

Then Joaquín said, "How much more, for six. For six to eat in the cabin, yes. And to have the steerage for us, private for the Murietas."

Jake thought a moment, looked down at the sheaf of dirty notes, and then said, "One hundred, on top of this."

"Ah..." Silence. Then Joaquín said, "The boat."

"What?"

"The whaleboat. She is yours. At that price. Good boat, worth lot more than just one hundred. Take it, and give us the steerage. With meals at the cabin table."

Silence. No one moved. Then Charlie Martin went to the side, looked at the boat, jumped down into it. The thump and splash seemed very loud. After a long moment he came up the side again, and whispered in Captain Dexter's ear.

And Jake looked at Joaquín Murieta, and curtly nodded.

A steady sou'easterly wind and the northward current carried the brig well off land and continued fair the following days. Their passage bid to be speedy, which Jake considered no small blessing.

At no time was it possible for him to forget that he was carrying passengers, and at all times he remembered a vow he had made right from the beginning—that he might smuggle goods through borders, that he might take on cargoes that were forbidden by local authorities, that he might trespass on foreign soil to spy for money, or go fortune-hunting on a hunch, but he would never touch the slave trade, and he would never carry passengers. Now, he wished most fervently that he had kept the last part of the resolution, because his cargo of Argonauts had proved to be just as arrogant, noisy, quarrelsome and dirty as Bodfish had predicted.

At the very first dawn they picked a fight with the watch, which turned into a brawl that Abner and Charlie had to quell with fists as well as shouts. The grievance, apparently, was that the Argonauts had chosen to sleep on deck, and the watch were careless with mops, water, and buckets when they washed down the planks. It was a brawl that set a pattern. The South Americans fought with each other as well as the *Goslings*; they spat everywhere, and fired pistols into the rigging, and carved in the woodwork, and stole each other's wine and tobacco.

If Harriet had not broken his pattern of not carrying passengers, he wouldn't have this chaotic situation, Jake brooded, ignoring the guilty truth—that the idea of carrying the Argonauts had been his own. And, worst of all, he didn't even have the privacy of the mess cabin, because the Murietas were always there. They had the steerage to themselves, but still they haunted the cabin.

Jake had made it plain and clear that they had no place at the table until he and Charlie and Miss Gray and Abner had eaten their meals, but every time he went down the companionway the Murietas were sprawled on the benches, with Joaquín arrogantly taking over the captain's chair. They passed the time digging into the table top with their knives, and smoking and card-playing, and when they ate they used those knives, and after eating they used the same knives to pick their teeth and fingernails. When Jake snapped at them to get to the steerage, they moved, but as soon as he left, they sneaked down again.

He had a word with Charlie, who protested that he did his best to keep them out of the mess cabin, too. "But, to tell the truth, sir," he said. "It's almost better that they're in here, because when they're not here, they run a gambling saloon."

"They … *what!*"

"They've turned the steerage into a gambling saloon, and what goes on in there causes still more fights."

Jake frowned. "What kind of gambling?"

"They call it monte, but it ain't the three-card game you see at Valparaiso. They throw down a serape, and mark it into four quarters, and they throw down four cards, face up, and bet on what the next card will be."

"That is monte as I know it," said Jake, and sighed. "Do our men play, too?"

"Crotchet does, in his watches below."

That, thought Jake, was no surprise. "Does he win?"

"He seems to win a lot, sir, yes."

"Good," said Harriet passionately, and Jake looked at her, startled, because she had been so quiet of late.

In fact, he had wondered if she had been avoiding him. The instant Charlie or Abner left the table, she would leave, too, going through the passage into her stateroom and pulling the latch string to her side of the door. Now, when their eyes met, she smiled, looking a little like her old self.

Jake lifted a crooked brow in return, and then, with another sigh, he stood and headed up to deck. His black mood deepened as he opened the door to see the usual lot of dirty Argonauts huddled all over his decks. It didn't occur to him for quite some moments that Harriet had stood too, when he left the table, and had gone into her stateroom, leaving Charlie by himself.

Next noon, it was Abner who left the table to relieve Charlie, who had the watch on deck, and Harriet, again, immediately stood. She was in her room with the latch clicked shut and the string pulled through before Jake could ask the reason. Then, before he could tap on her door, Joaquín Murieta came down the stairs from deck.

Jake said, "What the hell are you doing in here?"

"You, you're not finished yet?"

"No," said Jake flatly.

"Ah…" Joaquín looked furtively about and lowered his voice. "There is trouble, yes, with the pretty *gringita*?"

"*What?*"

"The señorita, such a pretty gray filly, yes. One pretty girl alone, so many men. She is yours? You are …" He hunted for the word. "Protector?"

Anger hit Jake in a jolt. He said stiffly, "Miss Gray is a passenger, señor. She is a passenger with all the rights of someone who has paid a fare."

Joaquín frowned. "But she actress, they say. Woman of the stage, yes."

"I don't know what the hell you're talking about."

"Ah, Capitán, beg pardon, señor." But Joaquín's expression was not at all apologetic.

Jake set down his mug with a bang, stood up, and left without another word.

Similar stupid stares filled his decks, however, and he thanked all Providence when he took a sighting and went down to his transom cabin to work out their position, and saw how close they had come to California. The fair wind had served him well. He'd be grateful for a tempest, he thought, if it would get them to San Francisco faster.

At the noon meal next day, a foreboding of that tempest arrived, in the form of a squall that whirled out of a peaceful blue sky. Jake left the table in a lunge, and made for the stairs with Charlie close on his heels.

But Abner had proved, yet again, that he well deserved his promotion. The courses were hauled up and the topsail reef tackles hauled out before Jake clambered up to the afterdeck. The brig was dancing and pitching her head, but Jonathan and Joseph Fayal were out on the boom furling the jib. The canvas was slatting, but the squall spent its strength with no damage, and within minutes the *Gosling* was back under all sail.

But the weather was going to deteriorate, Jake decided. There were clouds building high in the sky, and there was a harsh feel to the wind that told him that the squall had been a warning of what was to come. He gave instructions to both Charlie and Abner, and went down to the transom to check his charts.

When there was a tap on his door, he took a moment to answer, being absorbed in calculations. He expected it to be Charlie, come for more instructions, but instead it was Bodfish, who was looking extremely agitated.

"Sir," he said. "Miss Harriet."

"What's wrong with her?"

"She's ... She's in the foc'sle, Captain."

"She's ... *what?*"

"And ... and I think she's in a passion."

Jake said, "Oh Jehovah," and launched himself out of his room.

He ran through the empty mess cabin and up the stairs to deck. It was growing very gusty. Spray spat over the weather rail and the lee scuppers foamed. The sky was scudding with thickening cloud. Yet, despite the unpleasant conditions, the decks were even more crowded than usual, and the grins wider and even more stupid.

He was forced to jostle through groups of men to get forward, and then, to get to the forecastle hatch, he had to shove past the Murietas. What the hell were they doing on the foredeck? He didn't stop to ask, because he heard Harriet shouting inside the forecastle.

"For God's sake, Royal!" she shouted. "You're my brother, not a worm, so try to find a backbone!"

Jake plunged into the seamen's room, but despite his abrupt entry no one paid him any attention. Harriet was standing in the clear space at the foot of the foremast, facing her brother, who stood in the front of a huddle of *Gosling* seamen. The seamen were all staring raptly at her, but Royal had his hands covering his face.

Jake roared, "What the hell is going on?" — and Harriet turned.

Her hair was down in a tangled mass, half-covering her face, and for a horrible instant he thought she was weeping blood. Then she thrust the hair away with one hand, and he saw the long cut high on her cheek, running a thin red stream.

She said fiercely, "No doubt you're very angry with me, Captain, but don't be angry with your men, because the fault is not theirs."

"But what the devil ...?"

"The Murietas were tormenting her, sir," said Crotchet. "We all know it's improper for Miss Gray to come in here, but she came to us for refuge, sir, on account of her dire need."

The Murietas. Biting out the words, Jake demanded, "Why the foc'sle?"

"Because I came to that — that *worm* for support and defense!"

Royal winced. "For God's sake, Hat — "

204

"All that was needed was for you to show some spirit, brother! You know what bullies are like—all you have to do is raise your hackles and roar like a lion and they retreat in disarray, sir. My God," she said. She seemed on the verge of flying at Royal, and when Jake gripped her arm to keep her still, he could feel her trembling with rage. "Those goddamned Murietas, those bastard *bandits*, they caught me in the cabin alone—they insulted me!—they called me a gray *filly*, for God's sake, as if I were an animal! And Joaquín pulled at my hair, and threatened to cut it off if I didn't come to the steerage and pleasure their desires, and when I pulled away he cut my cheek. They called me an *actress*!"

"But you *are* an actress," Royal protested, and Harriet's arm jerked in Jake's grip as she tried to lunge at her brother, who put up his hands and said plaintively to Jake, "She wanted me to fight a duel for her honor, sir, she asked the impossible!"

Jake was seething with his own rage, remembering Joaquín's sly query. *Such a pretty filly, yes ... she is yours?* Damn it, he thought, *he should have said yes!*

Now, he said nothing, but urged Harriet out of the forecastle and onto the foredeck. The Murietas were still there, smirking, the passengers all gathered behind them, smirking too.

Jake shouted at them all, "You may be passengers, with agreed rights, but by God I tell you all that the next man who lays a finger on Miss Gray will be flogged!"

The sniggering silenced, and men began to retreat. Joaquín Murieta was slower to move, and Jake reached out and shoved him so hard that he stumbled backwards and then tripped and fell in the scuppers. No one helped him up. As Jake led Harriet to the afterhouse door, men hastily got out of the way.

He took her down the end of the passage, through the lobby, and into his transom cabin. Jake said, "Sit," and she sat on the sofa, watching warily as he got out his medical chest. Then he dragged out his chart desk chair, and sat down on it, facing her with his knees on either side of hers, holding her in place.

When he touched her face she tried to wince away, so he cupped her chin in his left palm to hold her head still. The cut was even deeper than he had thought, dangerously close to her left eye. She could have lost half her sight, he thought, and anger twisted again. There were tears of fury and pain on her lashes, and he brushed them away with a wad of clean cotton before moistening the wad from a bottle.

"Not brandy, Captain Dexter!"

"Hush." When she yelped and flinched as the wet cloth touched her cheek, he said, "Don't be such a baby."

"Then stop treating me like an infant!"

But she submitted, and sat quietly as he sponged carefully, drawing out blood, thinking of the Murietas' filthy knives, how they used those knives to pick their teeth and fingernails.

He said softly, "I wondered why you always left the table so fast."

"I couldn't risk being caught alone. They had poor Bodfish so scared."

And yet she was right. All bullies were cowards underneath. He demanded, "Why didn't you scream? All you needed to do was cry for help."

"If I screamed they would have known I was frightened, which would have made it worse. They were trying to force me into the steerage, like—like a filly in season, Jake."

Like a filly in season. Jake said savagely, "I'll kill them."

She merely smiled faintly. He finished cleaning the wound, and then pulled the edges together with tiny strips of adhesive plaster, before smearing on simple ointment. He drew back and studied her, hoping that it would heal without a scar, knowing that if he tried out his herringbone stitches she would end up looking like Abner. Then, when he had finished, she curled up against the cushions, and seemed to go to sleep.

Her eyes were shut, the long lashes lowered. Jake sat, and watched her, wanting to touch her again—but not just to dress her wound. He wanted to lean forward and kiss her on the cheek below the dressing, and then to move his kiss to her mouth. *Such a pretty filly, yes ... she is yours?* Yes, he thought emphatically. *The señorita, such a pretty gray filly, yes. One pretty girl alone, so many men. She is yours? You are...*

Her lover? Yes, he thought again, yes.

Then he roused, mindful of duty. The movement of the brig was growing increasingly uneasy, and he heard Charlie shout out for assistance.

"Stay here," he said, hoping she was listening. Then he went out on deck.

TWENTY-THREE

BY noon next day the brig was pitching as if she would jump the sticks right out of her. All hands were on deck, taking in sail piece by piece until they were running under double-reefed topsails and jib. Even with reduced canvas the *Gosling* was making twelve knots, bounding towards 'Frisco with every surge and splash.

The wind was rugged, but the wind was fair—and the Argonauts were in no condition to appreciate it. "They're travellin' by rail," quoth Valentine Fish with glee.

The Murietas, like most of their Ecuadorean fellows, had their heads over the lee rail, having learned the hard way to avoid the one on the weather side of the ship. Like the rest of the Argonauts, too, they were beseeching the unforgiving saints for mercy.

"Some of them are hiding themselves in lockers so the storm won't find them," said Charlie with a guffaw. Even Royal Gray wasn't seasick, nor the placid llamas in their pen. Harriet, however, was a-bed—not because of *mal de mer*, but because Jake Dexter, as medical officer, had ordered her to stay there.

At nine the next night she opened her eyes and blinked at Jake, who was standing at the head of her berth, hanging up a lit lamp. When he let go, the lamp swung wildly. Then he picked up his medical book and frowned from the pages to her.

She said, "Oh, go on deck and nurse your brig."

He grinned, but looked weary. She listened to the creak and the thump of waves and the wind in the rigging, and thought he would spend the night on deck, just as he had the night before.

Then she said, "Where are we?"

He said nothing for the moment, but squatted down and set to dabbing at her cheek with a cool solution on a cloth. She winced, but the cut was not really sore. She smelled his scent of salt and soap and warm leather.

Then he said, "It looks good. I've done well."

He sounded as smug as he had when he had baked good biscuit. However, when he straightened she smiled up at him.

He lifted a brow, and said at last, "We'll be in San Francisco tomorrow, thank God. With grace and favor and our cargo of prayers the wind stayed fair for California."

California, she thought. It still seemed unreal. She still felt as if they should be on the way to New South Wales with the livestock pens full of alpacas, but instead they were heading for an unknown future in California. She found it impossible to imagine what they would find there, so instead of answering she shut her eyes, and the next time she opened them, it was morning.

The brig, however, was scarcely moving. The *Gosling* wallowed, making little headway, and the view outside Harriet's row of portholes was gray and drifting. Fog. The lee shore of California was hidden in thick mist.

Harriet crept out of bed and got dressed, expecting to be scolded, but when she looked through the double doors the mess cabin was empty. At the top of the passageway steps she eased open the door to the deck. Mist clung stickily to the rigging. She could hear breakers, and everything dripped. The sails loomed ghostly gray, uncannily close because of some mirage-like effect. The varnished oilskin coats the seamen were wearing were black and shiny with wet, and there was not a sign of the Argonauts.

Harriet closed the door again, and went back into the afterquarters.

Three hours later, she was sitting on the sofa in Jake Dexter's transom cabin, eating dinner from a tray, when the door opened and Jake came in. His brows shot up as he saw her, but he made no comment. He had taken off his foul-weather gear and there were droplets like cobwebs in his hair. He looked tired, but not as played out as most men would look after forty-eight hours with no sleep, she thought.

He sat down beside her and picked up the book she had been reading. Then he said, "So you've been raiding my shelves."

It was Captain Schouten's journal. She said, "I've been trying to puzzle out the letters at the top of the map."

"L A S?"

"Yes. You said once that the L might be half of a D, and I've been thinking about that, wondering if the A is truly an A. Do you think it might be an H?"

He frowned. "L H S?"

"If the L was an I, it would be I H S. The Greek symbol for Jesus."

"But that doesn't make sense."

"I know." She sighed, and Jake put the book on the chart desk, then settled back and began to help himself from her tray, eating with his fingers, and reaching across her to pick up the pieces of food. Again, as in the pantry, she was beset by a sense of intimacy. To counter it, she lifted the tray and put it firmly on his knees, and then shifted to the far corner of the settee, where she curled up comfortably before looking back at him.

Then she said, "But Jesus is the opposite of Judas."

"It still doesn't make sense."

"I know," she said again, and watched him demolish all the food that was left.

There was a tap on the door, and Bodfish came in with hot coffee. He inspected them with his long benevolent face, picked up the tray, and went out. Harriet remembered that Royal had said that the men were laying bets on when she would become their skipper's mistress, but for some reason she couldn't make herself care about it.

When the door was shut, Jake said, "Perhaps all three letters are suspect. Do we trust the S?"

His drawl was amused. She was being teased, she knew, and merely smiled mysteriously.

Then he said, "*Las* is the plural Spanish for *the*."

"But the ... what?"

"What indeed? Mystery upon mystery, young Harriet."

Then, while she was trying to feel vexed that he wasn't taking her seriously, he moved.

It happened before she knew it. Jake put his emptied coffee mug on the floor, and stretched out, full length, on the long sofa. His head was in her lap.

He instantly fell asleep. Harriet sat utterly still, listening to her heart thump. His long legs were crossed at the ankle, the lower foot propped on the far arm of the settee. He was wearing rough woolen socks ... how great-aunt Diana's Mrs. Pink would have disapproved, because the appearance of decorum had to be preserved always, whatever the reality of the scandal...

Jake looked so weary, more tired now that he was relaxed than when he was awake. He shifted in his sleep, turning his head so the side of his face was buried in the apex of her lap. Then he was still, and when he breathed, deep inside her, there was a terrifyingly responsive warmth.

She wanted desperately to lie down beside him, stretch herself around him, and pull his face to her breasts, which suddenly felt so tight. It was the way she had felt in the pantry, but a thousand times magnified.

She had never felt anything like this wanton, overwhelming longing, even when she had thought herself in love with Frank Sefton. After Sefton's cold, uncaring destruction of her innocence, she had never thought she could feel any desire for a man. And certainly never this — this craving for her bare skin to be touched and caressed, this demanding inner hollowing, this shocking heated longing to be filled. With him. With Jake Dexter. With the hardness of his body.

Is Jake Dexter your lover, Harriet? Oh my God, how I wish it were so, she thought, and struggled to keep perfectly still, while her errant thoughts flew.

There were times when … when, if she had acted differently, yes, she could have been Jake Dexter's mistress now. Right from the moment she had stepped on board the *Gosling*, she had found him attractive, even though she thought she hated him — and over the miles of passage she had come to admire him, appreciate his wry wit, and like him more with each day. But she had kept her distance. If she had come to his cabin after that passionate kiss in Valparaiso — if she had turned round in the pantry, and taken that one, small step into his arms, they would have been lovers long since. But even when she had teased him, she had kept her distance.

And because of that, she had never told him about her shameful marriage. Jake didn't know about Frank Sefton.

She had asked about divorce in Auckland. It had been one of the humiliations. Someone had told her that the wives of American men could sue for divorce in certain circumstances, so she had spent some hard-earned money to consult a lawyer. She may as well have saved it, as the counsel had been curt to the point of rudeness. She could divorce Sefton only if he created a public scandal, he said. And, as the lawyer had pointed out, desertion, no matter how heartless, was not considered a public scandal. It happened all the time. Thousands of men left their wives penniless while they hunted fortunes in other lands.

Oh, dear God, she thought again. How could she tell Jake that she was the discarded wife of a man who hated her — that she was a fool who had succumbed to a man who had pretended he loved her so he could use her for his own devious purposes? She had often cursed herself for breaking the family tradition of not bothering with marriage, but her regrets had never been as intense as they were right now — because she knew she had to tell Jake her squalid story, and she was scared of the contempt she might see in his eyes.

But Jake had been heartlessly deserted himself, so surely he would understand ... and accept that all she could offer was to be his mistress. That he would be her lover, never her husband — that they would live as her parents had lived. *It's just part of life as an actor or actress, dear Hat, and you know that even better than I do.* How true, she thought, remembering her great-aunt Diana.

In Paris, the romances of the bohémiens — men and women who lived and loved without the restrictions of respectable society — were becoming immensely popular themes for music and drama. Could real life — the life that normal people lived — be like the stage? The poets and the playwrights said so, she thought hopefully, and touched Jake's eyebrow with one tender fingertip, tracing the crooked line of it, caressing him with infinite gentleness as she waited for him to wake up.

There was an urgent shout through the skylight. Jake moved so fast she couldn't believe it. One minute he was sound asleep, and the next he was gone. He even thrust his stockinged feet into boots as he went, so that she heard his steps hurry through the lobby and along the passage to the afterquarters door. A moment's pause, as he climbed the ladder to the poop, and then his boots echoed on the deck above her head, accompanied by a chorus of shouts from the rigging.

When Harriet went to the afterhouse door herself, it was

to find that the fog had lifted like a theater curtain. And the Golden Gate to Eldorado lay ahead.

End of book one

LOOK OUT FOR THE NEXT BOOK IN THE SERIES

A Promise of Gold

Book Two

CALAFIA'S KINGDOM

Chapter One Follows . . .

ONE

IT was the first of September in the year 1848, and the gate to Eldorado lay ahead.

Captain Jake Dexter's charts were inadequate now, and when a sloop beat out and hailed them he negotiated for a pilot with some relief. He turned out to be a grizzled old customer with a seamy face and not many teeth, but Jake had been told that a deserter from some whaleship named Richardson had acted as the pilot here for the past fifteen years, and while he hadn't introduced himself, this fellow's deep knowledge seemed to mark him as that man. "Haul in port mainbraces," he said, and Jake was content to leave him to his work.

The entrance to the Bay of San Francisco was framed by a grand vista of hills and mountains that marched boldly down to the sea, creating a panorama that Jake Dexter found unexpectedly dramatic. The water was like a glinting jewel, set in a coronet of peaks and valleys, reflecting stands of cypress trees, the golden-browns of rounded hills, and the heavy granite-gray of cliffs. Waves dashed up against the rocks, splashing rainbows, and seabirds flew in patterns close to the sea. Another tack, and the brig *Gosling* sailed into the great curve of the bay ... and Jake stared, astounded.

He had heard that about twenty whalers called here each year to load with firewood and fresh water at an island called Yerba Buena, but that otherwise the bay of San Francisco was usually deserted — but today many more than twenty ships were riding in the harbor. And the way they were riding was strange... A chill lifted the hairs on the nape of his neck as he stared from one vessel to another. The unexpected fleet was huddled untidily, as if the whims of the winds and the currents had more to do with the way the craft lay than the decisions of men. And they looked more like derelicts than ships.

The *Gosling* seamen, who had been exclaiming loudly from aloft, were now eerily silent. Every man was shading his eyes at he stared at the abandoned vessels — for abandoned they certainly were. The silent hulls were splodged with bird droppings, and streaked with rust stains beneath davits, catheads, and hawseholes. Their yards were struck or left hanging all awry, and there was not a sign of movement about any of the decks.

Then the brig passed the entrance to an inlet, and Jake saw the United States frigate *Savannah*, looking much as he had seen her last, in the harbor of Valparaiso, in June. This time, though, she was not flying a host of flags. For a horrified moment he thought the great man-of-war was as abandoned as the other craft, but then he saw a signal raised, and a boat begin to lower. Captain Mervine, it seemed, had recognized the *Gosling*, and was as anxious to see Jake as Jake Dexter felt to ask questions of him.

Wondering how long the frigate had been here, Jake turned to the pilot. The old man, it seemed, had been watching his grim expression, because he grinned and said, "The *Savannah* only keeps her sailors, sir, by the threat of flogging and worse. Ain't nothing else what anchors here but loses all his men, on account of they all run off to the diggin's. And the same'll happen to you, sir. Drop your anchor you may, but lose your men you will."

Jake said with confidence, "I don't believe that will happen."

"No? Ha, you'll see different, just like all the rest. A man can dig a thousand a month up in them fabled hills. You're sure you want to drop anchor, Captain Dexter?"

"Go ahead," Jake said curtly, and the old man went back to issuing directions, which Charlie Martin, the first mate, relayed to the men. A stream of orders, and the brig heeled to an anchorage seaward of the abandoned ships. The anchor hit the water with a splash.

Silence. Even the brig's disorderly Ecuadorean passengers were quiet, as every man on board studied what lay on the shore. Small squat buildings were scattered about the brown slopes, some of them clapboard, most of them adobe … and yet there was no sign of life. The only movement was the jerky swing of the arms of a distant windmill. It was high summer, but the air was dank with the after-chill of the dawn fog, and Jake shivered, despite his heavy pea-jacket.

Suddenly the passengers moved, in unison, as if they had come out of a communal spell. Shouting all together and jostling one another to get to the gangway rail, the South Americans demanded passage to shore, saying that they had paid to get all the way to San Francisco from the Tombez River, and not just to the harbor.

"Fine," said Jake, delighted to see the last of them, and the two whaleboats and the two dinghies were dropped into the water, piled up with bodies and their dunnage, and rowed to the beach. Three trips, and they were all gone. Never, thought Jake sardonically, had a rich man got rid of his poor relations with more pleasure.

Turning, he found the pilot at his shoulder, waiting for his money, as bargained. It was handed over, and the old man spat on the silver dollars, and tucked them away in the depths of his garments. Then he stepped to the gangway rail to drop down into his sloop, which had followed them into the harbor.

Jake stopped him, saying, "Are there any American whalemen here?"

"Aye, sir, the *Flora*—there she is, over there at Whalemen's Harbor. But it ain't no use going a-calling, for she be as deserted as the rest. See them empty davits? She come in June, the *Flora* did, and the captain saw the danger, tried to get away a-fore he lost his men, but too late. Crew mutinied, refused duty, gagged the watch, escaped off to the mines. Captain and mates saw naught could be done about it, so off they went off theirselves to the hills."

"Dear lord," said Jake, shocked. "They just abandoned their ship?"

"Aye, they did. Mind you," the old man said with an air of world-weary experience, "she was twenty-six months out, and had taken only seven hundred and fifty barrels of oil. Ah, the rainy season is nigh, and they'll be back. I'll warrant them chains and cables be sufficient strong to last till they comes."

Jake found that equally hard to credit. The deserted ships all looked as if they would never get to sea again. Then he saw that the boat from the frigate would be alongside within minutes.

Turning back to the old pilot, he hastily asked, "Tell me—you must hear talk—are any New Bedford whalemen expected here?"

"Not here," the old man said. "The *Minerva* was here, but the captain managed to get her away, with good luck, a good crew, and good judgment. He told me he intended to sail to Valparaiso to get rid of his oil and load merchandise, which he will carry here in the expectation of a grand profit—which he will get, believe me. The masters what have managed to bring off that trick have sold their entire invoices for very large money, and that's what that captain expects. But he won't be here for some weeks."

"What about other ports? Monterey, perhaps?"

"The *Isaac Walton* is lying in Monterey, or so Captain

4

Mervine told me, she being there discharging her oil while she still got some men. Then maybe her captain will go in for the provisioning trade, too. Others be plying the coast, carrying passengers in place of oil, and another one be up at Sutter's Fort, all done up for the boarding house business."

"The … *what?*"

"At the Embarcadero of Sutter's Fort — one hundred and fifty miles upriver. No need to be astounded," said the old man, dourly amused at Jake's expression. "The wind blows fair upriver from February to October, and the river be a noble one. She's navigable all the way up to the fork with the American River and after that to Pueblo San Marco on the Feather, when the wind is right. I've seen 300-ton barks sail up to the Embarcadero with ease — anything can sail the Sacramento what draws less than fifteen feet. This brig would make it easy, even now at the end of the dry season. I can pilot you there, if you want, and don't you doubt I can do it, for I were the first mate of that very same whaler that be a boarding house at Sutter's now."

Jake said blankly, "But I thought you were Captain Richardson?"

"What, me?" The old man found this very amusing. "No, no," he said. "Paddack's the name, late first mate of the whaleship *Humpback*, and I do think, yes, that I have seen this brig before. Off Judas Island, was it not?"

Jake shook his head. So here was the first mate of the ship that had brought Harriet Gray to Judas Island, and whose captain had tricked her into going on board the *Gosling* — coincidence beyond coincidence, he thought with disbelief. Then he thought about the call of the siren gold, and decided that maybe it was not such a coincidence, after all. Then he was distracted by the arrival of the *Savannah*'s boat, with Mervine himself on board, and when he turned back for another word, he found that Paddack had jumped into his sloop, which promptly tacked away.

Mervine was scrambling up the side, his face redder

5

than ever. "What do you think?" he cried. "Ain't it a scandal?"

Straightening as he arrived beside Jake, he swung out an arm and pointed. "See that bark?" he demanded.

Jake looked. The bark Mervine indicated seemed no different from the rest of the derelict fleet. He said, "Yes?"

"*Amity*, her name. She came in late yesterday, and this morning her master found but six men still on board. He's on the *Savannah* right now, laying a complaint. Oh, we'll punish the scoundrels when we find them, confiscate their gold, make spread-eagles of them all!"

"That's why the *Savannah* is here in San Francisco?" Jake said, astounded. "To catch deserters? But you told me in Valparaiso that you were on a mission to the Indian Ocean!"

"The need here is greater, Captain Dexter! We was summoned by no less than Colonel Mason himself, because deserters must be caught, and deserters must be punished!"

Then the frigate's commander lowered his voice. "I've lost more than a dozen men myself, and I am right ashamed to say it," he confided. "Scarcely half an hour had elapsed after dropping anchor before the officer of the watch noticed that the gig had disappeared, and with her the first half-dozen of our men. No sooner had he raised the alarm than there was a general rush to a lighter that was lying alongside, and off ten more men went, off over the side like so many eels. In vain was the guard turned out, because by the time another boat was lowered, than they had all shown a clean pair of heels. There's a seven-hundred-dollar bounty on each of their hides, and I assure you, sir, that they'll be sorry for themselves when they are handed in."

"Jehovah," said Jake Dexter, and then saw that Harriet had come on deck, freed to come out of the afterquarters by the departure of the last of the Ecuadoreans. She was looking for him, Jake saw, as if she had something to tell him, but then she sighted their visitor, and her anxious expression turned into one of surprise.

6

"Merciful heavens, it's Captain Mervine," she said.

Jake said to Mervine, "You remember our supercargo, Miss Harriet Gray?"

"Of course I do, of course! The famous actress, the beautiful Titania! Good morning, Miss Gray!"

Harriet inclined her head and shook his hand.

She did look beautiful, Jake thought, her waif-like face pale, and her wheat-colored hair tumbled about her shoulders, but Captain Mervine had no trouble dismissing her from his mind. Turning back to Jake, he urged, "Come ashore with me, Captain Dexter."

"To shore? But why?"

"I'd value your opinion, sir. Tell me what you think."

The boat pulled for a narrow gritty beach. Some of the Ecuadoreans were there, wading through shallow water as they made their way along a bluff, but Captain Mervine led Jake directly up the hill. The wind cut to the bone, despite the warmth of the exercise, and Jake climbed with his hands in his peajacket pockets, listening to Mervine's heavy panting.

At the top of the hill it was even colder, and there seemed to be nothing in sight except short brown-gold grass on the slopes and brown-gold dirt exposed in the gullies. Then, as they walked, signs of habitation appeared — rows of houses, mysteriously only half-built, all at the same stage of construction. It was as if some strange pestilence had carried off all the carpenters, bricklayers, and roofers. There were even ladders left propped against half-built walls, and stacks of shingles alongside the eaves of raftered, gaping roofs. Dogs cringed at corners. Two Ecuadoreans who had made it this far were staring about with bewildered looks.

"Fifty!" Mervine barked in Jake's ear.

"I beg your pardon?"

"Fifty houses a-building — according to plan they were, rising according to a timetable when I left this place in May.

7

The price of manual labor in California has always been high—from one to three dollars a day, with master workmen being able to command five dollars. On the discovery of gold on the American River, this changed at once, wages being tripled and quadrupled by the minute. Soon, tradesmen were being paid eight dollars a day, the highest in the land, but where are they now? Up the mines, sir, up at the diggings! A few hung back, but then the news of a buster nugget got out—a nugget weighing four pounds, worth one thousand and sixty dollars! And that news, Captain Dexter, sent the rest on their way."

Jake stared about, his hands curled into fists in his pockets, thinking that the scene reminded him of the landing stage at Tombez, when he had called there in July. The village had been completely emptied of men, a mystery that had been solved when he had learned that they had all rushed to California on a ship that had called by for provisions, carrying the news of gold. And here, in San Francisco, there was the same sense of hurried departure.

He said, "Is anyone at all in town?"

"Only the traders who are making money out of supplying the miners as they stream into the port on the way upriver to the hills, along with their clerks and servants, who are only kept pinned here by high wages. Do you have any idea what salesmen and shopmen demand from their employers?"

"No, I do not, Captain Mervine."

"From two thousand, three hundred dollars per annum, to two thousand, seven hundred dollars—with board and lodging! And mere boys have the sauce to demand pretty much the same, their seniors being all up in the hills—it's a scandal, Captain Dexter, a scandal! The officers at the garrison in Monterey are forced to go without servants, not being able to afford the outrageous rates—they have to cook their own dinners! Even Colonel Mason has to take his turn to cook! Is it any wonder, sir, that the general aspect of this town is so forlorn — that stores are shut, buildings abandoned? Houses empty? Businesses dead? Tell me what you think."

Jake grimaced, thinking that the abandoned ships in the harbor had certainly looked forlorn, and said, "Those seniors — the tradesmen and artisans who were building the houses and printing the newspapers. Did they leave the town all at once, in a body?"

"In a flood, Captain Dexter. Two thousand men left this budding city in June, sir, two-thirds of them American. Then after that, in July, another two thousand followed in their wake. And is that latest two thousand American? No, sir, that they ain't. The men who flood through here on the way to the diggings, Captain Dexter, are men all intent on robbing the territory of rightfully American gold, and they are not Americans, sir. They are Peruvian, Chilean, Ecuadorean, sir, Russian, French, and — for God's sake, and pardon me, sir — the miserable Mexicans and bloody arrogant English. Our natural-born enemies, sir, come to steal our rightfully won treasure, come to loot the territory what was won with American blood! They expect to leave amazing' rich in just a few months, and they have no intention whatsoever of becoming United States citizens. Barefaced robbery of what is rightfully American, Captain Dexter!"

"Dear me," said Jake.

"We fought a war, beat the Mexicans, made California rightfully American — for this?"

"It's certainly ironic."

"Worse than that, Captain Dexter, it's a scandal!"

They were walking again, more slowly, and the streets widened and became uphill and downhill, often with one side of the road a full few feet higher than the other. There was a deserted market, fenced with rawhides on wires, stinking most foully, and then substantial buildings, many made of stone ... but still, still no sign of life.

9

So where were the traders who were making a fortune out of supplying the miners? Behind their counters and inside their warehouses, Jake supposed — unless they were in the mines themselves, having run out of stocks. Or maybe out of customers, he mused, the season being so late. It was beyond belief, this silence and sense of desertion, almost dreamlike in its weirdness.

Jake shook his head, and said, "And yet, in Valparaiso, Captain Mervine, you swore there was no gold."

"Well, there is." Mervine made it sound like a personal insult. "Colonel Mason and Lieutenant Sherman went into the hills to make a survey — and Colonel Mason has just come back with a report of what the gold in them hills is like."

Jake waited. "And?"

"You've no idea," Mervine said sourly. "Sir, you ain't got a notion. Two ounces is a usual day's work. While Mason was watching, two men dug seventeen thousand dollars' worth, just in the space of an hour."

Jake said softly, "Jehovah." Even now, it didn't seem possible that the wild tales he had heard in Tombez did, after all, have such a solid foundation in truth. "In one hour?"

"And that was with naught but Indian baskets for sieving the nuggets out of the dirt. Them with machines like gold-washing pans and dirt-washing cradles can work out even more."

"And all this is in Colonel Mason's report?"

"He writ everything down and tomorrow we sail for Monterey, to escort the schooner *Lambayecana* out of Monterey to Paita. There will be a loyal lieutenant on board that schooner, who will carry that report, along with a tea caddy of gold samples, all the way to Washington."

"So Colonel Mason can ask for reinforcements?"

"I beg your pardon?"

"You told me in Valparaiso that if the gold did indeed

exist, Colonel Mason would claim it all as the property of the United States government."

Captain Mervine coughed, a loud sound that echoed among the deserted stone façades. "If we capture any deserters — and we will board all outgoing ships to search for deserters, I assure you of that! — then we will certainly confiscate their ill-gotten gold, and make spread-eagles of them all, sir, flog them till their bones are chalk! But," he added with vast distaste, "Colonel Mason has been forced to admit that that be the extent of our powers. The placer has proved to be fully five hundred miles in length — and there's the problem of desertion, too. He can't trust his troops, I am ashamed to say. But what allurement is a private's pay of six dollars a month compared to the tales coming out of the mines? Colonel Mason's force is small enough to start with, but his count of loyal officers and men diminishes by the day."

This was exactly what he himself had predicted, Jake remembered. However, he kept his counsel.

For a moment the only sounds were the thud of their boots, and the echoes that came back from the blank buildings. He saw some more Ecuadoreans, these men in a group, consulting together. As he watched, a couple of men he didn't recognize joined them, and waved their arms as they talked in a knowledgeable kind of way. They were locals, he supposed, because they looked so Spanish, being dressed in gaudy jackets and calcineros, with high-crowned sombreros on their heads. He hadn't seen a man who looked like an American yet. They were all, he supposed, in the hills.

Mervine's thoughts were running in the same direction, it seemed, because he growled again, "It's a scandal, Captain Dexter, a scandal. Back in April the place I left was bustling and American. Why there were two newspapers, two! Now both have failed, sir, and from what? Starvation, that's what, for no paper can survive when the writers, editors, printers

11

and readers have all gone off to the mines. Gold fever," he mumbled like a curse. "A disease, that's what it is, a disease."

San Francisco certainly looked as if it had been emptied by a plague. Jake wondered what other towns on the coast had been left deserted like this. Monterey, evidently. Perhaps Paita, Callao and Talcahuano were in the same state as Tombez and San Francisco, emptied by the fever. And what about Valparaiso? When he had left there, in June, the rumors were just taking hold.

"The October rains will fetch all the men back," Mervine prophesied, but the prospect didn't make him look happier. "The town will be bustling again—until February, when the rains stop. Then they'll all head back to the hills, and more foreigners with them. Damn it, sir, and beg your pardon, Captain Dexter, but it sure bites hard that the gold in this territory should be taken away by the very men we fought to keep out!"

"But it seems impossible to stop the South Americans from coming in, Captain Mervine," said Jake. He was thinking of the load of Ecuadoreans he had carried here—at what he had expected to be an immense profit.

"You think so? But that's why Colonel Mason is sending that report to Washington!"

"It is?"

"Of course! Once red-blooded American boys hear about that gold, then they will come in their thousands, and kick the foreigners out."

"You're expecting another war?"

"Wa'al," said Captain Mervine, and coughed. "Mebbe they won't actually kick them out, being too busy digging all that gold, but the American boys will dilute the multitudes, sir, outnumber the foreigners, make California American, the way it should rightfully be."

Jake contemplated the devious notion. After the loyal lieutenant arrived in Washington with his enlivening yarns and his tea caddy of gold, would New York and Boston be emptied out, too? On one hand, it was unimaginable, and yet … yet, looking around, it seemed eerily possible.

Mervine barked, "And it is your patriotic duty, sir, to do the same!"

"I beg your pardon?" said Jake, astonished.

"Your duty as an American, sir, is to take your brig upriver, and add to the quota of American citizens in the Sacramento valley. Show the flag, sir, wave it high!"

"Jehovah," said Jake, having trouble not to laugh. The crew of his brig numbered just fourteen — not including Harriet's brother, Royal Gray, who by Mervine's logic should not be counted, because he was English. His men were an energetic and virile lot, but the amount of diluting they could do was very limited.

But Mervine was perfectly serious. "The Sacramento is a mighty stream," he said. "Fully navigable for a hundred and fifty miles, sir, all the way to Sutter's Fort, on the fork with the American River. That's where the news of the gold was first bruited about, sir, the first gold being found on Sutter's ground, at his mill, which is about fifty miles up the fork. Most vessels go no further, because most of the business goes on at the Fort, or on the Embarcadero, but it is possible to sail as far as Pueblo San Marco, an old town half a day upriver, on the junction of the Feather River and Cache Creek, famous in the region as the gateway to the mines."

Jake was silent, thinking that if Sutter's Fort was as busy as Mervine said, it could be ideal for the scheme he had in mind. Then he wondered about duties and taxes — items that he was always anxious to avoid.

He said, "What's the state of law and order there?"

"Shocking, Captain Dexter, shocking! The alcalde, Robert Ross, is nothing better than an English adventurer what was appointed by the Mexicans, which is a scandal in itself. But he has his rules, sir, and his regulations, so Colonel Mason was forced to admit that he do the best what he can."

"Regulations? What regulations?"

"Wa'al, there ain't too many of those, Captain. Alcalde Ross has the same trouble with keeping deputies as we have with keeping sailors and soldiers, sir, and without deputies, what could even a proper American do, huh?"

"Interesting," said Jake, very thoughtfully.

"So you'll go, Captain Dexter—take your brig upriver to Sutter's or Pueblo San Marco? The season when the prevailing winds blow upriver is still with us—but not for long, so you'll have to make up your mind now. And face it, sir, there ain't no point in stopping here in 'Frisco."

Jake Dexter looked around again. A shut door in the imposing façade of the store to his right carried a tattered notice. It read, CLOSED ON ACCOUNT OF GOING TO THE MINES.

"You're absolutely right," he said.

End of Chapter One

AUTHOR'S NOTE

Many books, newspapers, and journals were read in the quest for background for the *Promise of Gold* trilogy. The following were found to be particularly useful.

Kelly, William, J.P. *An Excursion to California over the Prairie, Rocky Mountains, and Great Sierra Nevada, with a stroll through the Diggings and Ranches of that Country.* London: Chapman & Hall, 1851.

Robinson, Fayette, *California and its Gold Regions,* in, *The Gold Mines of California.* New York: Promontory Press, 1974.

Ryan, William Redmond. *Personal Adventures in Upper and Lower California in 1848-9.* New York: Arno Press, 1973 (first published 1850-1851).

Shaw, William. *Golden Dreams and Waking Realities.* London: Smith, Elder, 1851.

Street, Franklin. *California in 1850,* in, *The Gold Mines of California.* New York: Promontory Press, 1974.

Taylor, Bayard. *Eldorado, or, Adventures in the Path of Empire.* New York: Putnam, 1850.

The Friend, Honolulu, December 1, 1849, pp. 81-83. Account by a Hawaiian missionary (probably Rev. Damon) of a tour in Alta California.

Tyrwhitt-Brooks, J., M.D. (Pseudonym of J. Vizetelly, printer.) *Four Months among the Gold-finders in Alta California.* London: David Bogue, 1849.

Woods, Daniel B. *Sixteen Months at the Gold Diggings.* London: Sampson Low, 1857.

www.oldsaltpress.com

Old Salt Press is an independent press catering to those who love books about ships and the sea. We are an association of writers working together to produce the very best of nautical and maritime fiction and non-fiction, and invite you to join us as we go down to the sea in books.

From other Old Salt Press authors

Alaric Bond

Honour Bound
—In this, the tenth book of the Fighting Sail series, Commander King is seized by the enemy. In an atmosphere of mounting tension, he is forced to survive in hostile territory.

The Blackstrap Station
— Christmas 1803, and there is nothing to celebrate, as the shipwrecked crew of HMS *Prometheus* are forced to pit their wits against the enemy force sent out to hunt them down.

HMS *Prometheus*
— In the eighth book of the Fighting Sail series, HMS *Prometheus* sets sail from the shipyard at Gibraltar, to face the greatest challenge yet.

The Scent of Corruption
— Sir Richard Banks is appointed to HMS *Prometheus,* a seventy-four gun line-of-battleship which an eager Admiralty loses no time in ordering to sea — a non-stop nautical thriller in the best traditions of the genre.

The Torrid Zone
— She's a tired ship with a worn out crew, but **HMS Scylla** has one more trip to make before her much postponed re-fit — a trip fraught with unexpected dangers.

The Guinea Boat
— Set in Hastings, Sussex during the early part of 1803, *Guinea Boat* tells the story of two young lads, and the diverse paths they take to make a living on the water.

Turn a Blind Eye
— Autumn, 1801. Newly appointed to the local revenue cutter, Commander Griffin is determined to make his mark, and defeat a major gang of smugglers.

Linda Collison

Rhode Island Rendezvous
—— Adventure on the high seas in New England and the West Indies during the early days of Revolution. The third book in the popular Patricia MacPherson series.

Water Ghosts
—— *"I see things other people don't see
I hear things other people don't hear"* — a paranormal thriller set on board a junk peopled by troubled teens.

Rick Spilman

Evening Gray Morning Red
— A young American sailor must escape his past and the clutches of the Royal Navy, in the turbulent years just before the American Revolutionary War.

The Shantyman
— A gripping tale of survival against all odds at sea and ashore. A Kirkus Best Indie Book pick.

Bloody Rain
— A novella of blood and madness on the Hooghly River.

Hell Around the Horn
— The ordeal of a captain, his crew and his family in an epic doubling of Cape Horn.

Antoine Vanner

Britannia's Gamble

— It's 1884. A fanatical Islamist revolt is sweeping the Sudan and General Charles Gordon's hold on Khartoum is tenuous. There is only one way for Dawlish to come to the rescue — by an antique steamer, on a hostile river.

Britannia's Amazon

— A Victorian melodrama in which Florence Dawlish, left behind in England, risks her life to save the lives of others.

Britannia's Spartan

— A gripping yarn of convoluted diplomacy and bloody conflict in the Sea of Japan.

Britannia's Shark

— A maritime thriller set in the time of America's Gilded Age.

Britannia's Reach

—The action-packed second volume of the Dawlish Chronicles naval fiction series, in which Dawlish is forced to face his own conscience in a conflict of morality, in the midst of South American chaos.

Britannia's Wolf

—**An exciting debut that** introduces a naval hero who is more familiar with steam, breech-loaders and torpedoes than with sails, carronades and broadsides.

Joan Druett

Joan Druett is a maritime historian and writer, married to Ron Druett, a highly regarded maritime artist.

In 1984, while exploring the tropical island of Rarotonga, she slipped into the hole left by the roots of a large uprooted tree, and at the bottom discovered the grave of a young American whaling wife, who had died in January 1850 at the age of twenty-four. It was a life-changing experience. Her immediate interest in whaling captains' wives at sea was encouraged by a Fulbright fellowship, which led to five months of research in New Bedford and Edgartown, in Massachusetts, Mystic, Connecticut, and San Francisco, California, and resulted in her study of whaling captains' wives under sail, *Petticoat Whalers*.

The success of this book, and a companion volume, *She Was a Sister Sailor*, was followed by *Hen Frigates, Wives of Merchant Captains Under Sail*, which was given a New York Public Library Best to Remember Award, while *She Was a Sister Sailor* won the John Lyman Award for Best Book of American Maritime History. Joan Druett's ground-breaking work in the field of seafaring women was also recognized by a L. Byrne Waterman Award. Her non-fiction account of a double castaway experience in the sub-Antarctic, *Island of the Lost*, has become a classic in the genre. Then her strong interest in the stories of the Pacific Islanders who sailed on Euro-American ships led to a biography of an extraordinary Polynesian star navigator, *Tupaia*, which won the general nonfiction prize in the 2012 New Zealand Post Book Awards.

Joan Druett is also the author of the popular Wiki Coffin mysteries, which have a half-Maori, half-Yankee hero.

Her books have been translated into Chinese, French, Italian, Russian and German.

www.ingramcontent.com/pod-product-compliance
Lightning Source LLC
Chambersburg PA
CBHW070919180626
46817CB00003B/1131